HOT SHADOWS

Hostile Operations Team® - Strike Team 2

LYNN RAYE HARRIS

Printed in the United States of America

First Printing, 2023

For rights inquires, visit www.LynnRayeHarris.com

HOT Shadows

ISBN: 978-1-941002-75-9

Prologue

"It's an ambush! Abort, abort, abort!"

"Fuck," Jax "Gem" Stone swore as the explosion reverberated down the line. Ryder "Muffin" Hanson was behind the wheel of the armored car carrying members of Congresswoman Ellen Fairhope's staff. He rolled the wheel hard right and spun the vehicle, same as everyone else in the line did.

Gem grabbed onto the overhead handle until the spin stabilized then drew his weapon and prepared for a fight. He threw a look behind the car, but all he could see was a cloud of dust flaring into the air, obscuring his view.

He wasn't a fan of desert details. Not in the fucking least. He'd done his share, but they hadn't grown on him over the past few years. Even when shit was normal, it was fucking hot and the sand blew in his eyes and made them even grittier than the typical lack of sleep did. An ambush was some next-level bullshit, though.

As he twisted forward again, he glimpsed the wide eyes of the woman who'd introduced herself back in DC as Everly. A lawyer or something on the congresswoman's staff. He wasn't clear on that. She was pretty, with dark gold hair and intelligent brown eyes behind her glasses. She wasn't his usual type, but he had to admit he'd felt a tingle of interest when he'd first seen her. That was *before* they'd boarded the plane to Qu'rim.

He'd lost that interest when she'd looked down her pretty nose at him. Or up, since he was taller. She'd still made it look like she was looking down on him, though. He didn't care for that. He might not be a doctor or a lawyer, but he was damned good at what he did.

And what he did was going to save her ass right about now.

"Gem, you still there? Report."

Gem touched the mic control on his helmet. "Copy that, Saint. We're here. Taking the civvies back to the rendezvous point."

"Roger. We're moving that way too. See you there."

"Fucking hell," Muffin muttered as he glanced at the dashboard. He'd jammed the pedal to the floor, but the car wasn't going any faster.

"What?"

"Red line. This baby isn't going to make it much farther."

The car slowed as Muffin worked to keep the inevitable from happening. Damn desert heat. Gem gripped his pistol and swore to himself. "Take us as far as you can. We'll go on foot if we have to."

"No way. Keep driving."

Gem turned to look at the women in the back seat. His eyes met Everly's. Two other staffers were crammed in beside her, but he knew it'd been her by the way she glared at him. Damned if that flare of interest didn't happen again. He crushed it like an ant at a picnic.

"Excuse me?"

"I said no. Wendy has fibromyalgia. She can't walk through sand."

The woman in question gave him a weak smile. "I'm sorry," she whispered.

"Nothing to be sorry for. We'll carry you, ma'am."

Everly's brown eyes flashed at him, but he wasn't sure if it was anger or gratitude. Hard to tell with her prissy attitude. He turned away and touched the mic again.

"Got a situation in car three, Saint. Muffin says we're redlining. This vehicle isn't going to make it, and we've got someone with a medical condition onboard."

They were already falling behind if the cloud of dust in front of them was any indication.

"Copy that. How much longer?"

Gem arched an eyebrow at Muffin and nodded at the dash. "Any minute," Muffin replied.

Gem repeated the info to Saint as well as their location.

"We'll have to make a transfer then. No choice," Saint said. "We'll stop at the mile marker and wait for you—"

A woman's voice spoke in the background. Gem wasn't sure what was said, but a moment later Saint was back, sounding pissed. "The congresswoman doesn't want to stop. Cars two and four will wait for you there. Should be enough room for everyone."

Gem could hear the anger in Saint's voice, but disobeying a congresswoman who was also the chairwoman of the House Armed Services Committee wasn't really an option. Ellen Fairhope could make life hard for HOT if she wanted. None of them would willingly do that to General Mendez or Colonel Bishop. Or to their teammates.

Piling into the other two cars would make things tight, but they could do it.

"Roger," Gem said. "It's enough. We'll make it. Get her back to base and we'll join you soon."

Muffin glanced at him. He didn't look happy. "Seriously? Fucking civilians."

"Agreed."

Gem didn't know if the women in the rear of the car heard or not. He didn't care. They were in this mess because the congresswoman wanted to take a tour of Qu'rim and meet with a warlord who was supposed to be on the side the Americans were backing. Gem didn't know if the guy was or wasn't, but it was a little suspect that someone had planned an attack on her convoy when she was an hour into the journey.

The car slowed some more, and Gem looked behind them. They were the only ones throwing up dust now since they were in the rear, which meant it cleared faster than before.

"Shit," Gem growled when he could see. "We've got company. Two trucks and men on horseback closing in."

Muffin pressed the accelerator. The car surged forward before sputtering and slowing. "It's no good. This bitch is about to die a quick death."

Gem reached onto the floor for his rifle. There wasn't enough time to call for air support. No way was he letting these women fall into the hands of the enemy. If they were captured, it wouldn't be pretty for any of them.

Gem powered the window down and thrust himself through, leaning on the door frame for support and lifting the rifle to his shoulder. He fired at one of the trucks, aiming for the engine bay.

A second later, his bullet found its target and the truck lurched to a stop. He aimed at the next truck. He heard the clang of full metal jacket impacting, but the truck didn't stop. The bullet must have glanced off a steel support instead of tearing through the radiator or shredding the fan.

Gem sighted through the scope again, pulled in a breath to steady himself as the car lurched forward, then squeezed the trigger on the exhale.

Boom!

This time the round connected, and the truck's engine blew white smoke as the vehicle skidded. The driver slammed the brake and the top-heavy truck tipped onto its side, spilling men and guns into the sand. The horses scattered as their riders peeled off to whirl back the way they'd come.

Thank God.

Gem slipped into his seat. Cars two and four came into view ahead. Muffin somehow got their limping vehicle to the other two and they piled out, pulling the women from the rear and helping them toward the waiting vehicles as dust swirled and the sun beat down hard.

Wendy and the other woman ended up in one of the cars with Muffin. Gem hauled Everly to the car guarded by Zane "Zany" Scott and Mal McCoy. There wasn't enough room for both of them to have a seat and Gem didn't ask questions. He piled in and dragged Everly down on his lap, one arm banded around her waist as Zany hit the gas.

She was stiff as a board as she leaned against him. He tried not to inhale the sweetness of her shampoo or the tang of her sweat, but she was too close and it was a losing battle.

He clenched his jaw and told himself he'd smelled plenty of women before. And in better circumstances.

She wiggled her ass on his lap and he practically groaned. He tightened his arm around her a little roughly. "Stop moving."

"Your gun is digging into me," she grated at him.

The other staffers in the car didn't react, but Mal threw him a smirk. Gem snarled silently at his teammate. In different circumstances, sure, he might get a woody with a woman sitting on his lap as the car hurtled down the road, the entire frame vibrating with their speed.

But it wasn't his cock poking into her. It was the gear strapped to his body, specifically the tactical vest with ammo, weapons, and other items he might need in a protracted fight.

"Sorry," he said, shifting sideways to allow her to move off the offending piece of equipment.

She sniffed but didn't reply as she leaned away from him. The ride lasted another thirty minutes before they reached the safe zone they'd left only a couple of hours ago. Everly tried to throw herself off his lap as the car door opened from the outside, but her foot got caught on the way out and she went down. Gem grabbed her before she face-planted in the dirt.

Her long hair had flipped over her head, her feet

were still on the floorboards, and her breath heaved into her body as she clutched his arm tightly.

"Hang on, I've got you," he said. He tugged her back up so she could brace against him and get her feet out of the car. When they were firmly planted on the ground, he eased his hold and she stood on her own.

She turned to face him, her cheeks flushing as she shoved her wild hair behind her ears. "Thank you."

"You're welcome."

She hesitated. Her coworkers trudged toward the hotel they'd quartered in, but she didn't move to follow. "What happened out there?"

He got to his feet and she tilted her head back to gaze up at him. She looked young and scared and he had an urge to hold her. Not that he'd act on it, though.

"I don't know." Yet.

"Do you think it was aimed at her?"

"By her you mean the congresswoman, right?"

She nodded.

"Can't say."

She thrust a hand at him, and he realized she wanted to shake hands.

"Thank you for what you did back there," she said when he took her small hand in his. "I know Congresswoman Fairhope appreciates your quick thinking."

"More like training," he told her, fascinated by the

way she seemed to go from vulnerable to stick-up-the-ass formal in a heartbeat. "But you're welcome."

She nodded again, then dropped his hand and walked away. He watched her go then swore to himself as he rushed to catch up with her.

"Hey," he said.

She stopped, blinking in surprise. "Yes?"

"You got someone back in DC?"

"Um, no."

"Maybe we could go out sometime. See if we like each other somewhere more normal."

What the hell are you doing, Gem? This woman is way too annoying.

She frowned for a second. Then she pulled a card from the satchel she'd slung across her body and thrust it at him.

"My number is on here."

Gem glanced down at the piece of white card stock. There were two numbers—office and mobile—but it was her name that had his attention.

Everly Fairhope, Esq.

"Fairhope? Like the congresswoman?" The woman who wouldn't stop for her own staff when they were in danger?

Her lips seemed to flatten a moment. "She's my mother."

She was still holding the card out. He took it, reeling with that information. "Thanks."

"You won't call, but it's okay."

"Why do you think I won't?"

"It's complicated. Anyway, thanks for everything you did to keep us safe."

"You're welcome."

She nodded. "It was nice meeting you, Sergeant."

This time when she walked away, he didn't go after her.

Chapter One

Six months later...

GEM'S TEAMMATES got quiet when he walked into the locker room. Saint nodded. Wolf dropped his gaze to his range bag and started rummaging through it.

Gem's senses twitched, but he wouldn't let on that he suspected they were up to something. It wouldn't be the first time Strike Team 2 pranked one of their own. Just last week, they'd pranked Mal by putting warm pickle juice in his coffee cup. Since the lid had been on, Mal hadn't noticed the pungent aroma until it was too late and he'd taken a swig.

Hysterical. Gem could still see Mal's face screw up. And then the spray when he spewed the juice everywhere. They'd fallen over laughing, Mal cursing them the entire time and threatening retribution.

Gem glanced around, wondering what he was about to find in his locker. He shouldn't have been the last one in today. Not that it could have been helped. He'd had an appointment with the team doctor over at Riverstone for a follow-up about a knife wound to the leg he'd gotten almost two months ago. It hadn't been a deep wound, but HOT was nothing if not thorough with their people.

"How's the injury?" Zany asked, looking concerned.

Gem stood as far as possible from his locker door and tugged it open. Nothing jumped out at him.

"All better. Just gonna leave a scar is all."

Easy's phone dinged. He took it out and snorted. "So cute." He turned the phone so they could see his niece, soon-to-be daughter, sleeping on the floor with the two cats he and his wife Jenna had adopted. The cats were curled around Alice, all three sound asleep.

"When's the adoption hearing?" Saint asked.

"Next week," Easy said. "Jenna's nervous, but I keep telling her it'll be fine. We're already Alice's guardians."

"Just a formality."

"That's what I told her."

Gem got his range bag out. There were no rubber snakes, no gooey substances, no pickle juice lurking inside. What the fuck were these guys up to anyway?

He looked up to catch Mal's gaze. If anyone was planning a prank, it was fucking Mal. Especially since Gem may have been the one to suggest pickle juice to the others. But Mal smiled wanly and glanced away again.

Gem spread his feet apart, folded his arms, and locked his stance. "All right. What's going on with you guys?"

"Going on?" Muffin said. He opened his locker. A thin sheet of newspaper fell out and he picked it up and crumpled it. "Nothing."

Gem frowned. "I don't believe you."

Hacker groaned. "Just tell him. He's going to find out anyway. Hell, he might already know."

Gem's skin prickled with dread. "Know what? Did I get orders? Am I being sent to another unit? What the fuck is going on?"

Wolf snatched the newspaper from Muffin's fingers. "Everly Fairhope is engaged. It was in the paper this morning."

Ice washed over Gem's body. He took the piece of paper calmly and smoothed it out to glance at it. "I didn't know you read the wedding announcements, Muffin. Secret hobby?"

"No way, man. It was in the politics section. Not quite a formal announcement."

"Who reads an actual newspaper anymore?" Mal asked.

Muffin gave him a look. "I grew up with two

reporters for parents and I still read newsprint. Sue me."

Gem stopped listening and took in the headline.

CONGRESSWOMAN ELLEN FAIRHOPE'S DAUGHTER RUMORED TO BE ENGAGED TO J. STUART MORRISON OF MORRISON, MORRISON, AND FREDRICKS

His blood was icy enough to make him numb. Good thing, because he suspected rage was simmering below the surface, just waiting for an opportunity to erupt. Not that it was any of his business what Everly did. She'd made that clear two months ago when she'd broken up with him.

Everly Fairhope. He'd called her about a month after they'd returned from Qu'rim. They'd dated for three months, and he'd really liked her. Liked her so much he'd taken it slow. Hell, they'd just worked their way up to some heavy petting when she broke up with him.

He'd been pissed, not because they hadn't had sex, but because he'd started to care. He'd thought she cared too. He'd taken her to his teammates' homes for parties and get-togethers, and she'd fit right in. Everyone liked her. Everly wasn't stiff or formal with them, not like she'd been in Qu'rim. She'd seemed more herself, even if she didn't ever let the prim and proper side of herself go completely. She was Congresswoman Fairhope's daughter and she never let it all hang out. Too risky, she'd said. He hadn't argued with her, but he'd thought she was the most buttoned-up woman he'd ever known. He'd also thought she'd drop those barriers with him eventually, and it would've been so worth it.

He hadn't even minded that she didn't formally introduce him to her mother. He'd figured there was time for that. He'd been wrong.

"Okay, so she's getting married," Gem said, hoping he didn't sound as angry as he felt. "I wish her the best."

"Really?" Mal asked. "I thought you'd be pissed."

Gem shrugged and handed the clipping back to Muffin. "Why would I? We dated for three months. It didn't work out. Happens."

"Yeah, guess so. Just thought it might bother you."

"Nah, it's fine. Everly's a grown woman. If she wants to marry some guy she's only been dating a month or two, who am I to tell her she can't?"

Not that he knew she'd only been dating this J. Stuart Morrison guy for a month or two. For all he knew, she'd been with Stu—he totally didn't know if that was the guy's nickname, but that's what he was going with because it sounded stodgy as fuck—before she'd met him. Maybe Everly and Stu had been on a break. She'd said she hadn't been dating anyone for over a year, but that didn't make it true. Maybe they'd reconnected and there were fireworks.

Gem didn't like the knot in his gut. He'd thought there were fireworks between him and Everly, and he'd been willing to wait for the right time to make them explode, but it'd never happened. Fact was he was a shitty judge of female character. He had an ex-wife to prove it, and an ex-girlfriend now engaged to someone else. If that didn't make him clueless in the love department, he didn't know what did.

"Sorry anyway, brother," Zany said, clamping a hand on his shoulder. "I liked Everly. I hope she'll be happy."

"Me, too," Gem said, turning back to his locker for his gym clothes. First they had PT, then it was the range. Plenty of stuff to keep him occupied.

It wasn't until Gem was done with his fifteen miles and getting into the shower that it happened.

Grape jelly squirted out of his shampoo bottle, which he didn't realize until he'd already smeared it in his hair. Should have kept his eyes open when he got the shampoo. He might have seen it then.

"Mal, you fuckwit!" he yelled.

The shower enclosure erupted in hoots followed by howls of laughter. Gem couldn't help but laugh with them, even if his heart wasn't really in it.

"CONGRATULATIONS, EVERLY."

"Thank you," she called back to the person who'd spoken while zipping by on a golf cart. Everly strode briskly through the tunnel leading from the Capitol to the Rayburn House Office Building, smiling until her face hurt and thanking people for their congratulations.

She felt like her heart would never stop pounding again, her stomach never stop twisting like a wounded animal. She made it to her mother's suite of offices, somehow got through the pleasantries, and finally burst into the inner sanctum where Ellen Fairhope was closeted with her Chief of Staff. A position she'd said would one day be Everly's. *Before* she was expected to step into the family dynasty and run for political office of her own.

"Darling," her mother said, looking up with a pleasant smile on her face. "Congratulations on a fine catch. I think Stuart is wonderful. Just wonderful. He will make you very happy, sweetheart."

Everly's face ached with the strain. She didn't believe her mother's faux surprise for one moment. "Yes, I'm sure. I need to speak with you, Mother. Alone."

Bob Schaffer picked up his iPad and stood. "I've got some things to take care of anyway. I'll see you at lunch, Ellen."

Everly waited until Bob had gone before she dropped the facade. "What are you doing, Mother?"

"Doing, sweetheart? I'm making sure you fill all the boxes so you'll be ready when the time comes. Stuart is a good friend, a good supporter, and he's single. You can't afford to wait any longer before you get a proper husband, my dear."

Everly's stomach twisted again. "Stuart and I have only been dating for a month. We've never discussed marriage! How did we get engaged?"

She air-quoted the word *engaged*. She was trying so hard not to lose her temper, but it wouldn't have mattered anyway. Her mother was adept at handling people. She steered you where she wanted you to go, and she didn't bat an eye. By the time Ellen Fairhope was done, Everly would end up thanking her profusely for the honor.

Her insides knotted tighter. No. No damn way was she saying thank you for this stunt. She'd gone out with Stuart because he'd asked, and she'd thought, why not? She'd needed to get back out there after breaking it off with Gem. Her mother had certainly approved, despite their thirteen year age difference. Now they were supposedly engaged? She felt like she'd been blindsided.

"Stuart is key to getting my legislative agenda through the House. He's from Virginia old money, and his connections are impeccable. He knows everyone in this town, and he can persuade Democrats and Republicans alike to support me. He's a key player, darling, and a perfect partner for your ambitions."

Everly didn't *have* ambitions. Not like her mother did, but that didn't stop Ellen Fairhope from orchestrating Everly's life the way she saw fit. Everly felt as if a noose were tightening around her neck. She liked

Stuart well enough, but that didn't mean she wanted to marry him.

"Okay, but what does any of that have to do with *my* future?"

Her mother looked exasperated, as she so often did when faced with Everly's questions. "Stuart is the perfect husband for your *political* future, my dear. He's only forty, plenty of life left for marriage and family, and you have to admit he's handsome. He'll be a good partner."

Everly wanted to scream that there was no way her mother could know that. But she didn't. Stuart was definitely handsome, though. His dirty blond hair didn't sport even a hint of gray, his smile was glaringly white, his manners were impeccable, and his suits were bespoke. He was a perfect gentleman, and most women sighed when he entered a room. Being seen on his arm in Washington circles had often been gratifying, especially for someone like her. She didn't have curves, and she didn't stand out. She was smart, though, which she'd always told herself was more important than pretty.

Still, no matter how handsome he was, Stuart wasn't the man she really wanted. "Stuart is attractive, but what has that got to do with anything?"

"Nothing. But it could always be worse," her mother said matter-of-factly. "Take this gift and run with it, Everly. Stuart is a good man."

"Did he know about this announcement before it

happened? Or is he going to be calling me and wanting an explanation?"

"My dear, you underestimate me."

And that was all the answer she needed. "What if I send a correction to the press?"

Her heart hammered. All she'd ever wanted was to make her mother proud, but this was crazy town even for her.

"You can do that, of course. But why don't you keep going out with him and see if you don't change your mind when you realize how perfect he is for you. I only want what's best for you, Everly."

"What about love?" she asked, her voice smaller than she would have liked.

She pictured Gem—Jackson Stone, known as Jax, Gem to his teammates and close friends—the man who'd saved her life in Qu'rim. The man she missed with all her heart. She'd had to let him go. It had been the *right* thing to do, before he got tangled up in things he couldn't control. If she hadn't stopped seeing him, her mother would have had him posted halfway around the world, doing something he didn't want to do. Separated from his team, the men he considered brothers. She wouldn't be the cause of that.

She'd told him goodbye and she hadn't looked back. She'd thought he might call her, try again, but she'd done such a perfect job sending him away that he never had. Which was good because she might have had a weak moment and told him her fears. She had a feeling that telling Gem her mother was a control freak and a snob who would never think he was good enough for her would have had the opposite effect of making him understand why she couldn't risk seeing him anymore.

Gem was a fighter, and he would have wanted to fight. She couldn't let him do that. It would be career suicide. He might be a badass when facing down terrorists, but he wasn't going to win a fight against her mother.

"Honey," her mother was saying. "Love can grow. Your father and I weren't in love at first, but look how that turned out. We built such a powerful dynasty together, and when he died, the people chose *me* to take his seat. And they've kept choosing me, haven't they? Because your father and I were in perfect agreement about what needed doing."

Everly's eyes stung. Her dad had been nothing like her mother was now. Everett Fairhope had possessed a heart. A heart that had stopped beating way too soon when his ALS killed him. If not for Everly's memories of that moment when he'd died and the way her mother screamed like her heart was dying too, Everly might think her mother incapable of emotion.

It wasn't true, though. Her parents had been devoted to each other. She was only twelve when her dad passed, but she remembered with blinding clarity that it was the moment her mother began turning herself into the emotionless being she was today. She'd had fifteen years to smother her feelings, and she'd done a fine job of it.

Her mother must have sensed the turmoil inside Everly because she rose gracefully and walked over to where Everly stood. Then she took Everly's cold hands in hers. "Give him a chance, honey. If it doesn't work out or you don't feel he's the right man for you, we'll find someone else."

We.

Everly swallowed as she looked at their joined hands. Her mother's were elegant, with long fingers and trim nails. Everly's hands were dry from the cold weather. She badly needed a manicure. She always felt like an ugly duckling inside a swan's nest. A real duckling, not a baby swan.

"Okay, Mother," she said, her throat tight.

Ellen Fairhope squeezed her hands and smiled before turning away and going over to her desk to put papers in her briefcase. "That's a good girl, Everly. I can always count on you to make me proud. Walk me out? I need to meet Bob in the Members' Dining Room."

It wasn't until Everly was alone again that she realized she'd never asked her mother what Stuart was getting out of the deal. She'd ask him herself. She took her phone out and scrolled through her contacts. Gem's number stared back at her, along with a photo she'd taken of him the day they'd gone sailing on the Chesapeake.

Stuart was handsome in a debonair way, but Gem was startlingly hot, with muscles that rippled in the sun and abs that could make a woman senseless. His mouth was open in a wide grin that lit up his entire face. He'd had his cap on backward and a twinkle in his eye. She'd asked what he was thinking about after she snapped the photo.

"You," he'd said.

Everly's eyes stung and her throat dried up. Anger swirled hot, followed by despair. She wanted to call him. Just to hear his voice. To tell him she was sorry, yet again, for letting things go too far. For wanting what she could never have. She should have walked away in Qu'rim, not given him her card. Not that she'd really believed he would call her. Even with sweat rolling down his face, greasepaint under his eyes, and his hair soaked and flat to his head after he'd ripped his helmet off, he was the best-looking man she'd ever seen. Why he'd been interested still puzzled her, but it was the best three months she'd had with anyone.

She tucked the phone away and swallowed her tears. She was in no mood to talk to Stuart, and Gem probably hated her. She told herself that was a good thing. It was safer for him.

"Everly?"

She spun, resisting the urge to swipe at her eyes. "Oh, hi, Wendy. What can I help you with?"

Wendy looked pale, her blue eyes wide. "We got another one."

Ice formed in Everly's gut. "What's this one say?"

Wendy turned her phone, the photo of the note clear. *You're running out of time, Ellen. The world will know what you've done. Their blood is on your hands, and you will pay for your crimes. I am coming for you.*

"Did you call the FBI?"

"They're on the way. Michael bagged it when we realized what it was. We were going through the mail, and it was just there." Wendy shivered. "They're coming more frequently."

"That's a good thing," Everly said, not certain she believed it. "This person might make a mistake if he or she keeps sending anonymous notes to the Capitol."

They hadn't made a mistake yet, though. The notes came in envelopes, printed on cardstock like an invitation, and always said that her mother would pay. They were postmarked from various places, sometimes within the city, sometimes the suburbs, and other times from out of state. Everly had asked her mother about it, but she'd waved it off.

"If I got upset over every crackpot who sent anonymous emails and letters, I'd never get anything done, would I?"

It was true that members of Congress got a lot of

messages, some of them not so nice, but Everly wished her mother would take these more seriously than she did. She still insisted on appearances and meetings, and though she took a security detail with her, Everly couldn't help but think how it'd only been Gem's shooting that had saved them in Qu'rim. Logically, she knew it was more. It was the team. But that moment when the convoy was attacked and the car she was riding in was failing, she'd thought it was over. Until Gem shot out the motors of the pursuing trucks.

Everly's fingers itched to call him. To get his team to come help her find this person and stop them before they could harm anyone. It wasn't an option, though. It would never be an option again.

"You go back to the office and wait for the FBI," she said softly, patting Wendy's arm. "I'll go tell the congresswoman her stalker is still at it. If we're lucky, they'll find him this time."

Chapter Two

GEM DIDN'T WANT TO GO HOME. HE MAY NOT HAVE ever gotten Everly Fairhope naked, but they'd done plenty of heavy petting on his couch and he didn't want the reminder of sitting there with Everly draped across his lap, his hand up her shirt, his cock as hard as stone beneath her sweet little ass. He'd wanted, with every fiber of his being, to get lost inside her body, but he hadn't wanted to push. He'd been determined *not* to push.

Hell, if he could withstand the deprivation and hardship a Special Operator often did on a mission, he could damned sure endure a slow buildup to what he'd been certain would have been some next-level sex. That's what he told himself every time they started a make-out session. And every time it ended, he adjusted his dick in his pants and walked her to her car, his balls aching while he told himself it would happen when the time was right.

Of course he finished the job when he got back inside, coming hard and groaning as he thought of Everly's mouth beneath his, her tits in his hands, his cock stroking deep inside her.

He shook the memories from his head, slid the key in the ignition, and headed over to Buddy's Bar & Grill to join Muffin and Zany for wings, beer, and pool. They were the only three left on the team who weren't in relationships. The rest of the guys had gone home to their women since it was almost Christmas and there were couple and family things needing doing. As much as Gem told himself he didn't envy them one bit, he did. Deep down, he did.

By the time the evening wound to a close, he'd somewhat pushed away the thought of Everly being engaged to the mysterious Stu. It cropped up every once in a while, but not constantly like it had all day. He thought about texting her. About sending his congrats, but then he decided fuck that shit. Last thing he wanted was for Everly to know he thought about her *at all.*

She'd been the one who'd broken up with him. Why should he give her any indication he even remembered her name?

Gem drove the twenty minutes back to his apartment complex, parked in his spot, and stared at the building for a few moments. Some of his neighbors had strung lights on their balconies, and he could see Christmas trees in windows.

For the longest time, he hadn't cared where he lived so long as it met his requirements and was in a decent area. But after all the weekends spent at teammates' houses with backyards, barbecue grills, and signs of domesticity, he'd started to hate coming home to an apartment complex where all the buildings looked alike and there was no yard to chill in with his friends or a date.

Maybe he should have put up a tree, but what would be the point? He was going to Saint and Brooke's place, along with several of his teammates and their spouses, for Christmas dinner since he wasn't going to his parents' this year. He'd enjoy his friends' hospitality and decor then go home and not have to take anything down and put it away.

He turned off the car, grabbed his duffel, and headed for the stairwell leading up to his apartment. Top floor because he didn't want to make it easy for anyone to get in, and he wasn't worried about getting out if he needed to. Dropping over a balcony four floors high was nothing for a guy like him.

The stairwell and landings were open, which meant nobody could hide in them. He didn't sense the presence of another person until he hit the third-floor landing. It didn't stop him though. Could be his neighbor from the apartment across the stairwell heading out. Just in case, because he was who he was, he put his hand over the KA-BAR knife at his waist.

Wasn't until he was halfway up the last set of stairs that Gem saw the person waiting at the top of the landing. Blond hair gleamed in the florescent light, and her breath frosted in the air. She had on her glasses tonight which meant her eyes were tired and she was giving them a rest from contacts. She wore a cream-colored coat that went to her bare ankles, high heels, a cream scarf, and black gloves that could only be the finest leather. Calfskin, or ostrich probably. Her mother sent her to a personal shopper who picked her clothes for her. Had to keep up the Fairhope image, after all.

Gem didn't like the way his heart leapt at the sight of her. He scowled hard and hoped his face conveyed his displeasure. Everly's lips disappeared as she rolled them inward. A sign of discomfort. He'd seen it often enough when she'd been around her mother on the plane home from Qu'rim. And whenever she spoke about something that upset her when they'd still been seeing each other.

Didn't melt his resolve, though. He took the rest of the stairs up and stopped a couple feet away. He was wearing his ACUs and he wanted to get inside, shuck them off, put on some sweats, and collapse in his recliner for the rest of the evening. He had some TV watching to do and the next couple of weeks off, provided the world didn't go crazy.

"I hear congratulations are in order," he said, and then wanted to bite the shit out of his tongue. Why had he let her know he was aware of anything to do with her?

Her head dipped a little. He thought she was embarrassed, or maybe it was shame she felt. Shame that she had the nerve to be here when he got home.

"Thank you."

He could smell the vanilla and brown sugar scent of her perfume. It filled him with longing. "What do you want, Everly?" he practically snarled.

Her head snapped up, her brown eyes searching his face. He got the impression she was drinking him in, but it was probably his own hurt feelings making him think so. Wishing it was true. Fucking women and their games.

"I, um, something's happened."

His skin prickled as every cell in his body snapped to attention. "What?"

Her gaze darted behind him, then over to the door belonging to his neighbor. "Could we, um, go inside? Please?"

The last thing in this world he'd ever thought he'd do again was go inside his apartment with Everly. The woman he'd begun to believe might be the one until she'd dumped him. She didn't even have the decency to call. Just didn't turn up the day they were going to Easy and Jenna's place for a Saturday afternoon barbecue. He'd thought something had happened to her. He'd been ready to jump in his Vette and go searching all the possible routes to his house when his calls went unanswered. He'd left her a message saying as much. He'd just started the engine when she finally called him back. What she'd said next was still seared on his brain.

"We can't see each other anymore, Gem. It's been fun, b-but you aren't the right kind of guy for me. I'm sorry."

"I don't think so," Gem said as ice solidified his heart. "You already said everything, didn't you?"

"I-I was terrible to you, Gem. And I'm sorry. But I need your help now. Please. It's a matter of life or death."

"And I care why?"

Her shoulders slumped a little. Her eyes were bright in the light. Tears, he realized. "Because you're a good man. A man who fights for what's right. I did you wrong, and I'm sorry, but you won't let someone die if you can stop it. I know that about you."

"You know nothing about me, Everly. Go away."

He went to the door and inserted his key, his heart hammering hot beneath the ice. He didn't want to send her away, but he had to. Her mother was a United States Congresswoman. The Fairhopes were rich. They could afford the best security in the world if they needed it.

Everly didn't need his help. She didn't need anything from him at all.

HE HATED HER. That was her first thought. Her second was that Gem was going into his apartment. He planned to close the door and leave her on the landing, freezing her ass off in a cocktail gown and heels.

She couldn't let that happen. Everly didn't think. She launched herself at him as he slipped over the threshold, grabbing onto his thick camouflage coat. He reacted instinctively, as she knew he would, jerking her off her feet and spinning her against the wall, his hand at her throat, holding her in place. She went limp, her toes scraping the floor as she stared up at him helplessly.

He let her go as if touching her burned and took a step back, staring at her with wide, angry eyes. She could almost smell sulfur in the air, but it was probably just gunpowder from the range. "Don't *ever* do that again."

"Please, Gem. If you cared about me, *ever*, even just a little, please listen to me. If you tell me to get lost after you hear what I have to say, I'll go and you won't hear from me again."

He closed his eyes and dragged his palm down over his face, growling as he did so. "Fine. Fucking fine."

He shoved the door until it closed, then turned and stalked away like an angry lion. Everly swallowed.

Being with him again overwhelmed her senses. In this apartment where he'd kissed her so thoroughly, made her so incredibly hot for him, she'd wanted him badly, but he never would take that next step. She'd told him she didn't fall into bed with guys because of her position in her mother's political life, and he'd taken it so literally their physical relationship had progressed at a snail's pace.

A very hot, very sensual snail's pace.

Gem ripped off his jacket and flung it over the back of the couch. Then he turned and glared at her. Everly unbuttoned her coat with shaking fingers and removed it. Then she peeled off her gloves and scarf and laid it all on the chair nearest the door. Her dress had long sleeves and the skirt was tea-length, but it didn't protect her from the chill in the air. She wasn't sure if it was the frosty reception, or the fact she'd been waiting outside for nearly an hour.

Probably both.

"Who's dying and why are you here, princess? Your mother has more money than God. She can hire security or doctors, whichever one you need. Which means you don't need me. Or is it your boyfriend—Stuart, right? Is he in trouble? You want me to save him for you?"

Everly twisted her fingers together. She should have known he would be angry. But she was here now and she couldn't go back. She didn't want to talk about Stuart because she didn't know what to say. They were engaged, even if it wasn't official yet.

She'd spoken to him briefly since he'd been in meetings all day, but his position was that he wanted to marry her and he wasn't unhappy about the newspaper article. No, he hadn't expected it, but they could make it work. Have a long engagement. She'd agreed because she didn't know what else to do. There was time to figure that out. Or maybe she'd just get married and make her mother happy since being with Gem wasn't an option.

"No, it's not Stuart. It's Mother. You're right that she's rich and can hire security, but she won't. She isn't taking it seriously."

"If the threat is real, your mother is an idiot."

"She has a bodyguard and she thinks that's enough. The FBI hasn't found anything yet, and she's not entitled to Secret Service protection as a member of Congress. Only if she was the Speaker of the House or one of the party leaders or whips. Which she's not."

"Okay. And?"

"She's been getting threats." Everly fished her phone from her coat pocket and found the photos of the notes. She turned them to Gem. "Someone keeps sending these notes, saying time is running out and she's going to pay for her crimes. It started two months ago."

He closed the distance and took her phone,

scrolling through the photos. Then he handed it back with a shrug. "There's nothing specific, Everly. It looks like the usual stuff celebrities and elected officials get. Someone sees her on the news, takes issue with something she says or does, and fixates on her. They start sending notes. If the FBI can't find this person, what makes you think I can?" He shook his head. "There's nothing I can do."

"You can, Gem. I watched you shoot two trucks that were loaded with men who were coming for us in the desert. You stopped them, and you got us to safety."

"My team did that. It's not a one-man show."

"I know that. But I trust you. You won't brush this off or tell me it's not real. It *is* real, and you know people who can help you find the truth." She swallowed. "There's other stuff, too."

"Like what?"

"I think I'm being followed. Not here," she said in a rush when his brows drew down in an angry slash. "I was very careful. I didn't come straight here. I took my time, doubled back on myself, and made sure no one was following me before I came this way. I parked two blocks away and climbed over a fence to get into the complex."

If anything, he looked angrier. "You left your car and came on foot? Wearing white like a fucking beacon of light? And a party dress? Are you fucking crazy?"

Everly swallowed. *Damn it.* "I, um, I didn't think about the coat."

Gem blew out a breath and went over to the fridge. He took out a beer and popped the top. Then he flopped onto a chair, legs sprawled wide as he studied her. "Well?" he asked when she didn't say anything else.

"I keep seeing a black SUV. A Cadillac Escalade with tinted windows. When I go home, I see it in the rearview. And when I go to work, I see it again."

"Everly, there are a lot of fucking black Escalades with tinted windows. Someone who lives on your street could drive one. How do you know they don't?"

"I, um, don't. But I see it everywhere, Gem. There's a dent on the driver's side door. That's how I know it's the same one. I never manage to take down the plate, though. All I know is they have Virginia plates, and the first letter is a V. I think there's a three in there too."

He looked a little more interested. "Okay. Where else have you seen it?"

"I've seen it outside the House Office Building when I'm leaving work at night. At the grocery store just yesterday when I stopped to get a few things."

"How long have you been seeing it?"

"I noticed it about three weeks ago. I told myself it was a coincidence, but once I drove over to Arlington just to see—and they followed me there, too."

It had creeped her out more than she cared to admit. Being the daughter of Ellen Fairhope, being on her mother's staff and involved in the political arena, she was accustomed to scrutiny. Reporters sometimes followed her, looking for a story, but they didn't wait long to announce themselves and start asking questions. This was different.

"I don't know what you want me to do about it. I'm not a detective. I'm a soldier."

"I don't want a detective. I want someone who's going to look out for my mother. For me. Someone who knows what it looks like when something bad's about to happen."

Gem took a pull of his beer. "Everly, I'm sorry. I can't help you. You need to convince your mother to tighten her security—and you need a bodyguard, too, if someone's really following you. Maybe ask your fiancé to help out."

Everly's stomach did a slow dive to the floor. She'd known this was a long shot. Hell, she'd known she had nothing to go on other than a healthy dose of fear. And that wasn't enough for a man like Gem. Threatening notes the FBI was already investigating and a Cadillac Escalade that seemed to be everywhere wasn't enough to worry anyone other than her.

Everly swore to herself and picked up her coat. Her vision blurred. *Idiot.* She'd come because she wanted to see him. She'd talked herself into it, even when she knew he wasn't going to be persuaded, that her 'evidence' wasn't convincing. And what did she expect him to do, anyway? Strap on his weapons and act as her bodyguard for a few days? Talk to her mother and convince her to beef up her own security?

"Thanks," she said, shrugging into her coat and dragging on her gloves. "I'm sorry I took up your time. I'm going to be late anyway, so I won't keep you any longer."

She turned blindly to the door, needing to escape before she said anything stupid or broke down in front of him. She couldn't afford to break down when she needed to go to yet another party and smile for her mother's donors.

A hand closed around her arm and she stilled in the act of opening the door, her body trembling with his touch. She'd missed it so much.

"I can't let you walk two blocks in the dark alone in that outfit. I'll drive you to your car."

"I'd rather walk. And I'll be okay."

"Sorry, no can do, princess. I'm taking you to your car and watching you get in."

"You aren't going to take no for an answer, are you?"

"Nope." He grabbed his jacket and keys and pulled the door open. "I may not like you much, honey, but I'm still a gentleman. Here, don't forget your scarf. Wouldn't want you to have to come back."

He dangled it in his fingers and Everly snatched it, cheeks flaming. He no doubt thought she'd done it on purpose so she'd have an excuse to return. She wrapped it around her neck and glared. "Thank you. It was a present from Stuart. I'd hate to lose it."

His eyes hardened to chips of ice and she spun away before he could see she was lying about the scarf. She was a terrible liar, which was yet another reason she'd never make a good politician. They all lied, even when they were trying to do good. It was how things got done in this city.

She stepped onto the landing, and Gem locked the door before leading the way down the stairs. His strides were naturally long but he shortened them to match hers. She'd always appreciated it when they were going somewhere together.

They walked to his car in silence. The locks chirped and he opened the passenger door for her, like always. Everly brushed past him and maneuvered her way into the sports car. He got in and the engine purred to life, rumbling like a kitten.

"Which way?" he asked.

She pointed. "I came over the fence there. I didn't notice the street name." The fence was a white split rail, decorative not security. It was more appropriate to say she'd come through the fence since she'd bent down and slipped between the top and middle poles.

Gem backed out of the space and drove to the main road. He had to take a series of rights before he navigated around to the adjoining road where she'd left her BMW. It was there, the only vehicle in a parking lot that belonged to a real estate office. Gem pulled into a space facing her car. Everly dropped her chin and stared at her clasped hands. Her heart thudded. Disappointment soured her stomach.

"I'm sorry, Everly," he said, the first hint of softness she'd heard from him.

Somehow, that made it even harder. "Me too," she whispered past the lump in her throat.

He got out of the car and came around to open the door for her. The gesture made regret flare bright. Still, she swung her legs around and pushed up from the low seat of the sports car without taking the hand he offered. The top of her head came to his chin, and she tilted her head back to gaze up at him.

"I want you to be happy, Gem. So much."

His gaze shuttered. "I am happy, Everly. I've got the best job in the world, the best team, and what I do matters. You didn't break my heart."

Was it wrong to be disappointed about that? Of course it was, but she couldn't take it back. She'd wanted to mean something to him.

"Good," she lied. "I'm glad. Well, best be going."

He pulled open the driver's door for her. She hesitated, wanting to say something more, but nothing would come.

Until a red dot appeared on his jacket and her insides turned to ice. "Get down!" she screamed.

A moment later glass exploded, raining down like ash.

Chapter Three

GEM SAW THE RED DOT REFLECTED IN EVERLY'S glasses an instant before she screamed. He dropped, taking her with him, and glass exploded as a bullet impacted her driver's side window. Her fucking coat was like a beacon in the night and he wrapped himself around her as best he could, crab-walking them toward his car. He had to get her inside, and then he had to get them the fuck out of there.

He got her to the passenger side of his car, pulled the door open a few inches, and urged her inside.

"Stay down," he growled. "Your coat's a dead giveaway to your position."

She did as he said, lying half on the floor and keeping her head tucked. He went around the back of the vehicle, slid into the driver's seat, and put the car in reverse. Everly lay with her eyes squeezed tightly shut. She'd lost the glasses, or maybe she'd had the presence of mind to take them off and put them in her pocket. He doubted it though.

Gem floored the Vette then spun the wheel and hammered the clutch while shifting into drive. The tires smoked only a little before they were rocketing out of the parking lot and onto the road. He sat up straighter, gazing behind them, anger and self-recrimination throbbing behind his eyelids. He should have believed her.

No, he should have *done something*. Because he believed she'd seen an Escalade, but he hadn't thought that meant danger. Every suspicious car wasn't dangerous.

Except this was Everly Fairhope, Ellen Fairhope's daughter, and things weren't normal around them. Someone had leaked Ellen's itinerary in the desert, and armed rebels had nearly intercepted their convoy. Gem didn't know whose ass got reamed over that, or what steps for their safety had been taken once the congresswoman and her staff returned home, but he'd assumed it'd been handled. Maybe it hadn't. Maybe the threatening notes were related to the attack. Or maybe it was completely separate since they'd only started a couple of months ago.

Fuck.

"Are we being followed?" Everly asked.

"I don't think so. Can't be sure yet."

She eased up into the seat a bit more and snapped

her seatbelt into place. "When I saw that red dot on your chest…"

Her voice quavered. He reached over and squeezed her cold hand. "I'm fine. You warned me in time."

She squeezed back. "I'm so sorry I got you into this. I shouldn't have come."

"You did, though."

"I changed at the office. If I'd gone home instead of here—" The words choked off as she realized what would have happened if she'd been alone.

"It's okay, Everly. It didn't happen that way. You're alive and so am I."

"Oh God—what about my mother? What if someone attacked her, too? We were supposed to go to a party tonight. She might already be there."

Gem called up his phone and told it to dial his team leader. Cade "Saint" Rodgers answered on the second ring. "What's up, Gemstone?"

"Sorry to bother you, Saint. Can you find out if Ellen Fairhope is secure? She's supposed to be at a party—"

He shot a glance at her. "At the Ritz-Carlton," she whispered.

"At the Ritz-Carlton," he repeated.

"Yeah, I can do that. What's happening?"

"Everly came to see me. She has some fears for her mother's safety." He glanced at her pale face and wide eyes staring back at him. "Someone took a shot at me when I drove her back to where she'd left her car."

"Jesus," Saint said. "Yeah, give me a few minutes and I'll get back to you. Is Everly with you now?"

"She's here. We're both secure."

"Bring her here. I'll get answers for you."

Everly piped up. "I can't put you and Brooke in danger. But thank you. So much."

"It's good to hear your voice, Everly."

"You too," she said softly.

"Yeah, well get your ass over here. Gem knows how to get here without being followed, and we know how to keep you safe until we figure this out. Brooke would love to see you."

Everly glanced at Gem. He shrugged. "Better listen to the man, Everly."

"Okay. But not for long, Cade. I don't want to cause trouble."

Saint said a few more words and they ended the call. Gem flexed his fingers on the wheel as he kept making random turns, working his way over to Saint's place by the most illogical route possible. Whoever had taken the shot hadn't expected him to walk away or they'd have been better prepared to come after him. He wasn't sure if they'd been gunning for him or Everly, if it'd been a random attack or a planned one, but he was treating this like Everly was the target and making plans for how to keep her safe.

By the time they made it to Saint's place, he was

sure they were clear. There were no Escalades following them, no vehicles at all when he turned onto the residential street where Saint and Brooke lived. He drove past the house a couple of times, stopped at the end of the street to watch, then finally pulled into the drive and killed the engine.

The garage door rolled upward and Gem went around to open Everly's door so he could escort her inside. She rushed into the garage in front of him, hurrying over to the interior door that she was familiar with from prior visits. Before she could knock, it opened and Brooke cried out. "Everly! I'm so happy to see you, sweetie!"

Everly was swept into Brooke's arms while her German shepherd sniffed at Everly's coat. Then she was swept inside the house and along to the kitchen where Saint waited at the island, perched on a stool, phone in hand. He tipped his chin to Gem and smiled at Everly. Max panted happily and came over to lick Gem's hand.

"Hey, buddy. How you been?"

"Spoiled," Brooke said. "That's how he's been."

"Yeah, thanks," Cade said to whomever he was talking to. " 'Preciate it, man." He put the phone down. "Your mom is fine. She's at the party and security has been stepped up in light of the attack. She's been made aware, and she knows you're safe."

Everly let out a breath. "No one tried to get to her?"

"Doesn't look like it. This might not have been aimed at you. Could be Gem pissed someone off enough to take a shot at him," Saint teased.

"Never know," Gem said. "I can be annoying."

Everly's shoulders slumped a little, but she smiled. He thought it was probably relief, though exhaustion was another possibility. "You guys are funny, but you don't really believe that."

Saint shook his head. "Nope, just wanted to make you smile. We're going to do all we can to figure this out, Everly."

"Thank you."

Her white coat was dirty from where Gem had dropped her to the ground, and there were leaves and dried grass stuck to it as well. He slipped behind her and quietly removed the coat from her shoulders.

"Let me fix you a drink," Brooke said to Everly, beginning to pour ingredients into a cocktail shaker. "Sit down and keep me company while I work."

Everly complied. Gem walked to the back door, opened it and shook out the coat, brushing off the dirt, then placed it over one of the barstools. He returned and took Everly's scarf and gloves from her. He laid them over the coat, frowning at the scarf she'd said was a present from her fiancé. He took off his own coat and dropped it on top of the scarf.

"Man, you ain't been home?" Saint asked, tipping his chin at the uniform.

"I was home. Went to Buddy's with Zany and

Muffin first, then found Everly waiting for me. Wasn't there long enough to change."

"I see that. Tell me what happened."

He told Saint everything while Everly filled in her own details and showed Saint photos of the messages to her mother.

"Here," Brooke said, handing Everly a glass. "Cranberry martini."

"Thank you." Everly took a big drink and then coughed. "Smooth," she croaked out.

Brooke laughed and sipped her own. "Sorry. I thought you might need a strong one."

"Oh, I definitely do. Just wasn't expecting it. What do you think, Cade? Are the threats related?"

He shared a look with Gem before answering. "Hard to tell. Could be, if someone meant to make your mother pay by harming you."

Gem didn't like the way that made him feel. A crazed stalker going after Everly because they couldn't get to Ellen? He wanted to take her somewhere safe and keep her there until this was over. When he proposed it, however, Everly shook her head like he'd suggested they go skinny dipping in the frigid Chesapeake.

"No way. I have work to do, and I can't just disappear. Congress is in session, and my mother needs me."

Plus she had a fiancé to make plans with. Gem

didn't say those words aloud, but the thought twisted him up inside.

"She's right," Saint said. "So long as she's protected, there's no reason to go into hiding. We won't find who did this if she does."

"Someone took a shot at her," Gem growled. "And nearly hit me."

"I know that," Saint said as calmly as if he were talking to a child.

"I don't like it."

"She'll have protection. And she won't stay in her own house until we get answers."

Everly's head came up. He thought she might argue, but she seemed to think better of it. Instead, she took another swig of her drink. "I want Gem to protect me."

Gem's eyes bugged out. Shit, it's what he wanted too because he didn't trust anyone else, but he also wanted to say *what the fuck, Everly?* She was looking up at him as if she knew his thoughts. She probably did.

"I trust you," she said simply, and he knew the discussion was over. No way was he handing her over to a Secret Service detail or the FBI when she believed in his ability to keep her safe.

"What about your fiancé?" The words snapped out before he could stop them.

Brooke and Saint didn't say anything, and Everly seemed to squirm a little. "He'll be fine with it."

"Really? Your fiancé won't mind that a guy you

dated just a few months ago is the one staying close to you now?"

Her chin came up. There was the Everly who didn't back down from a fight. The one he'd been perversely attracted to in the desert when she'd been busting his balls about the escape plan.

"It's not his call. It's mine."

"Then I guess I'll do it," he grumbled. "I'm off for the next couple weeks." They'd returned from a mission a week ago and weren't due to rotate out again for a while.

"I'll talk to Viper and Ghost," Saint said. "I think they'll agree it's important. You'll need a safe house location to come and go from, though. Your place is compromised, even if they didn't see which apartment she entered. It's too close to where the shooting happened."

"Agreed," Gem said.

"It has to be utterly secret," Everly said. "I can't have the press tracking me down."

"It will be," Gem said. "Hey, what about Mal and Scarlett's apartment over the garage? Far enough from the city. Remote. As good as an official safe house, but with the added benefit of a second HOT operator on the premises for a couple of days. If we haven't caught the asshole who shot at us by then, we can move locations once Mal and Scarlett head to Galveston for the holiday."

Saint nodded. "Good idea. Let's see if Mal's onboard."

Gem knew he would be, but it was only right to ask first. "I'll do it." He took out his phone and called Mal, putting it on speaker so everyone could hear.

"Dude, you were hilarious with that grape jelly all over your head today," Mal greeted. "Too fucking funny."

Everly blinked.

"Yeah, yeah. We even now?"

"You and me, yeah."

Saint frowned, but Gem only grinned. Let his team leader wonder what was coming next and whether or not he'd be the target.

"Hey, got a favor to ask. You can say no. Oh, and you're on speaker. Saint's now worried about what you might do to him, by the way."

Mal snorted. "Reputation intact. Okay. Lay it on me."

Gem didn't leave anything out as he explained the situation. "Figured your place was best for what we need, but if you'd rather not, we'll use another location," he finished.

"Hell yeah, you can stay here. Apartment's clean and ready to go. You remember we're heading to my folks' in Galveston in a couple of days, right? Y'all can stay as long as you need to, though."

"Yeah, I remember. Hopefully we'll have caught

the bastard by then. Appreciate you agreeing so fast, but don't you need to ask Scarlett?"

"Nope. I'm the man of the house."

"Mal." Scarlett's voice chimed in, sounding amused.

"Okay, okay. Truth time," Mal said. "She heard everything and she's been over here nodding like her head's about to fall off."

"Now that part is true," Scarlett said. "Mal might be the man of the house, but all that means is he has a penis. I do enthusiastically approve, though. I like Everly."

Gem glanced at Everly. Her cheeks were red. He didn't know if it was the drink or the conversation. "She's right here, listening in."

"Hey, Everly! We've missed having you at our get-togethers," Scarlett replied.

"I've missed all of you too," Everly said. "Thank you for letting me stay at your place. I understand if you don't want the hassle, though."

"We've got you," Scarlett said. "You do remember what these guys do, right?"

"I do indeed," she said, and Gem knew she was thinking about that crazy car ride in Qu'rim when he'd levered himself out the window and shot at their pursuers.

"Okay, good. Case closed then. You're staying here, and the guys will keep you safe."

"It'll be a little while before we can head that

way," Gem added. "Need to make plans to get some of Everly's stuff, and mine as well."

"Gotcha," Mal said. "See you when you get here."

The call ended and Brooke eyed Everly's glass. "Need another?"

"No, I'm good. Thank you."

"What about food? Did you eat?"

"I had a sleeve of peanut butter crackers at the office."

Gem didn't have to say a word because Brooke did it for him. "Oh, honey. That won't do. Let me get out some pot roast and potatoes and feed you right. I just made it today, and we have plenty of leftovers."

"You don't have—"

"I do, and I will," Brooke said. "You can give me a hand if you like. Let these two discuss logistics."

Gem thought she might argue, but Everly sighed and joined Brooke in the kitchen. Gem followed Saint to the home office.

"You okay?" Saint asked when they were alone.

Gem didn't like the way his shoulders tightened. "Yeah, fine. Why?"

"Oh, I don't know. Maybe because you two broke up and now she's back, engaged, and wants you specifically to be her bodyguard?"

Saint knew Gem had been married before, and that his wife had allegedly left him because she couldn't stand the deployments. It wasn't the only reason. Monica had been the type who thought she deserved luxury. Her boss—now her second husband—was a doctor. Gem was a soldier. He didn't care anymore, but he'd been plenty pissed at the time. Hurt and pissed. She'd thrown his love, or what he'd thought had been love, in his face and made him feel like he wasn't good enough.

"I'm not thrilled about it, but I can do the job. She doesn't trust anyone else." Neither did he. Not now.

"Might be easier to let law enforcement take this one. Hand her over and let it go."

Gem thought about it. It'd be nice not to have to think about Everly, nice not to have to see her and be unable to touch her. Even nicer not to have to imagine her with Stu and falling in love so quickly she got engaged almost immediately after she'd broken up with him. But the idea of abandoning her stuck hard in his gut. "Can't do it. She asked for my help, and I almost failed. I won't fuck it up again."

"Brother, I'm telling you this because you need to hear it, but nobody could blame you for turning her away when she showed up like that. Everly Fairhope has resources. Trying to make her use them so you could protect your feelings wasn't the wrong move. Still isn't if that's what you want."

"It wasn't then, but would be now. I'm in this until we find who took a shot at her." He'd give her back to her fiancé in one healthy piece and feel good about it. Mostly.

"Coming in loud and clear. Just wanted to make sure."

"I'm sure."

"Then let's plan our next move."

EVERLY WAS SLEEPY, her eyes drifting closed from time to time as she huddled in the passenger seat of Gem's car.

It'd been a long day at the office and an even longer day once she'd decided to go see Gem. She hadn't known she'd be shot at and find herself under his protection by the end of it. She wasn't dumb enough to insist everything was normal and she should just go home, but she didn't like that she had to stay in Mal and Scarlett's guest apartment over their garage either. Not because she didn't like them, but because it felt like an imposition for someone they didn't know very well.

After Gem and Saint had left her alone with Brooke, she'd eaten a plateful of yummy pot roast with carrots and potatoes, and even let herself be talked into a slice of homemade pumpkin pie. She was full, and it was pretty much the best meal she'd had in a while.

She'd also spoken with her mother, who'd sounded strained. Everly had asked, again, that she please take the threats seriously. She'd promised she would. Her security had been stepped up, and she also promised to take a bodyguard wherever she went. She'd wanted Everly to stay at her house now that a security detail would be posted outside, but Everly had told her she had her own security. Her mother hadn't liked it, but Everly was still angry enough over Stuart to know she couldn't spend twenty-four hours a day in her mother's home and under her thumb.

Everly glanced over at Gem. Maybe she was being selfish. She should go to her mother's and let Gem off the hook. But whenever she thought about telling him to take her there and go home, live his life and enjoy his two weeks off, her throat closed up.

"You warm enough?" Gem asked, startling her out of her thoughts.

"Yes, fine. Thanks."

He'd blasted the heat on her since they'd gotten back into the car. She figured he must be hot as hell, but he didn't complain or turn the heat down. He'd taken his coat off before he got in, though. She was wearing hers, plus her scarf. Her gloves were in her pockets. Her bare ankles and her feet in her fashionable heels were a little chilled, but the rest of her was warm

She didn't have any clothes other than the cocktail dress at the moment, but Ryder and Zane were going to check her place out and grab some things, including her spare glasses since she'd lost hers during the attack. Assuming her home wasn't trashed and they didn't have to call the police. It wouldn't surprise her if someone had broken in. She still wasn't sure why they'd targeted her when all the letters had been aimed at her mother, but it must have made sense to someone.

She still had her purse, because it was a small evening bag with a strap that she'd worn crossbody beneath her coat. Her computer bag with all her papers and files were in her car. She doubted it would still be there, but the guys were planning to check that out, too, when they went to get Gem's clothes.

Her phone was a weight in her coat pocket. Gem had told her to use it sparingly. Cade and Gem had checked it for malware and found nothing, but they still wanted her to be cautious. She knew she could be tracked using her phone, but that would take someone with the kind of access Gem and his team had, not someone who'd sent crank messages to her mother. She resisted the urge to fish it out of her pocket and check email. There was always email, always something needing handled, and she couldn't face it right now.

"Tell me about this J. Stuart Morrison guy," Gem said. "He must be pretty spectacular if you got engaged so fast."

Her stomach tightened. She *so* didn't want to go there with him. Not tonight. Not ever. She worked to keep her voice even. "He's an attorney. He does a bit of work on the Hill, which is how we met. There's not really much to tell."

"I don't know. Must be more to it than that. It's a whirlwind romance, right? Unless you were seeing him on the side when we were dating. Or maybe I was the side piece. Can't quite figure that one out, if I'm honest."

Chapter Four

EVERLY WAS HORRIFIED. AND SHOCKED. THE IDEA OF her dating two men at once was laughable. "I wouldn't do that. I don't have time to do that, even if I wanted to! My job keeps me very busy."

"You say that like it's obvious, but it's not obvious to me. We dated for three months, never got past third base, and then you broke up with me on the phone. Two months later, your engagement's in the papers. You can understand why I wonder."

Everly's heart throbbed. "Yes, but that doesn't give you the right to accuse me of being dishonest. I knew Stuart because of the job, but I never went out with him until after we broke up. I'm offended you would think so."

He shrugged. "Wouldn't be the first time a woman I thought was into me was secretly seeing someone else."

She knew about his ex-wife because he'd told her, and it hurt to think he believed she was the same kind of person. But he clearly did.

"I am *not* that dishonest. We weren't right for each other, that's all."

"So I wasn't the *right kind* of guy, but I'm guessing he is?"

Everly's stomach twisted. She hated the anger in his voice, but she understood it. She'd chosen deliberately harsh words to push him away. She'd told herself she was protecting him, but maybe she'd gone too far. Maybe a simple *this isn't working for me* would have sufficed.

"Stuart and I have a lot in common. We're both attorneys and we both work on the Hill. And yes, it was a whirlwind once he asked me out. He swept me off my feet."

She made a fist in her lap, clenching and unclenching. She hated lying. It made her feel sick inside, especially when it was about something so personal. She couldn't deny she still had feelings for him. Which was why she'd gone to see him, and why she'd blurted she wanted him for her bodyguard. It would have been so much better if she'd found someone else.

And yet she still couldn't tell him to take her to her mother's house and put an end to this. She loved to torture herself it seemed.

"Stu has money, I take it?"

"I'm sure he does," she snapped, suddenly angry at the insinuation. "But I have my own job, and I do fine. I don't need his money and he doesn't need mine."

"How nice for you both."

"I guess it is."

They lapsed into silence. She was beginning to think the conversation was over, but then he spoke again.

"So how did Stu propose? Must have been a spur of the moment thing."

Her insides clenched. "Why do you say that?"

"No ring. Had to be impulsive, right?"

Everly wanted to escape the conversation, but it was impossible. She didn't seem to have the skill. "I'm not sharing that with you. It's personal."

Gem nodded. "Gotcha. Don't want to tell me how the most romantic moment of your life happened. Seems reasonable."

"Not everybody wants to share their private moments with the world. He asked, I said yes. We're going to pick out a ring later. *Together.* Satisfied?"

"Hey, I'm just making conversation. You're the one getting irritated."

"Because this feels like an interrogation instead of a conversation."

"Okay. Then I'm glad you're happy. And that your mother approves. She does approve, right?"

"Yes. She does. Can we talk about something else now?"

"What do you want to talk about?"

"Tell me about you. Seeing anyone?"

Great. Just great. Ask him the most obviously jealous question she could possibly ask.

He shook his head. "Nope."

Not the answer she'd expected. She'd imagined Gem going out with other women often. It always hurt, but she'd told herself it was her own fault. If she'd never given him her card, none of this would have happened. Her heart would still be intact, not fractured beyond repair.

"I'm sure the right woman will come along."

"Maybe. Then again, I don't have the best track record in that department."

His wife had cheated on him with her boss and then married him. Everly could never wrap her head around it, but sometimes relationships went sour. It didn't have to make sense.

She was still searching for something to say when Gem slowed the car. When he turned down a long drive, she realized they'd made it out to Mal's place. As they got nearer to the house, she could see Mal and Scarlett waiting on the porch, even though it was cold out.

Everly exited the car and stepped up on the front porch. Scarlett gave her a welcoming hug. "It's so nice to see you again, Everly."

Warmth glowed in her veins. She liked all the women who were engaged or married to Gem's teammates. They'd always made her feel like she belonged. It wasn't a feeling she'd had a lot of and she missed it. She'd worried when she first met them that her mother's shadow would stand over her and none of them would forget who she was or the fact she didn't belong in their world, but nothing had been further from the truth. They'd welcomed her, embraced her, and made her feel like she fit.

And so far they'd welcomed her back tonight like she'd never left, which made her miss them even more. She wished she hadn't left, except she'd had to do it to protect Gem. If she'd lost him because her mother intervened and caused him to be sent away to another part of the world, then she'd have lost them all anyway. And they'd have lost a vital part of their team with Gem gone.

"Thank you. It's nice to see you too."

"Come on and get inside where it's not cold," Mal said.

Everly followed them in, Gem bringing up the rear. "Thanks for letting us stay, brother," Gem said when they were inside the kitchen.

"You're welcome anytime. Here," Mal said, handing over the key to the apartment. "It's ready for you. There's a camp cot up there since there's only one bed, but you should have enough room. We'd offer you a room in the house, but I'm afraid we've been renovating and the upstairs is out of commission other than the master."

Gem folded his fingers over the key. "This is perfect. Thanks."

"Did y'all eat?" Scarlett asked. "We have some chicken and dumplings left over. Or I can order a pizza."

"Brooke fed me," Everly said. "But thank you."

"I was at Buddy's with Zany and Muffin before this happened. Ate wings and pizza, so I'm good."

"We put a new fridge in the apartment. It's stocked with water, beer, and some soda. There's also some basics like cheese and lunchmeat. I sometimes work on crafts up there," Scarlett explained. "Until we get my crafting room finished in the house. But I cleaned everything up so there'll be nothing in your way. Oh, and I keep some comfy clothes in the bathroom dresser, so help yourself to a change of clothes or a T-shirt to sleep in until your stuff gets here."

They chatted a little more, but when Everly yawned, Gem extracted them from the conversation. They exited the house from the back door and headed across the yard to the stairs leading up to the second-floor apartment over the garage. Everly climbed behind Gem, feeling the weariness of the day catching up to her with every step. She'd been at the office at six that morning because her mother had important meetings, and then she'd worked through lunch when Wendy showed her the latest note from the stalker. The afternoon had been intense, trying to talk her mother into postponing events and hiring more security, until she'd been left with a compelling feeling she needed to go to Gem before the day was over.

And now here they were. Not what she'd expected when she'd left her townhouse this morning. She waited while Gem unlocked the door, then followed him inside. The apartment was a single vaulted room with a kitchenette, and a bathroom that ran along one side of the building with a toilet, tub, and shower. The bed was a giant couch that Scarlett had bought second-hand, and there was a chair and coffee table too. It was cozy. Probably too cozy when she had to share it with Gem.

He shrugged out of his coat and hung it on one of the hooks beside the door. Everly did the same. "You can go to bed if you like," he told her. "I'll set up the cot and watch something on my phone until I hear from Muffin or Zany."

"I'm tired," she said. "But I'm too keyed up to sleep yet, if that makes sense. I'm going to go through email."

"Suit yourself." He walked over to where the cot lay against the wall, then moved the coffee table and unfolded it.

Everly shivered. There would only be about a foot

between them, but it was enough. Or so she hoped. She left him and went into the bathroom, intending to have a few moments to herself. And maybe find some socks since her feet were cold and she wanted to take her heels off.

She rummaged in the small dresser that lay against one wall and came out with a baggy sweatshirt and a pair of yoga pants and socks. And then, because she was cold and decided she needed it, she took a hot shower before dressing in Scarlett's clothes. When she was done, she felt marginally more relaxed than she had when she went in.

When she emerged from the bathroom, Gem was sitting on the cot, back against the wall, clad in his camouflage pants and a black T-shirt that stretched across firm muscles, legs crossed at the ankles. He looked up and their eyes met. She couldn't tell what was in his gaze before he looked down again. She realized that he'd shaken out the blanket and laid the pillows down on the couch for her, and she climbed in with a lump in her throat at his thoughtfulness.

"Thank you," she said.

He didn't look up. "You're welcome. Got a text from Zany. They were able to pick up some clothes and your spare glasses for you. Your home hasn't been broken into, but it's likely being watched. The police responded to the shooting, and they retrieved your computer bag from the car. You can get it back tomorrow."

Everly blew out a breath. "Thanks. I really thought it'd be gone."

"I don't think that was the point of the shooting."

"I don't either, but I thought they'd have looked in the car after we left."

"Nah. They were either attempting to follow us or they ran. The computer wasn't the objective."

"What do you think was then?"

"Someone either wanted to scare you and send a message, or they're a lousy fucking shot."

Everly shivered. "Thank God."

His head lifted, his eyes piercing into hers. "Got any enemies I should know about?"

"I don't think so."

"Maybe Stu has an ex who's pissed at the speed of your engagement."

Everly's heart thumped. "Even if he does, that's a pretty extreme reaction, isn't it? Killing me won't get him back. It'd land her in prison."

"Some people are unbalanced, Everly. It's a legit line of inquiry, though I admit it's unlikely. More likely, someone is pissed at your mother and targeted you as a means of intimidation or revenge."

"Which brings it back to the letters. Someone is counting down to the moment they act. Maybe tonight was the first strike."

He was frowning. "Hurting you would be one way to make her pay for these alleged crimes. Has she said anything about the letters? Speculated on what it's about?"

Everly shook her head. "She's in her fourth term. The number of people she's upset over the years has to be in the thousands, don't you think? Someone always loses when bills come to the table. Someone's district doesn't get the project, someone else's does. People are displaced because the jobs don't come, and they blame their representatives. Or maybe the hospital doesn't get built or the infrastructure doesn't get repaired before something fails. There are a *lot* of people with potential grudges. I doubt she has any idea, plus this person hasn't been specific. In a way, I don't blame her for forging ahead with her plans. If she let every accusing letter stop her, she'd never get anything done."

"And yet you were worried enough to come to me for help."

"This one feels different. More determined. More specific. He or she doesn't say what the issue is, but they keep talking about time running out. Other people are angry and make vague threats about karma, but they don't countdown to a shadowy date for retribution. I guess that's why it bothers me."

"It's good to listen to your instincts."

"Thank you." She hesitated. "You were mad at me for coming to see you. I'm sorry I dragged you into this, but you were the only person I could think of who would listen to me."

"Yeah, I was mad. I'm still not thrilled about it, but I'm glad you trusted me. And I'm sorry I didn't take you more seriously when you told me about the Escalade. I wish you'd gotten the plate. That would make everything easier."

"I know, and I'm sorry. I tried, but there was always a reason it was obscured." Everly nervously tucked a lock of hair behind her ear. "I don't blame you for not taking me seriously. We haven't spoken in a couple of months, and then I show up out of the blue, talking about things that have nothing to do with you. I could understand why you'd want me gone as fast as possible. I'm really sorry if I hurt your feelings, Gem. When we broke up, I mean."

His eyes flashed. "My feelings weren't hurt. I was fucking furious. You couldn't figure out in the three months we dated that I wasn't right for you? Or did you just enjoy slumming with me and my friends, a bunch of soldiers and their women who could never claim to have the kind of life you lead? Was it fun to drop into our lives and pretend to be one of us?"

Shock hit her like a physical blow. "Slumming? Are you really accusing me of pretending to be one of you for kicks?" Tears rose hot in her throat. Angry tears, she told herself, but they weren't really. The pit of despair and pain in her belly told the truth. "I would *never* do that. I loved being with you—being with *all* of you. But it wasn't going anywhere. It couldn't."

He studied her face, the way her chest heaved, as if he could divine her secrets. Maybe he could. When he opened his mouth, she feared he had. "Because of your mother."

"She doesn't run my life," Everly snapped back. "She's overbearing and controlling, but I still make my own decisions."

It didn't feel as true as she wanted to believe, and that bothered her more than she could say. But to outright admit her mother made decisions for her? That made her sound ridiculous. Maybe she was. Hell, she was the one engaged to a man she didn't love because her mother had planted the story in the media and Everly hadn't been brave enough to put her foot down and say it wasn't true.

"Doesn't she? She steers you where she wants you to go. I can't figure out why you let her. You're a grown woman with a life of your own. Don't you think it's time you told her that?"

"It's not that easy. It's been just the two of us since my dad died."

"It is that easy. Running your own life doesn't mean you aren't still her daughter. Except I don't think it's what *you* want. She wants you to run for office one day, to take her place like it's a fucking dynasty the Fairhopes are entitled to, and you jump to her tune because you want the same thing."

Everly felt like he'd slapped her. He could *not* be more wrong. It hurt that he didn't know it. But why should he? She'd done a stellar job of hiding herself from everyone. She'd had to, or she would have been chewed up and spit out by the meatgrinder that was political life. She didn't remember it being so bad when her father was the one in Congress, but after he died and her mother was appointed in his place, everything seemed to change.

Everly could remember when her mother had been less formal, less starchy. More soft and loving. When she'd cared about being at Everly's school plays and teacher meetings. When she'd baked cookies and played tea party with her only child.

All that had changed when Everly's dad died. She'd buttoned up her feelings that day and worked hard not to let them out again.

"It's not what I want," she said softly. She hadn't meant to say it, but she had a need to defend herself. "I hate politics."

He didn't look convinced. "If that's true, why do you work so hard to pretend you do?"

She pulled her knees up and wrapped her arms around them. What did it matter if she told him the truth? There were things she couldn't tell him, but at least she could share a little bit. "Because it matters to her. When my dad died, my mom swore she would fulfill his promises. He'd been a defense attorney, and then he'd been mayor. People loved him, and they voted him into Congress in a landslide both times. After he died, the governor appointed my mom to his seat for the remainder of his second term. She felt like she owed it to him, to the people of our state, to be the best damned representative we ever had. She threw herself into it, and when it was time to run for reelection, she made the decision to go for it. I was fourteen when she won the seat for herself. All she's ever wanted is for me to follow in her footsteps. It's our debt to the people of our state and to my dad."

Everly looked away, biting her lip to keep tears from coming. She couldn't believe she'd said so much. It was more than she'd told him before, more than she'd said to anyone.

"But you don't want to tell her it's not what you want."

She shook her head. She kept hoping her mother would *realize* it. That she'd be in office until she was in her late eighties, and when she retired, she'd be so satisfied at a job well done that she wouldn't expect Everly to carry on her legacy.

"She's sacrificed so much. Her version of service before self. Which you should understand, being in the military. For her it's a calling, and she takes it as seriously as you do your military career. Yes, she wants me to follow her, but only because she thinks it's the right thing to do."

His brow furrowed and she could tell he was considering her words. "I hadn't thought of it as a calling before, or as an act of service."

"Oh, I'm not implying it's completely selfless.

There's power in being in Congress. It's not an easy thing to let go."

"So tell her it's not what you want."

"You don't think I've tried?" Everly snorted. "My mother has a will of iron. She's positive I'll change my mind when the time comes."

"What if you don't get elected in her place? There are no guarantees."

"There aren't, but she doesn't believe it's not worth the effort. If I learn at her feet, position myself just right, etcetera, I'll be ready when the time comes."

"Hence the law degree."

"Hence the law degree."

He studied her. "What did you want to do before you went to law school?"

"Oh, don't get me wrong. I wanted to go to law school."

"Why, if not to run for Congress?"

Everly ran her fingers over the fringe of the blanket he'd spread on the couch for her. The night was cold and the room was warm, and she was telling him things she'd never told another soul. Not even when they'd been cuddled on his couch and she'd wanted to be as close to him as it was possible to be had she considered saying these things. Maybe it had everything to do with having nothing left to lose. At least as far as he was concerned.

Or maybe it was just that she couldn't stand the thought of him thinking poorly of her.

"My dad was in hospice at the end. He had ALS, aka Lou Gehrig's, and he needed care around the clock. He and my mom had determined that he wouldn't die at home for reasons you don't care to hear, but the result of that was that he was in a facility. People talked to my mom about how hard it'd been getting care for their loved ones—not hospice care, which was wonderful, but diagnostic tests and hospitalization. It's like when you reach a certain age, they write you off. Time to go die, my friend. I just—I wanted to help them, and I saw the law as a way to do that. I studied elder care issues in my spare time, and I've volunteered at an assisted living facility for the past five years. I don't get there very often anymore, but I try."

He was staring at her. "You never told me that before. You want to help old people?"

"Yes. Is that so hard to believe?"

"I'm not sure. I mean on the one hand, it's tailor-made for a political platform. On the other, you seem passionate about it for real."

Everly glared as hurt flared inside. "Jesus Christ, Gem. Do you really think I'm over here practicing my platform on you? You do realize that elderly people in assisted living homes aren't exactly a killer demographic, right? They have trouble getting to the polls, for one thing, because either they can't drive or no one will take them or voting absentee is too difficult. Some of them have memory issues, and they're more concerned with their day to day living than with voting for someone who might be able to help them in four years' time, assuming they're still alive to benefit from it."

"You really are passionate about it." He said it with some wonder, which pissed her off more.

"Yes, I am." She scooted beneath the covers and punched the pillow. "I'm tired. Thanks for keeping me from getting shot, and thanks for bringing me here. I appreciate the help. Good night."

She closed her eyes against the hot tears that threatened. She knew her burst of anger was slightly irrational, but it *hurt* for him to think she was working an angle instead of genuinely concerned about the people whose lives hung in the balance as they fought to get the care they needed.

She couldn't blame him, though. She'd let him think she was that kind of person when she broke up with him. The whole time they were together, she'd never really let him see too far beneath the surface. She'd always played the game the way she'd been taught, always kept him at arm's length. She'd never let him see too much. She'd been afraid to.

She was still afraid. What if he didn't like what he saw? What if nobody did?

GEM TRIED to watch a YouTube video on his phone, but his heart wasn't in it. He kept glancing at Everly. She lay on her side, facing him, one arm under her pillow, the other at her side, her fingers curled into a fist. Her facial muscles twitched from time to time. At first it was anger that made it happen, but then everything relaxed and she fell asleep. He could tell by the way her fist unclenched, the way her jaw slackened. The tiny whimpers that escaped her every now and then.

Sweet, feisty Everly. He hadn't realized she was so unhappy in her job, though he kept telling himself it could all be an act. He didn't know why she'd bother, though. They weren't a couple anymore, and they weren't going to rekindle anything. Even if his body was keenly aware of her so near. Even if he'd had an urge to tug her into his arms after she'd walked out of the bathroom in soft yoga pants and a sweatshirt. For a brief, insane moment, he'd wanted to tunnel his fingers into her hair while holding her close and kissing the daylights out of her.

He'd really thought there was something between them. She was pretty, but she wasn't the kind of woman who was so beautiful she knew it and used it to get what she wanted. Not like Monica. Everly was pretty and smart and reserved and kind. Until she wasn't.

Gem sighed and softly bounced the back of his head against the wall while he waited for his teammates to arrive. He needed to find out who wanted to hurt her and why, and then he needed to return her to her life. To her fiancé and the perfect future that awaited her. The kind of future a man like him could never be a part of.

Chapter Five

GEM WOKE THE NEXT MORNING WITH A KINK IN HIS neck. He glanced over at Everly, but she wasn't on the couch. The bathroom door was open but he didn't hear her moving around. He scrambled from the cot, his heart thudding, wondering if she'd skipped out last night after he fell asleep.

But where the fuck would she go? He'd been awake until midnight, waiting for Zany to arrive with Everly's suitcase and his duffel. Everly had been passed out when he'd crept from the apartment and gone downstairs to talk with his teammates. Muffin was there, too, and Mal came outside. The four of them discussed the attack and the game plan from there. They were off duty for the next few days, and they wanted to be involved. Except Mal, who was leaving town, though he offered to cancel if necessary. Gem told him no way.

Where the fuck was Everly? Gem dragged a shirt over his bare chest, slid his feet into his boots, and started for the door. When he found her, he was going to tan her ass. How dare she drag him into this shit, beg him for help, and then take off when she got mad at him for thinking she was as mercenary as her mother?

Yeah, it'd been a mistake, but shit, what had she expected after the way they'd ended?

Gem yanked the door open and stopped on the landing. His car was still there, which he would have known if he'd taken a moment to see if his keys were still in his jacket. Mal's truck and Scarlett's car were there too. He sniffed the air. Was that bacon?

Gem texted Mal before he went off half-cocked and made a fool of himself. *Everly down there with you?*

Mal: Yep. I'm makin' bacon. Scar is frying potatoes. Everly's whisking eggs. Get your ass down here.

Gem: Be there in a sec.

Gem blew out a breath before going back inside to brush his teeth and take a quick shower. He dragged on jeans, socks, hiking boots, and a flannel shirt over his tee. Feeling slightly more awake and less worried Everly had pulled a runner, he locked the door behind him and went down to join his friends. And Everly, since he couldn't quite call her a friend anymore.

She glanced up when he walked in, the warmth in her gaze cooling. "Morning," he said to no one in particular.

"Morning, sleepyhead," Mal replied. He turned, spatula in hand, sporting a *Will Cook for Sex* apron as he grinned like a bastard. "Did someone oversleep?"

"Mal, swear to God," Gem growled.

"Dude, I've got the bacon. Be nice."

Scarlett handed Gem a cup of coffee and patted his arm. "Ignore him. Drink your coffee. Speak when you're caffeinated."

Gem gave her a grateful smile and took a big sip. A few minutes later, he was beginning to feel human again. Everly leaned against the counter, a bowl in hand, presumably with the eggs. She wasn't whisking it anymore. Gem studied her from beneath lowered lids.

She looked fresh and pretty this morning. Her blond hair was pulled back in a sleek ponytail, and she wore black pants with black boots and a black turtleneck. The only thing that relieved the stark black was a gold necklace with a small locket that hung between her breasts. He knew it'd been a present from her parents when she turned ten, and he knew she'd put a picture of her dad in it.

But there were a lot of things he didn't know, as that conversation last night proved. She volunteered at an assisted living facility? He wouldn't have guessed, though maybe he should have. Everly had never particularly struck him as possessing the same mercenary personality her mother had. Until the day she'd told him he wasn't right for her and she didn't want to pursue a relationship. Then he'd decided she was just like Ellen Fairhope but better at hiding it.

"Bacon's done," Mal said, turning with a plate he plopped on the table. Gem snagged a piece. Shit was good and crispy, that's for sure.

Mal ignored his filching and went back to the stove to move the heavy cast iron skillet he'd been using. He poured the bacon grease in a jar then set the pan back on the stove. "Just enough to cook eggs," he said. "Baby, you want any for the potatoes?"

Scarlett shook her head as Everly started to pour eggs into the skillet. "Honey, you can have too much bacon grease in your life, you know."

"No way, sweetness. Bacon grease is good with everything. My granny said so."

"Mm-hmm, I know. I've seen Granny McCoy's coffee can of grease next to the stove and I'm telling you, no, we're not doing that. Save your jar, put it in the fridge, and you can use it for flavoring when appropriate."

"You are one serious killjoy, babe. Lucky I love you anyway." Mal gave her a loud smack on the cheek. Scarlett playfully pushed him away.

"I love you *and* your arteries, Malcolm. Which I tell you every time we have this conversation about bacon grease."

Mal grabbed a slice of bacon and crunched it dramatically. "Bet you won't tell her you disapprove of bacon grease when we're in Galveston for Christmas."

Scarlett scowled at him. "Malcolm, if you insinuate anything of the sort to your sweet granny, I'm going to put my foot up your behind."

"Rawr," Mal said. "Kinky."

"When are you leaving?" Everly asked. She was scooping scrambled eggs onto a platter at the counter.

Scarlett carried a bowl of potatoes to the table and set them down. "Day after tomorrow. We're going to spend some quality time with Mal's family."

Mal grinned and looped an arm around her hip, tugging her close. "Yeah, it's gonna be great. And I'd never tell Granny you disapprove of the way she cooks damned near everything with that grease. Gotta agree with you anyway when it comes to her cupcakes, babe."

Scarlett laughed. "Help me refill the coffee cups."

Scarlett and Mal carried the cups to the counter while Everly sat down beside Gem in the only seat those two had left vacant for her. She seemed rested enough, but he knew she'd gotten up a few times during the night. She'd cried out once before she'd snapped upright, gasping, and he figured she had to be dreaming about the shooting. He'd wanted to comfort her, but he hadn't known how to do that.

"You sleep okay?" Gem asked.

Everly didn't look at him as she shrugged. "Well enough. I heard you leave around midnight, but I fell asleep again once I realized it was Zane and Ryder. I appreciate them bringing my clothes. They did a good job."

Gem hadn't liked the idea at all of those two going through Everly's underwear, touching the silk of it, handling it. But how else were they going to bring Everly any clean clothes? Fortunately, neither man had even hinted at how silky or sexy Everly's lingerie was.

Gem had touched her panties, but only to slip his fingers beneath and tease her. He'd never gotten to drag them off and see her spreading her pretty legs for him. Never got to lick his way from her tits to her pussy before feasting on her clit and making her scream.

And, shit, he was going to get hard if he didn't stop thinking about the things he'd wanted to do to Everly before she'd told him it was never going to work between them.

Maybe a relationship wouldn't have, but he was pretty sure the sex would have been amazing if the way she responded to his fingers that one time had been any indication.

"They were glad to do it," Gem said roughly.

"How about you? Did you sleep well?" Everly asked, spooning eggs onto her plate.

"After they left, yeah." Not quite true, but he wasn't going to bring it up if she didn't. He shrugged his shoulder, still feeling the kink.

"I tried not to wake you this morning. You seemed pretty out of it, though."

Mal pulled Scarlett's chair out for her and then sat beside her. "You slept through Everly getting dressed and leaving? That's not like you. Maybe you're losing your touch."

Gem stabbed his fork into the eggs he'd put on his plate. "I'm not losing my touch. I was tired, and Everly's apparently quieter than a feather."

Everly looked pleased. "I can be *very* quiet. I sometimes sneak out of meetings my mom's having because they can be so mind-numbing and I'm not needed. I've had to perfect the art if I don't want to get yelled at later."

"I would've thought working on the Hill was amazing," Scarlett said. "I have this idea that everything they do up there is important."

Everly smiled. "It can be amazing. And a lot of it's important, but there are details upon details that are mind-numbing when they're working toward the important stuff. My mom loves every bit of it. I don't."

"Yet you keep working there," Gem said as he grabbed another piece of bacon.

Scarlett frowned at the sarcasm in his tone. "Just because someone doesn't like everything about their job doesn't mean they don't like their job. There are some days when I dread work because of the patient I'll be seeing, and other days it's a breeze."

"Like the day you met me," Mal said.

Scarlett gave him a look. "Oh yes, the day you were grumpy with me, you mean?"

"Hey, I got better. I wasn't always grumpy."

"You did, baby. Thank God."

"There are good days and bad days," Everly said. "With every job and every person. I work for my mother because she needs me and I'm good at it."

"Boom," Mal said. "Mic drop."

When breakfast was over and Everly said she needed to get to work, Gem was happy to oblige. He loved Mal and Scarlett, appreciated the hell out of them, but the way they looked at each other and the way they seemed to know what the other one was thinking only made him more keenly aware of what he didn't have.

They made the trip to DC in silence, Everly scrolling through her phone and typing out replies. He was burning to know if any of those messages were from Stuart Morrison, but there was no way he would ask. Instead, he turned on the radio and jacked it up high enough he couldn't hear the clicking of her thumbs flying over the keyboard. Everly turned her head to glare at him. He pretended not to notice. She eventually went back to her messages.

Saint called while they were on the way, informing Gem he'd find a parking pass and access ID at the guard station in the designated parking garage. The right people had been briefed to expect him.

"I wish I knew what that meant," Everly said when Saint hung up again. "Who are the right people?"

"Guess we'll find out," Gem said, turning the radio up again.

"That's what I'm afraid of," she practically shouted.

By the time they made it to the parking garage, it was nearly eight and Everly was fidgeting like a kid who had to pee. But they got into the garage, parked in the designated spot, and before Everly could pile out, Gem reached over and pressed an arm against her abdomen.

"Stop," he said. "Now."

Brown eyes flashed at him but he didn't relent. "I'm your private security for the next few days. You asked for me, and you're damned well going to listen to me. If you don't, Everly Elizabeth, I'm walking off this job and you'll be finding someone else to keep you safe and stop any attacks on your mother. You got me?"

Her jaw worked for a second, but she nodded. "Loud and clear, Jackson Jeremiah."

"I mean it, Everly." He hated that name and she knew it. "Push too hard, argue when I make a call, and I'm gone. If I'm protecting you, it's my ass on the line too. You do what I say or this is over now."

She nodded again, though the look in her eyes

said she'd gut him herself if she had a blade. "I'm beginning to regret that I went to your apartment."

He snorted. "Beginning? Honey, I'm already there."

EVERLY FUMED, but she wasn't stupid enough to rebel. She'd do what he told her to do because she *did* trust him to keep her safe. He came around to help her from the car, then locked it and led her to the elevators. When they entered the building, he flashed the credentials he'd been given, and they waved him through as if he'd been there every day of his life.

They walked down a long hall, heading for her mother's office, and Everly spoke to people she knew as they passed. There were a few stares, but she pretended not to notice. Gem, for his part, was silent and hulking. Just the way a bodyguard was supposed to be. He wasn't dressed in a black suit with a head set, but he'd put on dark jeans and a blue Henley that highlighted his eyes more than she'd like.

His hair was a little longer than usual, but that was because he'd been deployed on a mission and just got home again. It was more subtle than a military cut, at least around here, so it was probably a good thing he hadn't headed straight to the barber. He wore a leather jacket over the Henley, and he had a gun in a holster beneath his waistband. He looked the part of badass, but he also looked like the kind of man women would sell their souls for a night in bed with.

That fact was brought home to her with every stare sent his way, every woman who stopped dead in her tracks to watch him walk past. Everly pushed down on the kind of irrational jealousy she was not entitled to any longer. If she ever had been.

When they reached her mother's suite of offices, Everly stopped and took a deep breath.

Gem studied her. "You okay?"

"No. It all seems so surreal, you know? Like last night was a dream and this is overkill."

"It's not overkill."

"I know it's not, but right now I'm struggling to reconcile it with how normal everything seems." If she worked anywhere but a secure government building, she knew she wouldn't be at work today. The heightened security was the only thing that made her able to walk in through those doors on the lower level and not have a panic attack.

"I understand. How's your mother going to react when she realizes I'm your ex-boyfriend?"

Her stomach clenched. "Honestly, I don't know. But I'm not sure she will. She only saw you in the desert when you had on a lot of equipment and a helmet, not when we were dating."

Because she'd tried to keep it a secret. She'd learned what happened in high school when she'd fallen for Brady Moore. She'd been looking forward to homecoming, prom, all the things a girl should enjoy, when her mother swooped in and took her out of public school. She'd gone to an all-girls school for the rest of her high school years, and she'd never spoken to Brady again.

Two months and one week ago, her mother had started to ask questions about Gem. Everly had known she was busted. More, she knew what she had to do. Break up with him so his life wouldn't be adversely affected from getting tangled up with hers.

"Yeah, I know she never saw me when we were together. Doesn't mean she doesn't know what I look like, though. Your show," Gem said, shrugging.

Everly heard the condemnation in his voice. He was wondering why she'd never brought him around to see her mother when they were dating. She didn't have an explanation she could give that he would understand, so she pushed her way through the door and into the office.

The receptionist greeted her warmly, her gaze sliding over to Gem and lingering. "Hi."

"Hi," he said, his voice sounding deep and sexy. Everly wanted to kick him, but she went to her office instead. He was right behind her. She ignored him as she sat and started to power up her computer.

There was a knock on the door and Wendy peeked her head in. "Everly—oh, um, hi. I didn't know you had, uh, company."

Everly didn't know how much the staff had been told about the attack, so she kept it vague. "I've hired a bodyguard for personal protection. This is—"

"I've seen you before. The trip to Qu'rim. You were one of the soldiers who escorted us."

Great. If Wendy recognized him so quickly, his identity wasn't going to be a secret for long.

Gem took Wendy's offered hand. "That's right. You can call me Gem."

"Gem." Wendy giggled, and Everly tried not to roll her eyes. "I'm Wendy."

"I remember. How have you been?"

"Fine, thanks." Her cheeks were pink. "Did you leave the military, Gem?"

"Not yet, but I do private security on my own time."

"Maybe I could get your number. Just in case."

Everly busied herself with the papers on her desk, mentally rolling her eyes as she did so.

Gem didn't miss a beat. "Of course. I'll have Everly give it to you."

Everly wanted to grab his sleeve and drag him away from Wendy's flirtation. Then she wanted to put her foot in Wendy's backside. The woman was shameless.

"Is Mother with Bob?" Everly asked, cutting through the sugary nonsense.

"I believe she's alone. Bob isn't in yet."

"Good. I need to talk to her. Gem?" she said,

standing.

"Yes, ma'am. Great seeing you again, Wendy. I'll look forward to hearing from you should you need me."

Everly was going to kill him. Kill. Him.

But what right did she have? If he wanted to flirt with Wendy, if he wanted to take Wendy out, it was none of her business. She didn't have a claim to him anymore. She'd let him go. No, she'd shoved him out the metaphorical door and slammed it in his face.

Her mother's secretary wasn't at her desk, so Everly knocked on the door.

"Come in," her mother said.

Ellen Fairhope was at her desk, her head bent over the papers she was studying, but she looked up when Everly walked in. Her eyes coolly assessed her daughter then slid to Gem.

"Is he competent, dear?"

They were getting straight to the point, apparently. "Yes. Mr. Stone is highly recommended."

Her mother looked down again. Turned a page. Ran her finger over a few lines. "I think you mean Sergeant Stone, Everly."

Everly's stomach tightened. She'd made a mistake. She'd excised him from her life so her mother wouldn't have him posted somewhere remote, but she hadn't considered that pulling him back in for a protection detail would put him in her mother's crosshairs again.

"Okay, yes, Sergeant Stone. He was competent enough to stop two truckloads of terrorists from seizing our convoy, so I trust him to do the job right."

"Yet you were almost shot last night."

"If not for Gem's quick thinking, I'd be dead."

Her mother's eyes narrowed. "Why were you with him in the first place? You're engaged now, Everly. Appearances matter. I don't have to tell you how damaging it could be for you to get caught in a scandal."

Everly could feel Gem behind her, feel the weight of his stare. He hadn't made a sound, but she knew he was angry as surely as she knew her name was Everly Elizabeth Fairhope. Her mother wasn't totally unfeeling, but people who didn't know her well didn't understand how she coped.

"There's no scandal, Mother. I went to see him because you wouldn't take my concerns seriously. He and his team saved our lives once before. I was hoping they'd do it again."

"It isn't your place to advise me on security procedures. I'm taking all the precautions necessary, and my security team has been significantly beefed up after last night. I still won't be intimidated by threats, and I won't let anyone think I can't handle them. It's important I don't appear to be frightened."

"I understand that but—"

"Quiet, Everly. I've been sitting in this chair for fourteen years, and I have two more left on this term.

Do you have any idea how weak it makes me look if I appear to give in to a terroristic threat? I'm a woman, and I've had a long career, but if I want to stay here, if I want to run for the Senate—or, yes, the presidency—then I have to be twice as tough as a man. We are *not* calling in a military team to take up residence in this office. The optics are bad." Her mother leveled a look at Gem. "And if you repeat anything I just said, Sergeant, you'll find yourself shoveling penguin shit across a glacier in Antarctica. Am I clear?"

"Yes, ma'am."

"Good. Now thank you for your service, but you won't be needed any longer. My team can handle Everly's safety as well as my own. She'll move in with me until this matter is settled."

Everly closed her eyes. Her heart hammered. She'd brought him back for nothing. Put him in the line of fire for nothing. Her mother was steamrolling him the way she steamrolled everyone who stood in her way.

"With all due respect, ma'am, I'm here on orders from my command. I don't answer to you. Your daughter was shot at by a sniper with a high-powered rifle. That person missed. I don't think they intended to hit her, if I'm being honest. It's a message. To you or her, I don't know. But I do know if you send me away and give her protection to someone else, you could be signing her death warrant. Is that what you want?"

Chapter Six

Ellen Fairhope arched an eyebrow. It was the only reaction she had as they stared at each other.

Gem had to give it to the woman. Nothing appeared to rattle her. She was as cool on the outside as that glacier she'd mentioned. She was cold on the inside too. She'd left her daughter and staffers in a broke down car in the desert while she got to safety. And though she'd just tried to bully him into relinquishing her daughter's protection so Everly could stay with her, what kind of mother didn't jump up and wrap her daughter in her arms, grateful for seeing her alive after such a near miss?

Ellen broke the eye contact and picked up the phone. "Get me the Chairman of the Joint Chiefs."

"Gem." Everly turned to him, her eyes wide and panicked. "Just go. It'll be fine. Mother's taking the threat seriously now, and that's all I wanted when I came to you."

"Not going, Everly," he growled. "Not until my commander tells me to."

"Hello, General Owen. How are you today?" Ellen said a few moments later. "I have a bit of a situation here. I was wondering if you could help me."

Gem figured he ought to be scared shitless right about now, but he wasn't. He was pissed and growing more so as the congresswoman laughed and schmoozed the highest ranking general in the Army while Everly stood trembling in fear about what her mother would do to him. Everly was in danger and so was she, but this was how she reacted. A power play meant to intimidate him rather than concentrating on the best way to find the person responsible and ensure their safety.

Cold-hearted bitch didn't begin to cover it. Well, fuck that. He didn't care if she sent him to Antarctica for the rest of his career so long as he got to finish the job of protecting Everly. Nobody deserved a woman like that for a mother.

"Oh, General, you are too funny. Yes, it's been a while, hasn't it? As much as I've enjoyed catching up, I need to talk to you about a situation…"

"Come on, Gem," Everly muttered, grabbing his arm. "I'm not going to stand here and listen to this."

He followed her out of her mother's office and down the short hall to her own, wishing he could tell her that she damned well mattered and she didn't have to take that shit from anyone. His parents weren't perfect but there wasn't anything they wouldn't do for him if it was in their power.

There was a small alcove off to one side of the hall, and Gem grabbed Everly's arm as they passed, spinning her into it. Everly gasped as her hands came up to rest on his chest. Her eyes were wide and wounded, and he wanted nothing more than to kiss away that look of sadness and pain.

He couldn't though. She belonged to someone else.

Gem took a step back and Everly's hands dropped like he was on fire. "Sorry. You startled me."

"I just wanted to say, before we get back to your office and people start interrupting again, that I'm not going to leave you hanging. If she successfully gets me removed from protecting you, I'll still do whatever it fucking takes to catch this asshole. My team isn't going to stop trying to figure this out, I swear."

Everly blinked a few times, and he knew she was fighting tears. "Thank you. It means a lot to hear you say that."

"You're welcome," he said gruffly. Because what he really wanted was to drag her into his arms and crush her lips beneath his. It'd been too fucking long, and he missed the way she tasted. There were all sorts of reasons why he shouldn't, starting with the fiancé and ending with wrong time, wrong place.

"I wish you hadn't stood up to her. She won't forget it."

"Someone needs to, babe. She's going to let her ego get in the way of doing what's best for you, what *you* want, and that's not good enough for me. Shouldn't be good enough for you either."

"She's not—"

Her phone dinged with a text, startling her. She scanned the words before shoving the phone into her pocket again.

"What's wrong? Am I facing a firing squad at dawn or what?" he teased.

"No. It's, uh, Stuart. He wants to have lunch together."

Gem's heart pinched. "I see. Have to say I don't recommend leaving the building until it's time to go back to the safe house."

"I don't think I'm going with you at the end of the day. Mother usually gets her way, and I don't think this'll be any different."

Gem stepped out of the alcove because he needed to put some distance between them. "Like I said, my team will step up. We'll do whatever it takes to find the shooter."

"I know they will, and I'm grateful for everything all of you have done so far. I… I feel as welcome as I ever did. You have a terrific group of friends, Gem. I don't want you to lose that because of me."

"Miss Fairhope?" Her mother's secretary stood at the other end of the hall.

"Yes?"

"Congresswoman Fairhope would like to see you again. Both of you."

STUART WALKED INTO THE MEMBERS' Dining Hall at eleven, drawing more than one gaze. He was handsome in a gray suit and blue shirt, and he moved confidently toward her. Everly's heart thumped. If she hadn't met Gem, maybe she'd be thrilled at the prospect of marrying this man.

As much as she wanted to, she didn't look over at Gem, who was seated at a table facing hers in order to give her and Stuart some privacy while staying near enough to protect her.

He hadn't been sent away after all.

When they'd returned to her mother's office, her mother sat behind her desk looking as cool and unflappable as always. Not a hair out of place, not a single emotion other than serenity displayed on her pretty face. For a woman of sixty, she looked at least ten years younger, if not more.

"General Owen has persuaded me that Sergeant Stone should remain, and that keeping Everly and I in separate locations outside of work is best. You will not speak to the press about this development, and there will be no obvious displays of force unless absolutely warranted. I demand subtlety in this matter or the press will have a field day. I will not give any satisfaction to terrorists. Is that understood?"

Everly had been so relieved she didn't argue. Gem had expressed the appropriate respect for her mother's wishes and they'd been dismissed.

"What the heck just happened?" Everly had whispered as they'd walked back to her office.

"General Mendez. And probably Ian Black, too."

Everly knew who General John Mendez was, but she'd never heard of Ian Black. Didn't matter since one or both of them had somehow performed magic. Gem wasn't going to Antarctica. Yet. She felt like she could breathe again, even if only for a little while.

"Hello, darling," Stuart said as he reached her side. He bent to kiss her cheek before taking the seat across from her. "I'm sorry I couldn't get away yesterday. We had a lot going on at the office."

"I understand." She leaned toward him, mostly so no one would hear. He put his hand over hers where it lay on the table. She didn't pull away, though she found herself wanting to. "I'm sorry for anything my mother said or did to pressure you into a rumored engagement, by the way. It's okay if you want to inform the press it's only rumor."

Her mother would freak out, but she had to give him the opening.

He lifted her hand and kissed it. "It's my fault,

Everly. I told your mother I thought there was a chance for something really good between us. She asked if I wanted to marry you, and I said I could see it happening. I didn't realize she'd take it as a go ahead to plant a story. I wanted to ask you first." He let go of her hand and picked up the menu. "We can have a long engagement, like I said on the phone. There's no need to rush."

Everly frowned. She didn't want to be engaged at all, but right now she couldn't see another way out of it that wouldn't anger her mother. She wasn't naïve enough to think she could be the one to break it off right after it'd been announced. She'd hoped he'd do so if given the opportunity, but she should have known better. Her mother was very thorough when she closed deals. She'd promised him something he wanted. Everly wondered what that was, but she wasn't going to ask. Not now, and not here.

A few minutes after they ordered, her mother entered the dining room and made her way over to their table, stopping along the way to speak to colleagues, looking every bit like the belle of the ball.

"Well, hello, you two," she effused when she reached them. As if it'd been an accident to bump into them. "How are my favorite couple today?"

Stuart rose and gave her mother a hug. "Care to join us, Congresswoman?"

"Thank you, that would be lovely," her mother replied, taking the seat Stuart pulled out for her.

Everly didn't speak much during the remainder of lunch, but her mother and Stuart had a lot to talk about. She tried to listen, but most of it was about Stuart's family and their plans for a grand steeplechase event on their property in the spring. Everly wished she could look at Gem, but she didn't dare. She knew he was still there because he wouldn't leave her unguarded, no matter how safe the building, but she hated that he couldn't be at the same table. She understood why, but she hated it anyway.

What must he think of her? By all appearances, she and Stuart were an engaged couple. She didn't know what sort of picture they presented to others, but she knew they didn't look like Mal and Scarlett had this morning or Brooke and Cade had last night. Those were people who were truly in love, and it showed. At least to her.

Her mother got a call and excused herself after she'd finished her salad.

"Can I walk you back to your office?" Stuart asked when their plates had been removed.

"Uh, yes. Of course." Everly shot a look at Gem when Stuart came around to pull her chair out. His expression was unreadable, but he stood when she did. Stuart offered his arm and they left the dining room together.

Gem was behind them, giving them privacy even though she didn't really want it.

When they reached her mother's suite of offices,

Stuart stopped at the door and took her hand. Everly's heart crashed around in her chest, but not from excitement or happiness. Gem was watching. She wanted to tell him it wasn't real. How pitiful would that make her? Instead, she kept her mouth shut and smiled at Stuart like he was the best thing since sliced bread.

"It was nice to have lunch with you. How about dinner tonight?" Stuart asked, leaning in close as he placed her fingers on his lapel and pressed his hand over them.

"I-I can't tonight. Mother has a big project due before Congress adjourns for the holiday break. I'll be working on it for the next several days."

He sighed. "We have a few things going over at the office, too. Everyone seems to be in a rush to finish before the break. Maybe we can do lunch again this week. I'll call you."

"Yes, that would be great," Everly mumbled. Stuart kissed her and strode away as Everly stared after him. He'd been so… affectionate. Almost as if someone had told him he needed to step up the game.

As if she didn't know who would have done that. Her mother had lost the battle with General Owen, but she wasn't finished fighting. She wanted Everly to marry Stuart Morrison because it was part of her grand design, and she wasn't taking any chances.

"Seems like a nice enough guy," Gem said, and

Everly jumped. He'd come up beside her and she hadn't even heard him.

"Yes. I like him."

"Obviously. Looks like your mom does, too. That can't hurt a bit. Certainly gonna make holidays around the table easier."

"I imagine so."

Gem let out a low whistle. "Yep, would have been pretty rough trying to bring me home for Christmas, wouldn't it?"

Everly gritted her teeth. She couldn't deal with this right now. It hurt too much. "Is there a switch so I can turn you back to silent mode?"

"Don't think so." He grinned at her, but it didn't reach his eyes. "You got the bonus plan, babe. Enjoy the ride."

Chapter Seven

GEM HAD HATED WATCHING EVERLY AND HER FIANCÉ together. He'd hated every moment of lunch when he'd had to sit at a separate table and watch them talk intimately. The way Everly had leaned toward him, the way Stu put a hand over hers, the low whispers and occasional laughs. Then her mother had joined them, and it'd been like a family reunion. Not that Everly had spoken much once her mother arrived, but he'd noticed she didn't talk a lot when her mother was sucking up all the air anyway.

He'd been off to the side so he couldn't read Everly's expressions head on, but nothing in her manner had indicated she was unhappy or uncomfortable. And then Stu had walked her back to the office and kissed her. It hadn't been much of a kiss, but it'd sat like a stone in Gem's belly to watch it happen. Everly had stared after Stu, unmoving, and Gem had thought he might explode if he didn't pop her bubble.

Which made him the asshole in this situation. Instead of apologizing for being a jerk, he'd told her she'd gotten the bonus plan when she called him on it. Double asshole.

He sat in Everly's office most of the afternoon while she worked. He'd never spent time in a congressional office before, and he had to admit it was fascinating. It was also fascinating to listen to Everly talk to lobbyists and other interested parties on the phone. She really understood how things worked on the Hill. No surprise since she'd been around politics most of her life. She'd interned as a teenager, and she'd sat in on House and Senate sessions since she was a kid. She might not think this life was what she really wanted, but she was good at it. Maybe not the being elected part, but working for a Member of Congress was definitely in her wheelhouse.

He'd met most of the eighteen people who worked for Ellen Fairhope in her offices today, and he'd gotten to observe them. Wendy flirted with him, but she wasn't the only one. Lisa, Sue, and Brenda smiled and made small talk whenever they came in contact with him. There were ten women and eight men. Most of them said hi and ignored him after, while one or two actively seemed nervous or hostile. He paid attention to them most of all.

Michael Franks avoided him, and Alan Blake was

openly dismissive when Gem was introduced as Everly's protection detail. A former military officer, he had opinions about everything to do with personal security, and most of them were wrong.

"Please tell me that man isn't in charge of your mother's security," Gem had said to Everly when Alan was out of earshot.

"He's not. He advises Mother on veteran's issues and liaises with veteran's groups for her. He's actually good at his job, if a bit overbearing about most other things," Everly said with a smile.

When Saint called in a bit later, Gem was ready for a break. He walked out of the suite and down the hall to the gallery so he could talk in private.

"Heard you pissed off the congresswoman," Saint said.

Gem snorted. "My presence pisses her off. I didn't help the situation when I told her she couldn't fire me, though. She snatched up that phone and got General Owen on the line like she was the damn president. I thought I was done for. Guess the CO is thorough, isn't he?"

As if Gem hadn't known it beforehand. You'd need a three-day head start to even stand a chance of getting one over on John "Viper" Mendez. Ellen Fairhope hadn't understood the odds. She'd be ready the next time, though.

"He anticipated she might be a problem. I'm

guessing neither he nor Ghost are fans after the clusterfuck in Qu'rim."

"They aren't the only ones."

"I don't know what he said to General Owen, but it worked. How's Everly doing?"

Gem shrugged his shoulders to ease the tension in them. "Seems all right. Had lunch with her fiancé while I sat at another table and watched."

"Ouch."

"I'm fine. We had fun, we broke up. End of story. Any progress on the shooter?"

"There were some traffic and business cams in the area, and Hacker's got the feed. We're searching for Escalades and anything else suspicious. It'll take some time to go through all of them. But we found something else you need to know."

"What's that?"

"There was a tracker on her car. They didn't follow her so much as tracked her down when they were ready. No idea how long it's been there."

Gem's gut twisted. "Jesus."

"Yeah. The congresswoman's security team has been alerted to look for trackers on all her vehicles."

"I hope to hell she takes this as seriously as it deserves." He'd heard her reasons this morning for being a hard ass, and while a part of him could appreciate the enormity of the pressure she was under, he couldn't give her a pass for being worried about optics. Fuck that shit.

"Me too. Zany and Muffin will be waiting when it's time to take Everly back to the safe house. They'll make sure you aren't being followed. We managed to get her laptop from the police and run a check on it. There's no malware or tracking devices."

Gem frowned as he watched people walking through the marble lobby below. "Someone is pissed at Ellen Fairhope and wants her to pay for whatever they think she did. Tracking Everly, shooting at Everly, is the leverage. In my opinion, whoever's doing this seriously miscalculated if they thought threatening Everly would make Ellen do the thing they want her to do. She's not nearly as scared as she ought to be, if you ask me." The anger and frustration that'd been simmering in him all day needed a way out. "The woman is made of stone, Saint. She's the kind of person who'd throw her own kid under the bus to get what she wants. She ordered you to leave us behind in Qu'rim. How fucking sick is that?"

"I know, bud."

He wasn't done. "Everly told me that it wasn't about what her mother wanted to do as a mother, but what she *had* to do as a government official. What would happen if a group of terrorists kidnapped a sitting member of Congress, *blah, blah, blah*? Makes sense, but I still think it's a pretty asshole thing to do to your own kid."

He hated like hell that Everly had excuses for the things her mother did to her, but he understood too. It pissed him off, but he wouldn't be the one to get between them. Not anymore. Maybe Stu would, but after watching him with Everly and her mother at lunch, Gem kinda doubted it.

"Don't disagree with you, but we're not in control of Ellen Fairhope. What we've got is a bit of leverage to work with Everly for now. We need to find out what's going on and put a stop to it before General Owen decides he'd rather piss off Mendez than a ranking member of the House Armed Services Committee. Gives us a few days if we're lucky."

"Roger that." Gem looked at his watch. "I'm about done with this place. I'm going to hustle her out of here at five. That work for everyone?"

"Works. Zany and Muffin will be ready."

Gem headed back to the Congresswoman's suite. He passed Christmas trees and poinsettias in the marble halls. Everything was decked out for Christmas. Congress was going on break in a few days, and people were rushing to get stuff done, but the prevailing mood somehow managed to be festive.

Gem didn't feel any of the joy, though. What he felt was dread.

GEM HUSTLED her out of the office at five on the dot. Everly hadn't wanted to go, but he'd insisted. There was snow in the forecast, and he didn't want to be on the road. When she'd said she had work to do, he'd arched an eyebrow. "You want my protection or not?"

Everly had fumed inside, but she'd shoved her papers into her bag, shut down her computer, and marched out of the office with Gem leading the way. Her mother had gone to a meeting with colleagues and wouldn't be in the office again until morning. Everly had seen the security detail she'd taken with her and felt reassured.

"Where's your car?" Everly halted beside a cream-colored Toyota 4Runner and looked around for the Corvette.

Gem pulled open the passenger door, like always, but Everly wasn't moving until he answered. "The Vette isn't subtle. Zany and Muffin moved it earlier. It's at HQ, sitting in the parking lot. This is our ride for the next few days."

"Whose SUV is this?" Everly climbed into the seat and dropped her bag behind her while Gem went around to his side.

He slid the keys in the ignition. "Yours. And mine. That guy's too," Gem said, pointing at a man walking through the garage.

"Gem," she groaned.

"It's a government vehicle, Everly. Belongs to us all, which is why we gotta be careful with it."

"It doesn't have government plates. You're fucking with me."

His eyes blazed for a moment. “No, believe me, you’d know if I was fucking with you.”

Everly’s skin heated. Of all the dumb things to say to him…

“Special program,” he continued, putting the 4Runner in gear. “Your laptop’s in the back seat.”

Everly spun. Sure enough, there was her computer bag. She hadn’t seen it before because she hadn’t turned far enough. “I thought we had to go to the police station and sign for it.”

“My guys pulled some strings. They also checked it for malware and a tracking device. There was nothing.”

A chill washed over her. “Your team thinks of everything.”

“It’s the job.”

While she’d been immersed in work today, it’d been easier to push away everything that’d happened since that gunshot last night. Not completely, but enough to do her job. Now, alone with Gem as they headed toward the safe house, she felt the fear closing in again. Someone had shot at her. Shot at them. It could happen again.

She found herself trying to be smaller in her seat as her gaze darted around the interior of the garage. Gem noticed.

“Bullet-resistant glass and a hardened exterior skin, Everly. Nobody’s going to shoot you.”

"Really? Are you making that up to make me feel better?"

He looked serious as he eased them through the garage and to the exit. "No, I'm not making it up. I wouldn't lie about something like that. We have cool toys over at HOT, and this is one of them. Not only that, but Zany and Muffin are close by. They'll follow us and run interference if necessary."

Everly's eyes stung for a second. "Thank you."

"It's what we do." He sounded gruff.

She glanced at him, but he wasn't looking at her. They made the forty mile journey from downtown to Mal and Scarlett's place without exchanging more than a few polite words. The radio took up the slack, pouring sound into silence. Thankfully not at ear-splitting levels this time. Everly was grateful, but discomfited too. She'd thought he might ask about Stuart, or make pointed comments about him, but he'd said nothing. So she didn't either.

The snow was starting to come down as they rolled up to the house, not a lot of flakes, but still pretty. Didn't mean they'd get a white Christmas, but she thought it'd be nice if they did. She was supposed to be in Virginia, at the Golden Acres Retreat on Christmas Eve, then services at the Episcopal Church, and then Christmas Day at her childhood home in Roanoke where her mother would host some sort of gathering and expect Everly to attend with a smile on her face.

Mal and Scarlett's trip to Galveston sounded a lot more fun.

"Are you going home for Christmas?" Everly asked when Gem opened her door. She would have gotten herself out of the car, but he'd told her not to make a move without him and she'd wanted to prove she could listen.

Gem stood over her, tall and handsome and much too appealing for her liking. "No. My parents are going on a fourteen day cruise this year. Fortieth anniversary. My siblings and I felt like a couple of weeks in the sun was more important for once. We all chipped in and surprised them with it at Thanksgiving."

"That's nice." She knew Gem had a big family. He was a middle child, third of six, and he seemed to get along with his brothers and sisters. There were so many things she still wanted to know about him.

"Hey, we've got spaghetti for dinner if y'all didn't eat yet," Scarlett called out the back door.

"You up for that?" Gem asked soft enough for only her to hear.

Everly nodded.

"Sounds great, Scarlett. Thanks!"

"Be ready in about twenty minutes if you want to drop your stuff or change."

"We'll be there." Gem dropped his gaze to her. "What are you doing for Christmas, Everly?"

She hadn't expected him to ask. "The usual. I

always visit the assisted living facility where I volunteer on Christmas Eve if possible, though sometimes it's a day or two earlier if Mother has something going on that I need to be around for. We have dinner at Mother's and she always invites a few people."

"What about Stuart?"

Everly stiffened a little. It was a reasonable question, but she didn't have a reasonable answer. "I don't know. We haven't discussed it. It's still so new and all."

Gem studied her, and she felt as if he could see more than he let on. As if he knew she was making shit up on the fly. "You know something, Everly? If I'd just asked you to marry me, and you'd said yes, nothing would stop me from making plans to be wherever you were that day. I'd want to be with you, and you wouldn't have a doubt in your mind about that."

"Stuart's busy," she said, but it felt lame. Lame and childish and pitiful.

"Everybody's busy, babe. We make room for the priorities in our lives though."

He turned and walked toward the stairs. Everly's eyes prickled with tears. One spilled over, and she swiped angrily at her cheeks before following him up.

Chapter Eight

Ellen Fairhope was livid. She had to be careful what she said and where she said it, which was why the call had to wait until she was in the back seat of her limousine with the partition closed between her and the driver. She took out the burner phone she kept in her purse for such things and dialed angrily.

It took three rings, but he picked up. "Hello, Ellen. I trust you got my message?"

"If you ever threaten my daughter again, you won't get a damned thing from me. Do you understand me?"

She might not be the best mother in the world, but she loved her child and only wanted what was best for her. The right job, the right husband, the right path through life. If Everly would listen to her, she could be even more powerful and successful than Ellen was.

It hadn't started that way, the need for power, when Ellen had first come to Washington, but she'd learned how things were really done. Without power, you were ignored, mocked, laughed at. These days, you were dragged through the press and across social media. She didn't much care about that, but she might have if those things had been a bigger part of the political landscape fourteen years ago.

He laughed. "That's not how this works. I'm the one holding all the aces here. You know what happens if I release the information I have to the press."

She closed her eyes, fury swirling in her brain and belly. "It takes time to make these things happen. You know that. I never said you'd have the contract immediately. I'm working on it. This is much bigger than anything else you've asked for."

"I've been patient. I'm tired of waiting. It's a new fiscal year, and the committee is dragging their feet."

She gripped the phone tight. "How do you know I won't report every bit of this conversation to the FBI? That I'm not wired now?"

He laughed again. "Sorry, but you aren't wired. Implicate yourself in a corruption scandal? No way, Ellen. You talk a big game, but you won't do it. Not without kicking up a shitstorm that would take you down hard. You know the things I have will bury you."

"And you."

He laughed. "I don't think so. I'm not an elected official, am I?"

"Leave my daughter out of this," she gritted through clenched teeth.

"Sorry, can't do that. You get me what I want, or your daughter will disappear. And if she comes home again, and I'm not saying she will, I can't promise she won't be scarred by the experience. You think about that. Then you get in there and convince your cronies to award my company the contract. If not, Everly pays the price. Then it'll be your turn. I can make you both disappear, Ellen. Permanently. Understood?"

Ellen's throat was a tight knot of fear and impotent anger. If she could get her hands on him, she'd rip his dick off and flush it down the toilet. Then she'd stab him in the heart and set fire to his body.

"Yes."

"Good girl."

The line went dead, and Ellen lay her head back against the seat and closed her eyes. No matter how powerful or important a woman was, there was always a man willing to demean and dismiss her. Problem was, she'd walked into the trap all on her own.

Now she couldn't get out. She'd made a deal with the devil, and he wanted a lot more than her soul.

WHILE EVERLY WENT to change out of her work clothes, Gem typed a text to Saint.

I think we need to do some digging in J. Stuart Morrison's life. Find out what kind of skeletons he may have.

Saint's reply came a few moments later. *Dude, you sure about that? They just got engaged and you want to dig up dirt on him?*

Gem frowned, his gaze lifting to the bathroom door. Everly had gone inside and shut it, but not before he'd seen the redness in her eyes. It'd punched him in the gut to think he'd caused her tears, but maybe it was more about her fiancé than about him. The guy had been affectionate enough with her, but it hadn't seemed genuine. Or maybe Gem just didn't want it to be genuine. That was possible too.

He typed back. *I want to be sure. She doesn't have an engagement ring, won't say how he proposed, and didn't mention spending any time at Christmas with her new fiancé. Wouldn't you want to be with the woman you loved on a big holiday?*

Saint: Point taken. I'll get Hacker on it. But Morrison isn't the focus here. Everly is.

Gem: Agreed.

Saint: What aren't you telling me?

Gem sighed. *I fucking made her cry by asking about Christmas with Stu. And yeah, I feel like a dick, but more than that I'm pissed. For her. Why doesn't she know where he'll be on Christmas? Why isn't he calling her all the damn time and why isn't she giggling into her phone while she tries to keep anyone from hearing what she's saying?*

Saint: Maybe she's not a giggler? Or he's not funny? I don't know. You're thinking too deep about this. Lots of explanations.

Gem: I'm not. We talked on the phone when we were dating, and she laughed and whispered when she was at work. If she wasn't, then we'd talk longer. Sometimes a couple hours. She's barely on her phone.

Saint: Uh, because we told her not to use it unless she had to?

He knew that, but it still didn't feel right. *She has a computer. Zoom or FaceTime or whatever. But she doesn't.*

Saint: Doesn't mean anything, but we'll look.

The bathroom door opened and Everly came out in a pair of jeans, hiking boots, and a sweatshirt.

Gem: Thanks. Gotta go. Scarlett made spaghetti.

Saint sent a thumbs up text and Gem slipped the phone in his pocket. "Everything okay?" he asked.

Everly nodded. "Of course. Why wouldn't it be?"

"No reason. Just a question. You ready to go to dinner?"

"Definitely."

The snow was coming down a little harder now, and the stairs were coated. He probably should salt them for the return trip, but for now he took the lead. They were almost to the bottom when Everly squeaked. He started to turn, but something heavy crashed into him and he lost his balance. He went down back first into the grass, which was barely covered with snow. Everly landed on top of him with an *oof.*

"Oh my God, I'm so sorry," she said, her voice muffled where her face pressed into his chest.

Gem lay on the ground looking up at the night sky, snow raining down, and started to laugh. His balls were intact, thank God, because her knee hadn't clocked him in the groin. But she sprawled on top of him in a tangle of limbs, and when she tried to push upright, her hand slipped from his chest to the ground. Her hair was in her face, and he lifted a hand to push it away as she sputtered.

Touching her was a bad idea, because his balls started to tighten. Or maybe that was because she was laying on top of him, her body pressed to his, and he wanted what he'd never had. His laughter died in his throat.

She stilled as he brushed her hair back. She'd taken her contacts out and her glasses were askew on her nose. He righted them as she stared down at him.

"You okay?" he asked, sounding gruffer than he intended. But damn, she was making him hard.

"Yes. Sorry. I don't know what happened..."

"I'd guess you slipped."

"I mean I know I slipped. I don't know how. I was being careful." She dropped her gaze, and he knew she was thinking about something she wasn't going to tell him.

"It's my fault. I should have salted the stairs."

"It's not that bad yet." She shifted. "Oh," she squeaked as his dick made itself known.

He wanted to grip her hips and thrust up against her center again. He didn't, though.

"Yeah. Sorry. Has a mind of its own sometimes."

"I— Um—"

"If you'd just get off—shit, not what I meant."

Her eyes widened a little, and then she moved her hips, pressing into him. Gem bit off a groan.

Everly's eyes locked with his. Their breath frosted in the air. Neither of them moved. And then he threaded his fingers in her hair, cupped the back of her head, and tugged her down. If he was going to Hell anyway, might as well go for a damned good reason.

When her mouth met his, her warm lips and hot tongue sliding willingly against his, he thought he'd died and gone to heaven. It was worth falling down a couple of steps, worth any bruises, worth having her land on him. Worth any discomfort he had to endure just to feel her mouth on his again.

He held her to him, cupped her jaw with his other hand, and kissed her like a man starved. She kissed him back the same way. His dick ached, his balls tightened, and he wanted nothing more than to turn her over on her back, slide their jeans down, and thrust inside her wet pussy until they both came.

He remembered Stuart with her at lunch today, his hands on her, the kiss he gave her afterward. Gem wanted like hell to ignore thoughts of Stuart Morrison, but he couldn't. *Fuck.*

Gem broke away, panting with need and fury and hurt all at once. He was kissing his ex-girlfriend, the woman who'd told him in so many words he wasn't good enough for her. The woman who was fucking *engaged* to be married to a fancy douche of a lawyer she'd only been dating a month. She wasn't chasing the money like Monica had, because she came from money, but it still fucking pressed against that vulnerable place inside him.

Everly frowned down at him, as frozen in place as he was. He could see the moment clarity broke over her. She gasped and scrambled backward, throwing herself off his body and pushing to her feet, sucking in big breaths as she stared.

"Breathe, Everly. Don't pass out."

She nodded, and Gem got to his feet slowly, brushing himself off. His dick ached like a motherfucker now that he wasn't going to get some relief. His own fault though.

"I think I forgot about Stu," he bit out. "But I don't think I'm the only one."

Everly's face reddened. He could see it in the light from the garage, but he didn't take pleasure in her discomfort. He thought she might say something, might cuss him, but instead she stalked toward Mal's back porch, yanked open the screen door, and disappeared into the house.

Gem growled his frustration to the wind. He wanted to follow her and demand answers, but he knew she wouldn't give him any. Instead, he stood in the cold, damp air until his blood cooled and he could walk inside without embarrassment.

EVERLY WAS STILL REELING from that kiss the next morning. Gem hadn't said another word about it. He'd come inside about five minutes after she had, and they'd spent the next couple of hours laughing and chatting with Mal and Scarlett, who were excited to be heading to Galveston for Christmas. When Everly started yawning, Gem said he'd go salt the stairs.

He'd come back fifteen minutes later and told her everything was good to go. She'd said her goodbyes to her hosts, wished them safe travels, and then followed Gem outside. He'd stopped at the bottom of the stairs to let her pass, and they'd climbed wordlessly to the top. She'd been extra careful so they didn't have a repeat of earlier.

She'd meant to say sorry for falling on him and sorry for kissing him and sorry for everything, but he'd been so closed off that she'd never found the nerve. She got ready for bed, climbed under the covers, and fell asleep in minutes.

Now they were in the 4Runner on the way into the city, and she stared out the window and replayed every moment in her head. The feel of his body beneath hers, the moment when she'd realized he was hard, the way pleasure streaked through her when she flexed her hips against his. His cock had been against her groin, and every press of his hardness there fired up the nerves in her clit. If she'd been alone in her own bed after all that, she'd have slipped a hand into her panties and taken care of business.

Why, oh, why had she never taken the bull by the horns when they'd been dating? He'd been careful, and sweet, and hot—and she'd let him go at that snail's pace because, well, she didn't quite know why. She should have stripped naked at some point during that three months, and then she should have climbed him like a tree.

Then again, maybe she shouldn't have. Because she'd have known exactly what she was missing last night and she'd have made an even bigger fool of herself than she had.

She could still feel his kiss searing into her. The sweep of his tongue in her mouth, the press of his lips against hers. Her body had responded with heat and wetness, her pussy aching with need. She'd been on fire for him, and the world had narrowed to just the two of them. She'd forgotten everything else.

Until she hadn't. And then shame and regret had threatened to swallow her whole. He'd told her to breathe, and she had, but for a minute she'd thought she was going to fall apart from the unfairness of it all. He'd assumed she was feeling guilt for kissing him when she was engaged, but that wasn't it at all.

She'd been angry and overwhelmed and she'd wanted to run all the way to DC, to her mother's house, where she'd rip open the door and tell her mother that she was taking charge of her own life and to hell with political ambition or agendas or old money or anything else her mother wanted to throw at her.

Breathe, Everly.

He'd said that, and she had. She'd soon settled into herself again. Into the path being carved for her, whether she wanted it or not.

So unfair. She wanted love and happiness like Mal and Scarlett had. The kind of relationship where someone intimately knew your innermost thoughts. Where a look could say everything without sound, and where a touch could convey a thousand emotions. It wasn't too much to ask out of life.

And maybe she wouldn't really have that with Gem, but didn't she deserve to find out for herself? Except she was engaged now, and though Stuart was nice enough, she already knew they'd never have a connection like the one she wanted.

Gem drove into the parking garage and they were plunged into darkness. For some reason, she felt the tension grow tighter than it had been in the light.

"I'm sorry about last night," she blurted as he wound through the decks to the designated parking space. "I shouldn't have kissed you, and I shouldn't have forgotten I'm engaged, and I shouldn't have demanded that you be the one to protect me in the first place. It's a mess, and it's all my fault."

There was silence until he pulled into the space and put the vehicle in park. Then he turned to her. "I kissed you, Everly. That's my fault, not yours. Once someone shot at us, I was all in with protecting you, so that's not your fault either. Can't help you on the engaged part, though."

"I know."

He faced forward, looking at the wall. Thinking before he spoke. "Why are you going to marry someone who doesn't make you giddy with excitement?"

"Excitement isn't everything."

He snorted. "Isn't it? You should want to be with the person you marry so badly that you can't imagine being with anyone else. That you aren't tempted by anyone else. I know shit falls apart between people, because I've been there, but when you're in that first heady phase of love? No, you shouldn't be capable of being with anyone else for even a second. If you are, then it's not real."

Everly felt like a balloon that'd been popped. Empty, deflated. There wasn't anything she could say. He wasn't wrong. "It's complicated."

Gem's hands tightened on the wheel. "Everything's complicated with you. Every move you make, every thought in your head. It all has to be measured against your mother's approval. You said I wasn't the man for you, and maybe I wasn't, but I think it's more likely I wasn't the man your mother could approve of. Clearly, good old Stu fits the bill." He swung around to look at her, his eyes blazing with heat and anger. "When are you going to stop letting her dictate everything and start doing what you want to do?"

"You don't understand, Gem," she whispered.

"Then make me understand. Tell me why her approval is so important to you."

A hard knot formed in her belly. These were things she didn't talk about, ever, but maybe it was time she did. Not everything, but a little bit. Because she wanted him to understand what it was like to be her.

"When my dad died, it was hard for my mom. She loved him, but she didn't get much chance to really grieve. Not that I understood it at the time because I was a kid. She had to be everything to everyone—she had to be my mother, a congresswoman, a widow, a passionate advocate for others. So many things were expected of her, and it was hard. I was twelve, and I didn't understand why she had to do any of it except be with me, so I made it even harder by acting out. But she sat me down one day and had a woman-to-woman talk with me. She told me I was a big girl, and that what I wanted wasn't as important as what the people who'd elected my dad needed. She said we had to make sacrifices, but it would be worth it." Everly's throat tightened, but she didn't cry. "I learned from an early age that what *I* want is secondary to the greater good. To serving the people."

Gem blew out a breath. "For fuck's sake, Everly, you were a child. And while your mom had a lot of shit on her plate, telling you that your needs weren't important—I'm sorry, but she shouldn't have done that. Not in such a way that's made you believe you have to put your needs secondary to hers—to everyone else's—for the rest of your life. You're allowed to want things. You're also allowed to be happy. So if Stuart fucking Morrison makes you happy, then good for you. But if he doesn't, don't marry the man just because it's what your mother wants. Find another man, someone who makes you happy. And if your mother doesn't approve of him, then fuck her. It's not her fucking choice!"

She loved his passion on her behalf. It wasn't just on her behalf, though. He was that way about a lot of things, and she thought it was part of what made him wonderful. When they'd been in that convoy in the desert and she'd challenged him about Wendy's fibromyalgia and how Wendy wasn't walking anywhere for long, he hadn't gotten mad. He'd changed the plan. He'd been considerate toward Wendy, and he'd made sure she knew she'd be safe no matter what. Then he'd proceeded to make them all safe by singlehandedly stopping their pursuers.

But no matter how much she wanted to do what he said and make her own choices, it wasn't that easy. Her mother would fuck his career if Everly chose him. It wasn't worth the risk. Everly could win some of the battles with her mother, but not a big one like that. Maybe she could back out of the engagement with Stuart in a few months, but now wasn't the time.

"Thank you, Gem. I appreciate everything you've said. And I don't disagree, but I still have to pick my battles. Maybe I'm not in love with Stuart, but he's the right choice for now."

He frowned hard then shook his head and reached for the door handle. "Fine, princess. Whatever you want. I've said what I had to say. Now let's get you inside so you can support your mother's career like a good daughter."

Chapter Nine

GEM WAS FUCKING PISSED. "SAY THAT AGAIN," HE told Saint as he paced back and forth in Mal's yard. It was dark and cold, but he hadn't wanted Everly to hear anything when Saint texted and said they needed to talk about Stuart Morrison.

"You heard right. Good old Stu has a girlfriend. She's married to a Congressman. Hamblin, also from Virginia."

"No fucking way."

"Yeah. Bliss called some of her contacts."

Bliss was married to Gem's teammate, Sky "Hacker" Kelly, and she had connections in private security that his guys didn't have. She was every bit as good a computer hacker as her husband. She did contract work for HOT, but she still did private work too. Which didn't hurt them when they needed someone to do the kind of things they couldn't do as active-duty military members. Technically, they didn't operate within US borders, but protecting Everly was private contract work on their own time.

"Thank her for me."

"Already did. You okay?"

Was he? No. He was breathing like he'd run ten miles in full pack, and he was angrier than shit.

"Yeah, just pissed."

"Understood."

It'd been two days since Everly told him she didn't love Stuart Morrison. She'd had lunch with the man today. Gem had sat at a distance, watching how the two interacted. Morrison was attentive and affectionate, but there didn't seem to be passion behind it. The more he thought about it, the more convinced he was that Ellen Fairhope had her nose firmly in the middle of the relationship.

But did she know about Stuart and his girlfriend? He wouldn't be surprised. He already thought the woman was a stone cold bitch for a lot of reasons. She was certainly capable of wanting her daughter to marry a man who didn't love her just for the connection. For the *optics*.

"What are his ties to Ellen Fairhope?"

"He's a lobbyist. Represents defense industry companies like Raytheon and Lockheed Martin, among others. He's also done work for other organizations without ties to defense, and he's lobbied for companies that are in her congressional district. They know each other well, and he's contributed personally to her campaign in the past."

Gem looked up at the garage apartment. The lights were on, and Everly was probably sitting on the couch with her laptop, going over research for her mother. He wanted to race up there and tell her what he'd learned, but he couldn't do it. He'd already given her shit about not being in love with Stuart. If he marched in and told her that her betrothed was fucking another woman, she'd think he was taking pleasure in twisting the knife.

He wouldn't do that to her, but fuck all if he wanted her actually marrying the guy. Still, it wasn't like they were getting married at the courthouse anytime soon. Her mother would demand a big wedding with rich friends and plenty of media coverage. A quick wedding would never work for the Fairhopes. Thank God.

"Shit," Gem said, raking a hand over his head. "This is bad."

"You gonna tell her?"

His breath puffed out in steamy curls. "She has to know, but I can't just blurt it out."

"Bliss can send you the photos and credit card receipts. Sometimes they go to a hotel, but often it's his place. She never stays the night. She's gone on a couple of trips with him, though. Her husband thinks they're girls' weekends with her friends."

"How long's it been going on?"

"About five months. He gets around, according to Bliss's sources. Never stays with anyone for longer than a few months."

Gem couldn't see straight he was so fucking angry. "Just what Everly needs. A guy who'll cheat every time the wind blows his dick up."

"She's not going to marry him, Gem. If you don't want to show her the evidence, I'll do it. Or Brooke can. Might be better coming from a woman anyway."

"Maybe so. Doesn't have to be tonight. We've got time. I'd rather find the shooter."

"Yeah, I know. We've got nothing to go on, though. It's like it didn't happen so far as the surveillance cameras are concerned."

"That's what bugs me most. Sounds like a professional. Or the luckiest fucking amateur in the world."

"Agreed. If it's a pro, means they missed on purpose."

"This time. Can't let them get close enough for a second time."

There was no usable evidence on the shooter, no clear shots of license plates or faces. Nothing else had happened since that night. No more notes had shown up at the congresswoman's office either. It was a good thing, but not so good when the shooter was still out there, biding their time. But for what? Why Everly?

"Just keep her at Mal's place this weekend. We've got surveillance on her place. Let's see if they get impatient and reveal something we can use to track them down."

"I'm on it. Thanks, Saint. Give Brooke my love. I'm hoping this'll all be over by Christmas. Been looking forward to her prime rib since you told me that was the plan."

Saint laughed. "I'll tell her. And don't worry, we'll figure something out even if we haven't found the shooter by then. You'll get your prime rib."

"Thank God."

They finished the call and Gem trudged back up the stairs. Everly looked up when he opened the door. Cold air swirled inside as he pulled it shut again. More snow was predicted for tonight, only this time it was supposed to come down hard. They could get up to three feet, which wasn't anything compared to some places, but since they didn't get that kind of snow often, there would be problems with roads being cleared this far in the country. They had a stocked refrigerator, though, and they had access to Mal and Scarlett's house if they needed anything.

"Good news?" Everly asked, looking hopeful.

Gem shook his head and her face fell. "Nothing yet."

"How can someone shoot a rifle at people inside a populous city and no one see anything?"

She sounded frustrated. Not that he blamed her.

"It was dark and late, and they chose their

moment carefully. Doesn't mean no one saw them, just means we haven't found anyone yet."

Everly closed her laptop with a snap and got to her feet. She hugged her arms around herself as she stalked to the kitchenette and snagged a bag of pretzel crisps off the counter. "I hate not being able to go home and live my own life," she growled as she ripped the package open. "And now I'm stress eating, and that's not good either."

"Hey, it's the holidays. Eating extra is expected."

She didn't look amused as she stuffed a couple of the thin pretzels into her mouth. "Eating turkey with stuffing and holiday treats like cookies and fudge, yes. But I don't have any of those things because I'm here instead of home."

Gem cocked his head. "You've got turkey and stuffing at home?"

She flushed. "Not exactly. But I could have it! All I'd have to do is go to the diner a few blocks down the street. They make the best comfort food."

"Well, sorry, we didn't buy a turkey. Plus we have a toaster oven."

"Mal and Scarlett have an oven. They said we could use it."

"Everly. Even if we went to the store right now, we couldn't have turkey. They don't sell them pre-cooked."

"Some places do."

"Okay, fine, some places do. I doubt any of the

stores near here do. You aren't in the city, remember?"

She sighed and put the bag down, rolling it tight first. "I know. Sorry, I'm just frustrated. And pissed that someone can affect my life so much and I don't even know who or why." She gave him a hopeful look. "What if we go back to my house? Wouldn't it be a better way to catch this person? He might try again, but you'd be waiting for him. You could catch him, and then we'd find out what's going on. It'd be over and life could be normal again."

"No. It's not safe."

"But it is. *You're* with me." She sounded like she was pleading with him. "My mother is still in her house."

"Your mother wasn't the one shot at, and nobody's made a move against her. She has a security team, and she opted not to go to another location. You chose me, and so long as I'm responsible for your safety, you do what I say. I'm saying no. You want to go home while this asshole's still out there, you find someone else to watch over you."

She studied him. Then she blew out a breath. "Fine. I'm going to take a shower."

She disappeared into the bathroom and he stood there for a while, imagining her removing her clothes. When the water started, he pictured her stepping under it. Pictured himself stepping in behind her, wrapping his arms around her, kissing her neck.

Gem put his hands on the sides of his head and scrubbed back and forth, trying to remove the pictures from his mind. When that didn't work, he walked outside again, sans coat, and sat on the steps, letting the cold air do the work of leaching all the heat from his body.

GEM SNAPPED AWAKE, his senses engaging at the speed of a man who relied on quick reactions to stay alive. He pushed himself up, careful not to creak the cot and wake Everly. He could see snow falling through the window outside. He shouldn't be able to see it as well as he did, but the motion sensor light on Mal's house had tripped on.

Motion sensor light…

Gem was up in a flash, reaching for the Sig he kept beside the bed. Mal had lights on all four corners of the house, and there was enough wildlife to make them light up, but some sixth sense prickled inside, telling Gem not to chalk it up to deer before he'd investigated.

He moved to the window, flattening himself alongside it, then eased over slowly to peer out the edge. The light illuminated the drive coming from the road. A dark car without headlights sat unmoving about twenty yards from the house, just beyond where the circle of light reached. They must have stopped the instant the lights came on and backed up a bit. The car was still running because he could see the condensation from the tailpipe.

Son of a bitch!

Gem couldn't see anyone moving in the darkness, but that didn't mean they weren't there. Could be innocent. Could be someone got lost in the snow and turned down the wrong drive. Why weren't they moving now, if that was the case? Why no headlights?

Every instinct he had told him to get Everly out of there. The Toyota was parked around the left side of the garage. He'd done it purposely because of the way the snow was falling, and he was beginning to thank God he had. That side was the protected side.

Mal's garage was too jammed with stuff from the reno to park inside it. Gem was glad for it now.

He rushed back to the bed, dragged on his jeans with his holster and extra mags, then jammed his feet into his boots as he dragged his sweatshirt over his head. He thought about leaving Everly, going after the intruder himself, but he needed her ready to run if necessary.

He reached over to shake her softly. "Everly. Wake up."

Her eyes snapped open. "Wha—"

He put a hand over her mouth and she sucked in a breath. "Shh, honey. Need you to get up and get your clothes on. If you gotta talk, whisper."

He let her go and she jumped up and started

pulling on the rest of her clothes. She'd been sleeping in her sweatshirt and socks, and he was glad for that.

"What is it?" she whispered, tugging on her boots.

"Not sure. Someone's out there. Could be nothing, could be something. We have to act like it's something."

There was a popping sound outside and Gem's guts turned to ice.

"What was that?"

"Someone busting a door in, probably. Get your coat. Now."

Whoever it was had broken into Mal and Scarlett's house. Might be a crime of opportunity, but Gem had to assume it was someone looking for Everly. He didn't know how they'd found her, and he didn't have time to figure it out. He just had to get her out of there.

"I have to get my computer and papers first—"

"No time for that," he growled. She'd left it all spread out on the small table in the kitchenette. It'd take her a couple of minutes to gather everything and stuff it in her bag.

"But—"

He grabbed her arm tight and cupped her jaw with a hand. "Everly, we have no time. Follow me and do what I tell you. Coat, now."

"Okay."

He let her go and she shrugged into her coat. She grabbed her purse. He didn't stop her since it wasn't as heavy as a computer case with a laptop and a three-inch stack of documents.

"I'm going out first. When I tell you it's safe, then you follow."

"What if they see you?"

"You let me worry about that."

She nodded, her eyes wide. There was no time for it, but Gem tilted her chin up with his fingers and kissed her. It wasn't a sweet kiss. It was a hot, hard kiss that elicited a moan from her. It was a kiss full of promise, and he intended to stay alive and deliver on it.

He broke the kiss and slipped out the door. The motion sensor on the back of Mal's house would trip the light when he reached the bottom of the stairs, but he didn't intend to go straight down. Instead, he crept halfway, then dropped over the side and darted beneath the staircase, listening for movement. The Toyota was on the other side of the garage. He just had to get them there.

"Goddammit, they aren't here," a voice said, coming from the back porch of the house. "You said they'd be here."

Male. Talking on a phone since there was no reply.

"There's a garage. We haven't looked in there yet. Yeah, I'll let you know."

The door to the house opened and shut as the man went back inside. Gem thought about going after him, but he didn't know how many of them there were. His first priority was getting Every to safety. He ducked under the stairs on the opposite side and leapt over the bannister. When he was almost to the top, the door to the house banged again.

Gem ducked inside to find Everly waiting. There was a flash of steel as her hand moved. "Hey, it's me," he whispered. "Don't stab me."

"I'm sorry. I wasn't sure it was you. I took a knife from the kitchen a-and—"

"Shh, it's okay. Look, we've got to go out the window at the back. There's at least two of them, and they're looking for us. They're coming now."

"I don't know how to rappel down a building. I don't know what to do," Everly blurted.

"I got you. Come on, let's go. Quick before they get into the garage and hear the floor squeak."

He hustled them to the back of the room then pushed the window up, thankful it slid in the track without any squeaks or scrapes. He punched out the screen and stuck his head out. The garage butted out just a foot or so beyond the window, which meant there was a foothold. Not much of one, but enough to work with, though it'd be slick from the snow. The trees behind the garage were massive, and the branches reached to the roof. If he could get Everly out the window and to the tree, they could use it to drop to the ground and get to the 4Runner.

"Trust me, Everly?"

She nodded, but her hand gripped his coat tight, squeezing the fabric in her fist.

"You can do it, baby. I know you can," he whispered in her ear. "We're going out the window, skirting along the overhang, and then we're going onto that branch over there. See it? The nice, fat one. Follow me and I won't let you fall."

He went first then turned to help her. There wasn't a lot of room, and the snow was coming down thick. The wind was colder than a witch's tit, too. Everly was shaking as she put a foot out onto the ledge.

"That's it, honey. I got you." He held her hand tight, then eased her to a standing position against the side of the building, the asphalt roofing tiles helping provide a foothold. With his other hand, he shoved the window down until it clicked. Two reasons. One, it was Mal's property and he didn't want to damage it. Two, if the intruders came upstairs, they wouldn't see an open window and they'd spend time searching the apartment first, tiny as it was.

Every second counted in a situation like this. Gem slid first one foot and then the other along the ledge, urging Everly to do the same. She gripped his hand tightly, her breathing labored as she did what he said. He knew it was fear that made her whimper and he didn't admonish her. He was used to shit like this. She wasn't.

"Nothing but a bunch of shit in there," an irritated male voice said. "Goddammit, why did he want us to get this chick tonight of all nights? Jesus Christ. Better check upstairs."

The reply wasn't loud enough to make out, but that meant there were at least two of them. Could be more. In the house, waiting in the car, silently rounding the building. Gem prayed two was it. He'd fight, but he didn't want Everly to see it. Shooting was one thing. Using his KA-BAR to slit a man's throat was another. Wouldn't be pretty, and Everly didn't need that in her head.

He reached the tree branch he'd been seeking. The big mother that would hold their weight. He stepped out of the way and eased Everly into the tree, then followed, urging her to slide along the branch until their weight made it droop.

He pressed his lips to her ear. "We've gotta swing down, babe. I'll go first, then you. Copy what I do."

"Okay," she said.

Footsteps tromped up the stairs to the apartment. The door gave way as someone put a boot to it.

Gem swung down, holding the branch with both hands, the cold bark scraping his palms, then dropped the rest of the way to the ground. He rolled, coming up on his feet with his gun drawn. Then he was back under the tree a little farther down, jumping to grab the branch and drag it lower for Everly.

"Drop, babe," he said. "Roll when you land."

"Gem," she choked.

"You can do this, Everly." The branch was dragging at his arms, wanting to snap up again, and he couldn't hold it for too much longer. "Drop."

She eased her way down until she was holding on with both hands, then she closed her eyes and let go.

Chapter Ten

EVERLY HIT THE GROUND WITH AN *OOF*. SHE'D MEANT to tuck and roll like Gem had, but instead she sprawled face first in the snow. Part of her wanted to stay there. Just stay and pretend everything was fine.

It wasn't fine. Gem was at her side, easing her up, his breath against her ear. "I got you, baby. It's okay. You're fine. Let's go."

She slipped as she tried to find her footing, but Gem hauled her up and tugged her around to the side of the garage where he'd parked the Toyota. He didn't hit the fob to unlock it, though. Instead, he rushed her over to the passenger door and inserted the key in the lock.

"Get in and strap in," he said before gliding away from her side. She felt awkward and numb, and he moved with the grace of a dancer, as if he was completely at home in this environment. Maybe he was.

Everly dragged her purse over her head, tossed it to the floor, and then fumbled for the seatbelt. Gem jumped into the driver's seat, clipped his belt into place, and shot her a look filled with determination.

"It could get rough," he said. "But we've got protection inside the vehicle. Don't open the door for anyone. And hang on tight."

"Okay," she said, her voice strangled.

He shoved the key into the ignition and turned. The engine came to life. Before she could really understand what was happening, he jammed the pedal and whipped the wheel so they spun in a circle that made her belly leap into her throat. The tires spun as the engine whined, then they were shooting forward and down the drive. There was a car in the way, but he didn't stop. Instead, he went around, the 4Runner sliding and bumping in the snow. Everly may have screamed, or she may have imagined it.

She heard shouting and then something pinged against the metal of the 4Runner. Gem swore, but he didn't speed up. Everly turned to look behind them. Two figures were running in the snow, heading for the car sitting in the driveway. One of them stopped and there was a tiny flare of orange. When the metal pinged again, she realized the orange flare had been a bullet leaving the chamber.

"They're shooting at us," she cried out.

"I know. It's okay. Hardened skin, remember? Couldn't withstand a rocket launcher, but what they're shooting won't get through.

Gem skidded onto the road and pressed the gas. There was snow piling up on the roadway, but he didn't ease up on his speed except when they came to curves in the road. Everly kept looking for headlights behind them. When they appeared, her throat tightened with fear.

"Is it them?" she asked, hoping Gem would tell her it couldn't possibly be.

"I don't know. It's best to assume it is, though."

"Are we going to escape?"

"Yes."

She loved how confident he sounded. But was he doing it to make her feel safe? "Are you telling the truth?"

"The truth as I see it. They made mistakes back there, the kind of mistakes they shouldn't, which means they aren't as well-trained as I am. That gives me the advantage."

He hit the button on the steering wheel that brought up the computer voice that asked what she could help him with. "Dial Saint."

"Dialing Saint," the voice said.

Cade Rodgers picked up before the first ring had died. "What's happening?"

"They found us. Two men in a Buick sedan. We're away, but looks like they're in pursuit. No injuries. Heading south for now."

"Got it. Can you evade?"

"I mean to."

"All right, do what you can. I'll get with the guys and see where we can send you."

"Copy."

The call ended and Gem kept driving, increasing speed when he could, decreasing when the tires slipped too much. He kept glancing in the rearview, and she turned to look over her shoulder. The car behind them hadn't gained on them, but it was still there.

"How did they find me?" Her stomach churned and her throat was tight, but she had to trust that Gem would get them out of this. She *did* trust that he would. It was why she'd wanted his help in the first place.

"I don't know. Did you tell anyone where we were staying?"

"No. The only people who know are your people."

He nodded. "Do you still have your phone?"

"Yes."

"Give it to me."

She pulled her phone from where she'd tucked it in a pocket on her purse and handed it to him. Before she knew what he planned, he powered the window down and threw it out.

"Hey! Why did you do that?"

His expression was hard as he shot her a look. "Not taking any chances."

"You said there were no hidden tracking apps on my phone! Your guys checked it over. They also disabled the Find My app for now."

"I know. Sorry. There isn't a hidden app. And I don't know that anyone's tracking you by phone, but it seems most likely. If they are, then they've got access to phone records. Turning it off won't solve anything, so consider it lost. We'll get you another when this is over."

Everly knew he was right, but losing her phone didn't make her feel any better. It was her connection to work, to her life. Without it, she felt adrift. Not that she had time to think too much about it when they were currently running from someone who'd shot at them.

"Do you think they're planning to kill us?" she asked, willing her heart not to hammer. Didn't work, though.

"I don't think they're planning to kill you. Me, probably."

She didn't like the way that made her belly turn inside out. "Why?"

"You could be useful, assuming it's your mother they want to get to. I'm not."

She shook her head. “Mother can’t be pressured like that. She left us behind in Qu’rim, and she knew we could be captured. This is no different.”

“Maybe not, but I don’t think they know that.” He glanced into the rearview. “Shit, they’re gaining.”

He stepped on the accelerator and the 4Runner slipped and bucked before surging forward. The snow was coming down hard, giving her tunnel vision as she stared at the flakes pelting the windshield. When they came to a curve in the road, Gem slowed. There was a train bridge crossing the road at the end of the curve, and Gem hit the brake so they skidded to a stop.

Then he put the 4Runner in reverse and backed off the road, coming to rest beside the pilings. He flipped off the lights and then shut off the engine so the interior lights went out, too.

“What are you doing?” she gasped when he opened the door and stood on the running board.

He drew his pistol and steadied it on the door frame. “If they stop or turn, I’m shooting. If they keep going, then we’ll wait a few minutes and go back the other way.”

Everly’s heart was in her throat as she strained to hear a car coming in the snow. They hadn’t seen any cars on the trip south so far, but they were on rural roads that most people were probably avoiding tonight. When she heard the slushy sound of tires in snow, she held her breath. The headlights shined on the road in front of them, growing bigger. Eventually, a Buick emerged, not going too fast, but slipping as they tried to speed up.

Gem had parked them in a spot by the bridge pilings that couldn't be seen from that direction because of the angle. She kept expecting the other car to skid to a halt like Gem had. And then it hit her that he expected the same thing, no matter what he'd said. She could see the tire tracks in the snow the same as their pursuers did. It was obvious a car had stopped and gone off the road.

Sure enough, the Buick began to slow. Her heart lodged in her throat—and the boom of a gun split the night.

Everly jumped and bit down a scream. Gem shot again. She heard the tire blow. The car skidded sideways and down a small embankment until it was in the opposite ditch. Gem dropped into the seat, slammed the door, and turned the engine over. There was movement in the direction of the Buick, but it was too late.

The 4Runner was on the road, going under the bridge, and Gem took them back the way they'd come. "We're headed toward the city. The roads will get better there, and there are more places to hide."

THERE WERE other cars on the road the farther north they went, some crawling along, others in the ditch. Gem would have stopped to help under normal circumstances, but these weren't normal. The salt trucks were out doing their job, though, and first responders were helping those who were stranded.

Gem had lost his signal for a while but the minute it was back, he called Saint and informed him of the change in direction and the loss of their pursuers.

"Good job, man. Got an address for you," Saint said. "It's not far from your current location. I'll send the coordinates to your phone. The sit-rep on Ellen Fairhope is that she's secure. No attacks or attempts."

"Thanks, man. 'Preciate everything."

"You got it."

Everly lay against the seat, turned toward him, blinking blearily from time to time. He knew she was tired, and probably a bit in shock, but she'd be better with some sleep. He told her that the situation with her mother was normal in the hopes that it would take some of the worry away. She nodded.

He still didn't understand why she was the target. The notes were to her mother, the threats directed at her mother. And yet someone had sent two men after Everly specifically tonight. Had to be that someone intended to use her against her mother. It was the only thing that made sense.

It took about twenty minutes, but Gem pulled up

to a small ranch house on a quiet residential street. He found the key where Saint told him, unlocked the house and opened the garage so he could pull the 4Runner in. Once the door was shut securely behind them, he led Everly into the house and flipped on the kitchen light.

It was three-thirty in the morning according to the microwave clock, and they'd been on the move for over two hours. Everly flopped wearily into a chair at the kitchen table. "Whose house is this?"

"Safe house," Gem said. "Official, I mean. Saint got permission to use it or we wouldn't be here."

She nodded. "I don't even want to know how he did that."

"Pretty sure armed men breaking into a HOT operator's house and shooting at us was a factor. My team's on a private job on our time off, but that was an escalation our command can't ignore."

She shivered, weaving on the seat from lack of sleep. "Gem, I don't like any of this. I just want my life to be normal again. When I came to see you, I thought it was Mother who was in the most trouble. I knew someone was following me, but I thought it was because of her. But this… Why me?" she asked, her voice strained and frightened.

"I don't know yet. But I intend to find out."

Gem slid a hand under her knees and behind her shoulders, picking her up and cradling her against him. She stiffened for only a second before she relaxed against him. He carried her from the kitchen and through the house until he found the master bedroom. She'd curled a hand into his sweatshirt and her eyes were closed.

He lay her gently on the bed, then untied her boots and removed them one by one. When he unsnapped her jeans and dragged the zipper down, she didn't fight. She blinked up at him, her eyes red with weariness and nothing but trust in her gaze. That trust nearly undid him. If she only knew how difficult it was, and the raging hard-on he was fighting at the thought of removing her jeans.

"Lift your hips and I'll take them off," he told her gently. "Then you can get under the covers and sleep. You're safe here, Everly. I won't let anything happen to you."

"I know."

She did as he said, and he was careful to pull her jeans off her hips while leaving her panties in place. Then he dragged his gaze from that little scrap of silkiness and took her jeans off before folding them and laying them on the bench at the foot of the bed.

She pushed herself up and reached beneath her shirt. A moment later, she was pulling her bra from her sleeves and dropping it on the quilt. "Too constricting," she said, her jaw cracking with a yawn.

"Go to sleep, Everly. We'll talk in the morning."

He started to turn, but she reached for him, grabbing his sleeve. "Don't go. I-I don't want to be alone."

Gem gazed down at her, her blond hair mussed and dark gold in the lamplight, her brown eyes sleepy but scared too. He dropped his gaze to her pink lips, and then to the gap where her sweatshirt opened just enough to see a hint of cleavage as she leaned toward him. He put his hand on hers where she held him.

"Honey, I need to find a bed of my own. Because if I stay here with you, I'm going to want more than you can give me."

Her grip tightened. "Maybe I want that, too."

His lungs squeezed as he imagined holding her with nothing between them. Skin on skin. Her legs wrapping around his hips. Thrusting inside her warm, wet pussy like he'd wanted to do for months.

"You're tired and stressed, Everly. It's not the time for a decision like that."

She frowned. "What on earth makes you think I'm so weak I only just decided what I want? I've wanted you forever," she finished on a whisper.

The blood beat in his cock, his brain. *Take it. Take it. Take it.*

Gem shook his head to clear it. "Then you'll still want me in the morning, won't you?"

"Yes, I will. So what's stopping you from staying now? I'll put my jeans back on. Just don't leave me. I can't sleep without you here."

"Baby, you're barely awake as it is. Do you really think you aren't going to fall asleep the second your head hits the pillow?"

She blinked adorably. "Maybe I will, but I'll wake up soon, and you won't be here and I'll be scared."

Gem closed his eyes and blew out a breath. "For the love of— Fine. I have to go check the locks and windows. I'll be back."

Chapter Eleven

EVERLY'S HEART GALLOPED. SHE LET GO OF HIS sleeve, and Gem left to do his perimeter check, grumbling the whole time.

A little voice in her head asked her if she knew what she was doing.

"Yes," she whispered back. "It's time I let myself have something *I* want for a change."

She turned on her side and waited, her eyelids drooping. She was tired but also keyed up. Just when she was beginning to wonder if Gem would return, he strolled back into the room.

"Still awake."

She didn't think it was a question but she nodded anyway. "I'm not sleeping until you're beside me."

She watched him in the lamplight as he dragged his sweatshirt over his head. She'd seen him shirtless before, and it was quite the sight to behold. Gem had lean, hard muscles, tanned skin with a couple of scars he'd told her were knife wounds, and a profusion of tattoos that weren't visible until he was shirtless.

He looked every inch the bad boy her mother would completely disapprove of. Which only made the prospect of being with him more exciting, if she were honest. Not that it was her primary reason. Her primary reason was that she'd fallen for him months ago because of the man he was. Gem *was* a gem. He was worth more than ten Stuart Morrisons. She wished her mother could see that.

He lay a gun on the nightstand after he removed it from the holster at his waist, then pushed his jeans off until he was in his boxer briefs.

Oh God, boxer briefs. On a man with abs that didn't quit and thighs that filled them out to perfection. She could see the outline of his cock, and her pussy throbbed with need. It'd been too long that she'd been taking care of herself when she had the urge for release. Since moving to Washington and going to work for her mother, she hadn't had the chance to have many relationships that resulted in sex.

It'd been a long dry spell for Everly Fairhope, Esquire. A dry spell she wanted to end with this man.

Gem frowned down at her. "You sure you want me to get in there with you?"

She pushed the covers back. "Yes, I'm sure."

"What about Stu?"

Everly frowned. Of course he'd care about her

engagement. Maybe she should, too, but it wasn't real and Stuart didn't love her. He viewed it like an advantageous merger, same as her mother. "It's not real," she said, voicing what she'd sworn she wouldn't. Not to him, anyway.

His brows arrowed down. "Not real?"

"The engagement," she flung out. "He didn't ask, and I didn't say yes. It's my mother's doing. I don't know what he's getting out of it, but she'll have promised him something."

If she thought she'd seen Gem pissed before, that was nothing compared to now. "Your mother *arranged* a marriage for you?"

She was beginning to think she'd messed up. She shouldn't have said anything. "She only wants what's best for me—"

"No," he snapped. "She fucking doesn't. She wants what's best for *her*. Jesus Christ, Everly. This is America in the twenty-first century. You don't have to marry anyone you don't want to marry."

"Please," she said. "I don't want to talk about it right now. I just want you to hold me."

He closed his eyes, his nostrils flaring for a second. "Fine. But we're going to talk about this eventually, so don't think we aren't."

"I know."

He slipped into bed and turned off the lamp. Then he opened his arm to her and she took the invitation to tuck herself against his side. They'd done this before, on his couch, fully clothed. Never in a bed where the only thing between them was underwear. Everly put her arm over his waist, her cheek on his chest, and sighed.

Gem was home to her. If she went to sleep like this every night of her life, she thought she'd be a happy woman. Maybe it was just want and need, but she didn't think that was the only reason. His fingers skimmed her hip, and little sensations of delight exploded inside her.

"Go to sleep, Everly. You're safe, and I won't leave you."

"I don't want to sleep. I want to memorize every second of this."

His arm squeezed a little tighter around her. "It's been a long night. I think sleep would do us both good."

She hadn't considered that he might be exhausted too. She lifted her head to look at him. His eyes glittered in the street light coming in through the curtains. He felt the strain, too. He was so strong and commanding that she hadn't considered he'd be tired. She'd always thought of him as not suffering from exhaustion the way mere mortals did. But of course he did. He wasn't superhuman. He was just well-trained and capable of suffering deprivation in pursuit of a goal.

She ran her palm up his chest and cupped his jaw.

She wouldn't make him suffer more tonight. "Then I guess we should sleep."

He nodded, and Everly lay her cheek on his chest again. She didn't remember anything else.

GEM WAS HAVING a hard time going to sleep. Hard in more than one sense.

Everly had thrown her leg over his, her thigh perilously close to rubbing his groin, and he needed to adjust both her and himself. Because his dick was extremely interested in the near misses of her thigh.

He was still reeling from the news her engagement was fake. Certainly would make it easier to tell her that good old Stu was cheating on her. But how ethical was it to tell her about her fiancé and then fuck her until she couldn't walk straight?

Probably not very. And he was probably gonna do it anyway.

Unless she changed her mind, which she might when she was less exhausted and more angry with the situation. He wasn't sure how those men had found them at Mal and Scarlett's place, but he wasn't ruling anything out.

Someone tracking her phone—though they could have shown up at any point over the last several days. He would have thought they'd have chosen a night when it wasn't fucking snowing like crazy. He would have.

Could also be someone sharing information they shouldn't. Not his team, because that was impossible, but he didn't know who on Everly's mother's team had been made aware of her location. Everly said she hadn't told anyone, but that didn't mean she hadn't accidentally let a clue slip. To her coworkers or Stuart, maybe.

Gem sighed. He wasn't figuring it out tonight so he closed his eyes and tried not to think about the soft, warm body curled against him. He'd lain on his couch with her like this before and survived it, but in a bed where all he had to do was slide her panties down and bury his face between her legs until she sobbed his name?

Fucking torture.

When Gem awoke around seven, he was alone. He knifed upright and palmed his gun, then stalked out of the room and down the hall, checking rooms as he went. No Everly.

He told himself it was stupid to think someone had snatched her away without making a sound, but better safe than sorry. It wasn't until he reached the kitchen that he relaxed, dropping the gun to his side. She was standing at the counter, pouring coffee grounds into the machine, and humming something he didn't recognize.

When she snapped the filter basket in place and

turned to get water from the sink, she let out a little scream, her hand going to her chest. Then she stomped. "Good Lord, you scared me."

"Sorry, babe. I woke up and you weren't there. Worried me." He shook his head. "Damn, you're quiet. How did you leave the bed and I didn't know?" That was twice she'd gotten the jump on him. It was kind of unnerving considering what he did and how alert he typically was.

"You were sleeping, so I eased away then slipped out of bed to tiptoe in here. I carried my jeans out so I could put them on without you hearing me." Her gaze dropped over his chest and lingered on his groin. He could see the moment when she saw the fresh scar on his thigh. She blinked then returned her gaze to his face. "Rawr," she said, and he laughed.

"I'll put my clothes on."

"Not on my account, I hope." She batted her lashes and he laughed again.

"How about on account of it's cold and I don't want to freeze my nipples off?"

Everly sighed. "Well, if you must," she said, waving a hand.

Gem returned to the bedroom to pull on his clothes, stopped in the bathroom to take care of teeth and necessities, then went back to the kitchen. Everly was sitting at the eat-in table, drawing shapes on a pad of paper she'd found. She looked up and smiled. His heart did a little skip. Was it hope? Maybe so.

"It's so weird not to have a phone to scroll through. I feel like something's missing, but I also feel like no one's waiting for me to do something. It's kinda nice not to have to read the headlines first thing, too."

"We have a TV for that."

"I know. I didn't want to turn it on. I'd kinda like to pretend I'm a pioneer woman for a little longer."

"Isn't she on TV?"

Everly laughed and nodded. "Yes. *The Pioneer Woman.* She has a cooking show. It's not about pioneers or how they lived, for the record."

"Too bad."

"Right? If I cooked, I'd try some of those recipes. Maybe I will anyway. Worst that could happen is I burn everything."

"Nah, you're too smart to burn it. You'll follow directions perfectly."

She smiled again. He liked that smile. It was soft and sweet and a little shy. "Thanks."

The coffee pot beeped, and he motioned for her to stay seated while he got coffee for them both. Though she'd never woken at his house, they'd met for breakfast before and he knew she liked cream in her coffee.

"Thank you," she said, taking the mug with both hands.

On impulse, Gem bent over to kiss her. Her mouth met his without hesitation, a low moan escaping her throat as he slipped his tongue inside. She did not attempt to pull away or retreat. He almost didn't either, but he decided he should. There were still things to talk about.

"You're welcome," he told her a few moments later, taking a seat across from her.

"What was that for?"

"Seemed like the thing to do."

She sipped her coffee and smiled. He saw the moment it faded from her face and worry took over. "What happened to your leg?"

Not what he'd expected her to say. He'd thought she'd be more worried about the situation they were in at the moment. "Got stabbed by a tango a couple of months ago. It's healing."

"You mean a terrorist, don't you?"

"That's exactly what I mean. The mission's classified, but we were somewhere not in the US, and we got ambushed. I was on point—that's the one in the lead—and he surprised me. Slashed my leg before I knew he was there. Lost a bit of blood, but the guys got me out and back to the hospital. Doc said any deeper and he'd have hit an artery. I'd have bled out on the battlefield."

Everly swallowed. "Oh, wow."

"One of the perks of the job," he said.

Her eyes were shiny. "I'm glad you didn't bleed out."

"Me too."

"It had to be right after we broke up, right?"

He nodded. "Yeah."

"I'm sorry." Her chin trembled a little.

"Hey, it's not your fault. Shit happens. You didn't make it happen."

"I know. I just… I hate it happened to you, and I wasn't there for you after."

He gave her a reassuring smile. "It's all right, Everly… Hey, you want to tell me more about this engagement? You kinda dropped a bomb last night."

She sighed. "I know. But there's not a lot to tell. Stuart asked me out a month ago. I said yes because… Well, it doesn't matter why. I just did. We went on a few dates, and he seemed nice. A few days ago, the news of our rumored engagement was in the paper. That's how I learned about it."

"But you didn't deny it."

She dropped her chin and shook her head. "Mother was so happy about it, and it seemed easier to agree. I figured I'd find a way to back out later, once the initial interest died down."

"I'm not sure you will. Your mother will always have a reason why you can't refuse, until you find yourself at the altar, marrying a man you don't love and who doesn't love you. Is that what you really want?"

"Of course not. But it won't happen that way. I won't go through with it." She set the coffee cup down a little harder than she probably meant to, and some of the liquid sloshed over the side. She swiped at it with a napkin. "Why are you pressing me about this? You asked and I told you. Shouldn't you be more worried about how those men found us last night? How do we know they aren't on the way here right now?"

He'd touched a nerve. Good. She needed to think about it in the here and now, not imagine a shadowy future where she somehow got out of the wedding.

"We don't know that," he said truthfully. "But they can't sneak up on us the same as they did before. We have a house alarm that'll trigger a response, and there are weapons I can access. I could hold off intruders until help arrives."

She let out a shaky breath. "Wish you'd told me that last night."

"I told you that you were safe. I thought that was enough."

"A little more explanation would have been nice."

"Now you have it."

"I'm not ungrateful, Gem. I'm just frustrated."

"And scared."

She nodded. "Yes, and scared. I never thought I'd be the target of someone who was angry with Mother, but I guess I should have realized it could happen. Our relationship isn't a secret. People know I'm her daughter. I'm easier to get to, I guess."

He reached for her hand. "I don't know how they found us last night, but I know how the shooter found you the first time. There was a tracking device on your car. Someone, probably the person in the Escalade, used it to follow you."

Her eyes widened. "Oh my God. They could have killed me at any point, couldn't they?"

He squeezed her hand. The idea of her not here, of someone ending her life, filled him with anger and a devastation he couldn't begin to fathom. "But they didn't, which means they want something."

"How long have you known about the tracker?"

"A few days. I didn't tell you because you had a lot on your mind."

She pulled away. "You don't get to make that decision for me, Gem. That's the kind of thing my mother does all the time. If you don't think she should do it, then you don't get to either."

He hated to admit it, but she was right. Though he wanted to protect her from anything that could hurt her, he had to be someone in her life who told the truth. It was the least she deserved. "Fair enough. I'm sorry."

She nodded. "What else aren't you telling me?"

Shit. But if he kept it from her now, she'd never forgive him when the truth came out. Not that he'd blame her. "Something about Stuart, though it's not important to this situation. Just don't marry him, okay?"

She shook her head, determination written in her expression. He should have known.

"No. Tell me. Now, Gem. I'm tired of finding things out after the fact, tired of people making decisions for me and hiding things like I'm twelve instead of twenty-seven. I want to know."

He sighed. "Okay, but I didn't want to tell you because I don't need you thinking I'm taking any pleasure in this." He hesitated, trying to figure out if he could soften the blow somehow. But he couldn't. "Stuart's having an affair with a congressman's wife. They've gone out of town together, and he meets her at a hotel in Maryland when she doesn't go to his place. It's been going on for five months. She's not the first, either."

She stared. He didn't think she was going to say anything, but finally she nodded. "I see. Good thing I didn't think he really cared about me. Poor Mother. She'll be so d-disappointed."

She bent over at the waist, and alarm flared inside. He wasn't prepared for her to break down, and he didn't know what to say. Until it hit him that she was laughing. Those weren't tears making her double over.

"Aren't you upset?"

She wrapped her arms around her body and howled. "Are you k-kidding? I'm relieved as shit! My mother will be f-furious! Oh God, J. Stuart Morrison will rue the day!"

Everly laughed so hard her face turned red. Gem couldn't help but laugh with her, though he was more than a bit concerned tears might be around the corner once she was laughed out. Not because she loved Stuart, but because this whole situation was out of control and her life wasn't her own at the moment. He hated to see her cry. It broke his heart when he couldn't fix it for her.

"Not the reaction I thought you'd have," he said when her giggles died down a bit. The only tears on her cheeks came from laughing so hard. Maybe she wasn't going to cry after all.

She snorted again but quelled the laughter as she took a sip of coffee. "Me neither, quite honestly. Though I guess I should worry about Mother trying to sweep it under the rug. She's capable of it."

"Not happening, Everly. We have evidence. If she tries, send it to the media. Or at least threaten that you will."

"Oh, I will. She'll be livid, though."

"And? Do you want to marry a guy who thinks marriage vows are only suggestions that he's somehow immune to?"

"Nope." She spread a palm on the table. "I know my mother seems terrible to you, and she is terrible in some ways, but she wasn't always like this. She doesn't want me to be unhappy, no matter what you think."

"But you *are* unhappy."

She dropped her gaze. "A little bit."

He reached over and tipped her chin up with a finger, forcing her to look at him. "Baby, it's more than a little bit and you know it. You have to stand up for yourself, tell her you aren't going to be like her, that your path is different. She might get mad for a while, she might try to talk you out of it, but if what you say is true, she's going to back off and let you do what makes you happy. And if you're wrong, then you gotta insist and to hell with her agenda."

She nodded and his stomach sank a little. He wasn't sure she would stand up to her overbearing mother, but it wasn't his fight even if he wanted it to be.

"What's the plan for today?" she asked brightly, effectively changing the subject. "Are we leaving or staying?"

It was Saturday so he didn't have to take her to the office. Not that he would have anyway after last night. The Capitol was secure, but there was the getting there and back to worry about. Thankfully, it was a non-issue today. There was nowhere to be. They could stay put and wait for instructions from Saint.

"Unless I hear differently, we're staying."

"Okay. Good."

She finished her coffee and stood. And then she hesitated. He wondered what she was about to say, but she put her hands on either side of his face and kissed him. His body hardened at the way her tongue slid into his mouth, at the feel of her hands on his skin. He didn't move, though. Didn't know what to do, so he did nothing.

"I'm going to take a shower," she whispered against his mouth when she broke the kiss. "In case you want to come with me…"

Chapter Twelve

Everly's entire body was on fire as she walked into the master bedroom and tugged off her clothes. Maybe she should be angrier about Stuart's affair, angrier that her mother hadn't looked deeply enough into his background after all her preaching about marrying the right type of person, and angrier that Gem hadn't told her sooner about the tracking device HOT found on her car.

She *was* angry about those things, some more than others, but after everything that had happened the past few hours, there were more important things to focus on.

Like doing what she wanted for once and having sex with the man she'd never stopped thinking about. The man she'd given up for his own good, not for hers. The man she still loved.

She strained to hear if he was following—the

sound of his chair scraping, footsteps in the hall—but she couldn't hear a thing past the blood beating in her ears. Everly shed everything, down to the buff, and turned on the shower. It was a glass enclosure, not too big but big enough, and she imagined being under the spray with Gem, skin to skin.

Maybe he didn't want her the same way anymore. Maybe imagining was all she'd get to do. Probably best for them both since sex wouldn't change the fact they couldn't be together. Her mother would always be a danger to his career, and Everly wouldn't let him sacrifice his job for her. Not when it meant so much to him.

A part of her wished he would, though. For his own safety. That fresh scar on his thigh had brought it back to her how deadly it was to do what he did. To be part of an elite, secret Special Ops team that took the jobs nobody else wanted or could handle. How could she deal with that life? How could she do what Brooke, Scarlett, Bliss, Hayley, and Jenna did every time their men went away? How could she bear the waiting and the worrying?

They did it, but she didn't know how.

She waited until the steam began to curl before she stepped into the enclosure. He wasn't following. Her throat knotted with disappointment. But what had she expected? Gem had every right to stay angry at her for the way she'd broken up with him. Despite how hard he'd been last night, despite holding her as she fell asleep on him, that didn't mean he could forgive her enough to be intimate.

There was such a thing as too little, too late, after all.

She stepped under the spray, closing her eyes, and let the water slide over her skin. She wished she'd closed and locked the door so she could at least relieve this needy tension herself, but it was too late now.

"I need to know why you want this, Everly."

Her eyes snapped open to find him standing in the bathroom, still clothed, watching her. She fought the urge to cover herself. Didn't matter anyway because his eyes didn't roam. Maybe he didn't like what he saw. Disappointment raged inside her brain, her heart.

Be honest.

He needed that. Deserved it.

"I always wanted you, Gem. At first I denied myself because I had to be careful, and then it was you who denied us. I wanted you so much at the end, but you wouldn't go any farther. It was like we'd gotten stuck in the same groove, and you didn't want out of it."

He looked surprised. "You made it clear from the first that Everly Fairhope didn't have casual sex. I took you at your word. Besides, I knew that when I took you to bed, I wanted to keep you there with me all night. I didn't want you having to leave all the time because it didn't look right or you couldn't be caught spending the night somewhere. Fuck that shit. I wanted to spend hours with you, tangled up in the sheets, kissing and touching and, yeah, hearing you moan when I made you come. What I wanted from you was a lot more than casual, but I had to respect what you told me. I did that, and now you want to blame me for not pressing you to go farther?"

Everly swallowed. She hadn't exactly told him she wanted more. She'd thought he'd understood by the way she responded to him, how she didn't stop him from touching her, how she touched him, but it was clearly her who hadn't understood a thing.

"I'm sorry. You're right that I wouldn't have stayed the night with you—but I should have. I should have stayed as often as you wanted me to. It's just… difficult."

Her heart throbbed. Would he understand, or were they at an impasse?

"Only because you make it that way."

She snorted. It was almost a sob, but not quite. "You know who my mother is, right? Do you realize what she can do? You're a government employee. She's the government. How about that job in Antarctica she threatened you with a few days ago? How long do you think your General Mendez is going to protect you when HOT funding starts to dry up?"

He looked pissed. "That's not the way it's supposed to work. Are you really telling me your mother would hold HOT hostage because of me? That's fucking criminal."

"They all do it, Gem. This guy wants that project, the other guy wants a different one, so they hold things up while they fight over the details. And maybe the project goes through, but it probably shouldn't have after they've stripped it of everything that made it good. Maybe it would have been better in Ohio, but Missouri fought harder and had more leverage so they get the contract. Mother would never cut off HOT funding because of you, but she'd find reasons why it needed more scrutiny and she'd get her fellow committee members on board. And when you ended up in Antarctica like she wanted, the tap would magically open again."

He was staring at her. She could see the moment he understood everything. "What you're telling me is you broke up with me because you wanted to protect me from your mother, is that it?"

Tears stung her eyes. She'd never intended to tell him the truth, but maybe she owed it to him. "In a nutshell. I've tried my whole life to make my mother happy, not to rock the boat, to be the dutiful daughter. I'm beginning to realize that it's cost me too much of myself. But what other choice do I have? I can't let anyone else pay the price for my rebellion, so I stay inside the lines."

"Everly. Jesus Christ." His gaze dropped then, roaming over her body in a way that made her skin tingle. She wanted to cover herself, but she didn't. His eyes met hers again, heat blazing in their blue depths. "You think I'm going to let her intimidate me? Stop me from being with you? Fuck that noise."

Her tears spilled over, mingling with the water. "It's not worth it," she whispered. What she really meant was *I'm not worth it.*

Gem growled as he tugged his shirt off and unbuttoned his jeans. "Is to me."

He tugged open the shower door and stepped inside, and her heart rate kicked up. He was big and beautiful, all rock hard alpha male, and desire clawed through her, leaving a sharp ache deep inside. She loved him and she wanted him, and she didn't know how she was going to let him go again.

"You are fucking beautiful," he said as he stalked toward her. "And you're worth fighting for."

Everly whimpered as he palmed her ass with one hand before lifting her leg to wrap it around his hip.

"Tell me you really want this," he commanded, tipping her chin up so he could look into her eyes. "Tell me you aren't going to think about anything but us when we're naked together."

"I want you, Gem. And I'm having a hard time thinking at all right now."

His fingers skimmed her pussy. "Good girl. It's going to be my solemn duty to make sure you don't think of anything but your own pleasure."

He slid a finger inside her. She gasped at the same

time he pressed his mouth to hers, swallowing the sound. His finger stroked in and out as their tongues met, and Everly thought her knees would buckle if he wasn't holding her up. She slid her palms over his pecs and around his neck, gripping him tightly as the kiss deepened.

Gem was a warrior, relentless when he had an objective, and right now his objective was her. The kiss changed, grew harder and hotter. He kissed her like he needed her to breathe, like kissing was his only mission, until she was nothing more than melted butter in his arms.

Everly whimpered, wanting more than that slow, maddening finger, but he didn't stop kissing her. When he finally stopped stroking her pussy and pinched one of her nipples between his thumb and forefinger, her body lit up like the fourth of July. She wanted so much more, and she wanted it now.

But Gem wouldn't be hurried. She knew that. She also knew it had never felt this good with anyone else. No college boys or law school students had ever compared to how Gem made her feel now.

Hot. Horny. Like she'd do anything to get him inside her.

"Gem," she gasped when he dropped his mouth to her nipple. He sucked just hard enough to make her clench his shoulders. "So good, oh my God…"

His fingers skimmed her pussy again, this time finding the button that made her moan. Abruptly he stopped everything he was doing. She would have stumbled if he hadn't supported her. She gaped up at him, confused, but he only grinned.

"It's a shower, babe. Got to wash up, right?"

He eased her leg down and turned her away from him, then poured body wash in his hands and ran his slick palms over her back, down her spine, massaging her ass cheeks before sliding around to her front. He skated his fingers over her clit, but didn't press, and she thought she might die.

Then he soaped her breasts, squeezing and pulling on her nipples until she arched backward into him, her head thrown back. She'd barely gotten a look at his dick, but she felt it, pressing hard between her cheeks and up the small of her back.

She'd only gotten to touch him once before, wrapping her hand around him beneath his jeans. He'd felt big and solid, and she'd wanted so badly to slide his jeans down and see him, but that was as far as it had gone. She wanted to look now, wanted to turn and grasp him, lick him, but she didn't want him to stop what he was doing. She reached behind her, pressing the head of his cock to her, rolling her hand up and down his shaft.

Gem made a sexy noise in his throat that was half groan, half growl. Or maybe it was a plea.

His mouth was against her ear then. "Part of me wants to bend you over and fuck you right here, but the rest of me thinks you need to be pampered and taken slowly." He nipped her earlobe, then sucked a spot beneath her ear that made little shivers race down her spine despite the heat of the water.

"I want all of that," she said, turning in his arms because she couldn't take it anymore—the sensitivity, the need, the desire to be a part of him. "I'm still on birth control. Nothing has changed for me. I was never with Stuart."

His hands roamed down her back, pulling her in tighter. "Thank God for that," he muttered. "I haven't been with anyone either. I'm safe."

He lifted her up and she wrapped her legs around his waist. Their eyes were level, and she marveled at the strength of him. He took them beneath the spray, rinsing them both off before flipping the taps. Then he carried her out to the rug, set her down, and grabbed a fluffy towel to dry her off.

She felt completely cared for, cherished, but her heart ached because she loved him and wanted this to be a beginning, not an end. It was an end, though. It had to be, no matter what he said about fighting for her. She'd promised not to think about those things when they were naked, but it wasn't always possible to keep her dark thoughts at bay.

She was committing all these firsts with him to memory and wondering how long they had before it was over.

He dried himself while she stroked his cock, then tossed the towel aside, picked her up again, and walked her to the bedroom where he tumbled onto the mattress with her in his arms, careful not to crush her beneath him.

She spread her legs to wrap around his hips, but he didn't push inside her the way she expected. He kissed her until she was a puddle, until her brain was mush, then made his way down her throat to her breasts. He spent a lot of time there, licking, sucking, and kissing, before sliding lower still.

His tongue traced her bikini line, and then he dropped and shouldered her legs open. Everly came up on her elbows, heart racing, wanting his tongue on her *there* but not knowing if he would or not. She'd had a guy go down on her before. It had been awkward and embarrassing, mostly because he didn't seem to know what to do. And he hadn't asked, either. He'd sort of licked his way around the whole thing like it was a chore he had to perform, then he was done and thrusting inside her, and she'd been left wondering why it hadn't made her see stars the way everyone said it would.

What if Gem didn't make her see stars, either? What if he didn't like the way she tasted, or smelled, or how wet she was?

Stop, Everly. Stop the negativity.

"You have no idea how often I've thought about this," he said. "How many times I imagined tasting you and feeling you fall apart as I licked you until you screamed. Do you want that, Everly?"

"Yes," she forced out through the stricture in her throat. Everything inside her was wound tight. She wanted to come. Needed to come.

He opened her with his fingers, stroked her softly, and then tasted her like she was made of honey, his tongue dipping inside, swirling up and around her clit, then down again. Everly fell back on the bed, squeezing her eyes shut. It wouldn't take much to make her shatter.

She didn't want it yet. Not until she'd felt more of this, more of his hot tongue thrusting into her body, sucking her clitoris, making all the nerve endings in her skin flare bright and hot.

But what she wanted and what she got were two different things, because the wave suddenly crested and folded over, rolling toward her at speed. There was nothing she could do to stop it from crashing into her, over her, dragging her with it while she shook apart beneath him and gasped his name.

She hit bottom, a sharp, hard place where pain and pleasure mingled, then floated skyward again, all the tension in her body leaching away.

It didn't last, though. The ache was there again, sharper than before. The need. The want.

Gem slid up her body like a dark god emerging from the sea, all sleek grace and hard alpha male. He settled between her legs while she gazed up at him with a mouth that wouldn't quite form words.

He grinned. "That was fast. See stars?"

She nodded. Stars, sparks, explosions. So many of them, until the sky was blotted with light.

The grin widened. "Good. Hang on tight then, honey, because I plan to make you see the glory of the universe before we're through."

HE NEEDED to be inside her. As much as he wanted her to shiver apart while he devoured her warm, sweet pussy again, he wanted to be balls deep inside her even more. Maybe the foreplay hadn't lasted long today, but in his mind it'd been going on for the entire three months they'd been together. They'd been apart for two months now, but the long, slow build was still there, still simmering in the background for them both.

The way she'd splintered apart so fast lent proof to the idea.

Everly wrapped her arms around his neck and arched her hips up into him, opening her legs wide. He hadn't asked, but the gesture meant everything. It meant she trusted him, wanted him. It meant she was ready for this step and there was no going back now.

Gem's balls ached with need, his heart thrummed, and his pulse beat in his cock, urging him to get on with it. It'd been months for him, too, but he wouldn't slam into her and start grinding away. If he did that, it'd be over in ten seconds.

The way it had been for her. He loved that she'd come so fast and so vocally. He'd wanted to keep licking, nipping, sucking, but he wanted to fuck her even more. If he had his way, there'd be a lot more of his mouth between her legs. Sucking her tits. Kissing her.

He'd barely tasted her, and he already craved more.

Right now, though, he needed *this.* Gem positioned the head of his cock at her entrance then hesitated as doubt needled him. "You still sure?"

If she said no, he'd die of longing. And blue balls. But he had to ask. Had to make certain it was what she really wanted.

She gave him a disbelieving look. "Really? My legs are wrapped around you, I'm as wet as the Potomac in a downpour, and you just made me see stars. I think I'm pretty damn sure."

He couldn't help but laugh. "Point taken."

Gem glided forward, her body wet and hot and welcoming. When he was seated fully, he bowed his head to hers, their foreheads touching, breaths mingling. Hot, dark emotion threatened to overcome him. He didn't know exactly what it was, but somewhere deep inside, his blood was pounding out a rhythm. *Mine, mine, mine.*

"Gem," she whispered. "This feels amazing."

"I know," he answered. The emotion was still there, still whipping through him. He moved his hips, pulling out, then thrusting inside her warm, wet heat again. She made a noise in her throat that sounded like encouragement or satisfaction. He wasn't sure, but he didn't need any encouragement to do it again.

Gem moved slowly at first, deliberately, trying to make every single moment last. Wasn't possible though, not with a woman as hot and tight as Everly beneath him. She wasn't a virgin, but he'd bet every last dime he had that she wasn't all that experienced either. Not if her bullshit rules about her mother and reputations and all that crap had been a thing her whole life. Which, he suspected, it had been.

Gem shook those thoughts from his head. All that mattered was Everly and this moment.

So many things he wanted to do to her. He wanted to fuck her hard and fast, wanted to turn her over and mount her doggie style, wanted to see her on top, riding his dick like a wild thing, wanted to feast on her and listen to her moans grow hoarse as pleasure rippled over her again and again.

He increased the pace, and Everly's ankles locked over the small of his back, her body rising and sinking with every thrust. They moved together like magic, and he wanted to feel like this always.

When she spread her legs wide and started to moan, he lost the ability to go slow. Pleasure gripped him, his balls starting to tighten and tingle with every deep thrust of his body into hers. He was too close, too close. He had to make it last. For her.

Everly's moans grew louder, her hips arching up to

ride the top of every thrust, dragging the base of his cock against the nerve endings in her clit. He hooked an arm around her knee and drew her leg up high, changing the angle and putting pressure where she needed it.

"Gem," she moaned, her eyes closing.

He kissed her then, moving hard inside her. He felt the moment she came because she started to shudder, ripping her mouth from his so she could cry out, her pussy walls tightening around his cock.

A second later he was there, too, throwing his head back in a silent groan as wave after wave of ecstasy rippled from his balls to his toes to the top of his head. He didn't know how long it lasted, but when it was through he sank onto his elbows and sucked her nipples before he rolled to his back.

She lay beside him, staring up at the ceiling, and he started to wonder if she was regretting her decision. But her hand found his, fingers twining together. She gave him a little squeeze and he squeezed back.

"That was incredible," she finally said. "I want to do it again."

Of all the things he'd expected, that hadn't been it. He'd really thought she'd feel some regret. That she'd pull the sheets up and tell him it could never happen again while he climbed from bed and angrily tugged on his clothes.

He propped himself on an elbow beside her and

let his other hand wander over her nipples, down her abdomen. "As many times as you want, babe."

He strummed her clit and she gasped, widening her legs for him. He planned to get her off with his fingers, but it suddenly wasn't enough. His dick was hard, and she wanted it. Be a shame to waste the opportunity.

"On your hands and knees, Everly."

Her brown eyes glittered with excitement as she did what he said. He knelt behind her, pausing at the sight of his semen dripping down her leg. So fucking hot. He smeared it against her skin, over her ass cheek, needing to mark her as his.

He pinched her clit gently, and she gasped. "Oh God, that feels so good…"

"You want more?" He kept pinching, rubbing, squeezing, and her hips bucked as she groaned and dropped to her elbows, her ass in the air. Such a pretty little ass. He wanted to bite those cheeks, but he'd save that for another time.

"So much more," she said. "I—"

He waited. "What, Everly?"

"Nothing," she sighed.

It troubled him that she'd stopped whatever she was about to say, but he told himself that wasn't the important part. What was important was making her feel good. Giving her all the orgasms she could handle.

"You let me know if it gets to be too much," he

said gruffly as he positioned the head of his cock, sliding the tip inside her.

"Mmm, don't see that happening, but okay."

He watched his dick disappear, watched the arch of her back and the hiss of her breath, and something primal roared to life within him. The urge to possess and claim, to mark, to own. He wasn't like that with other women, but this one turned him into a caveman. All he wanted was to fuck and eat and fuck some more.

He took her slow, then fast, then slow again, listening to her moans building each time, until it was too much for him to bear, until he made her explode with a gasping, groaning shudder. He sank deep and shot his semen into her again, until they were both so utterly spent they fell asleep with his body curved around hers, one arm beneath her head, the other curled around her abdomen.

Protecting her. Shielding her. Cherishing her.

The way it should be.

Chapter Thirteen

Everly was alone in bed when she woke up again. Memories of the past few hours flooded her, making her squirm. In a good way, though. My goodness, the things she'd done with Gem. He made her feel safe, and he definitely made her feel sexy.

Every woman should experience what it felt like to have a man as strong and badass as Gem losing his control because of her, the corded muscles of his neck tight, his eyes closed and mouth open as pleasure overtook him.

She shifted, and her body protested. She was tender in some very personal places, but it was a good feeling. That's what happened when you hadn't had sex in forever, other than with yourself, and then had lots of it with a man whose dick wasn't exactly small.

But oh, what a fabulous feeling!

Everly lay cocooned in the sheets and listened to

the sounds of the house. That was when she heard voices speaking low. Gem must be watching television. She threw the covers back and sat up. She thought about strolling out there completely naked and enticing him back to bed, but her stomach rumbled.

First things first, then.

Everly riffled through the clothing in the closet until she found something that would work for her. A pair of black leggings and a man's gray T-shirt, along with clean underwear and a sports bra. Gem had told her that since it was a safe house, there was a small selection of men's and women's clothing in small, medium, and large sizes, including underwear. This place was meant to get someone through a few days before they moved on or before they were restocked.

She found a set of hair ties in the bathroom and she twisted her hair up and into a loose bun. Then she brushed her teeth, hopped into the shower for a quick wash, and went to find out what smelled so good. Gem must have made lunch, and she was starved.

Everly hummed to herself as she headed down the long central hallway to the small living room.

Three pairs of eyes looked her way when she emerged. Everly blinked. Zane and Ryder were sitting with Gem, looking as badass and sexy, *almost*, as Gem did.

He shot to his feet, his gaze raking over her possessively. She thought she shouldn't like that look, as a feminist and all, but holy hell, she did. So much.

"Hey, Everly," Zane said. "How are you feeling after everything?"

Everly didn't know what to say. Her gaze slid to Gem. Would he really tell his teammates about what they'd been doing? She knew they were close, but she didn't really think they were *that* close. Bragging hadn't seemed his style. Then again, now that she'd finally said yes, maybe it was completely his style.

"Um, a little, um—"

"She handled the escape like a pro," Gem said. "Went out the window, followed me to the tree, and dropped to the ground like she'd been doing it her whole life."

Everly's heart tripped. Oh, shit. The escape. Of course. Zany wasn't talking about sex, because Gem wouldn't have shared something so personal with him.

"Thank you," she said, finding the ground beneath her feet again. "I was scared, not gonna lie. I didn't sleep well, so when I kept nodding off this morning, Gem told me to go back to bed and get some sleep." She smiled brightly. "So I did."

A shiver rolled over her and she wrapped her arms around her body.

"You cold?" Gem asked.

"I am now. It was warmer in the bed." She felt her face turning red. Oh Lord, Ryder and Zane would know any minute what was going on if she didn't get herself under control. Then again, did she care?

"Here," Gem said, handing her a throw blanket he took from one end of the couch.

"Thanks." Everly wrapped it around her shoulders. "Much better."

"You hungry?"

"Starved. I forgot to eat breakfast before I went back to bed."

His eyes gleamed. He arched an eyebrow suggestively, and her belly clenched. "Gotta keep your strength up, Everly."

"I would really prefer *not* to go out a window again, if you don't mind," she joked.

"That's the plan. The guys brought pizza for lunch, along with some more clothing they picked up from my place and yours. Pizza work for you, or you want eggs or something?"

"Pizza is great. Thanks."

"I'll get it." He went into the kitchen and Everly followed, trailing after him like a lovesick puppy. But he was so gorgeous, and he made her so happy. She didn't want to let him go again. She wanted to find a way to see him, to let this thing with him happen. To keep him safe and keep her mother from interfering.

She didn't know how to make it work, though. Everly's shoulders drooped as she pictured her mother's reaction. Stuart was clearly out now, but that didn't mean her mother would give up the idea of a power marriage for Everly.

"You okay?" Gem asked softly as he opened the pizza box and plopped two slices on a paper plate.

Everly smiled. "Yes. Why?"

He glanced toward the living room. There was a wall between them and the other two men, but she liked that he checked anyway before he tugged her into his arms and kissed her. Everly sighed, lifting one arm to wrap around his neck while she held the blanket with the other. The first brush of his tongue, and her insides went liquid. She wanted more of him. All of him. Always.

Her heart thumped as he slid a hand over her ass and squeezed. Then he pulled away. "Damn, honey, you make me so hard. I want to take you back to bed for another couple of hours."

"I want to let you. But first, food."

He grinned. "You got it. Don't want you running out of energy on me."

She caressed his cheek. "Me neither. Pizza should do the trick."

"Good. 'Fraid the guys are both single, so they're gonna hang out for a while unless I tell them to get lost. They're here because of last night, not because I invited them, by the way. Standard procedure to check in."

Everly frowned. "I feel like they've given up their Saturday because of me. Don't ask them to leave yet. I'll feel bad if you do."

He kissed her forehead and handed her the plate.

"Go sit down. You want a bottle of water? Coke? Beer?"

"Water, please."

"You got it, babe. I'll bring it."

Everly took her food to the living room and sat on the opposite end of the couch from Ryder, draping the blanket around her shoulders like a poncho. She'd always wondered why his call sign was Muffin, but she'd never asked. Zany made sense because his first name was Zane.

"Are the roads bad?" she asked. Gem set her water on the end table and took the chair nearby. Her senses prickled with his nearness. They'd done that before when she was dating him, but it was amplified now. Sharper and brighter, like he was the sun to her moon.

"Bad enough," Zane said as Everly took a bite of pizza.

Ryder snorted. "No. I grew up in Buffalo. The roads are fine."

"To you," Zane replied. "The rest of us didn't take our driver's tests on snow-packed roads."

The two of them argued back and forth for a few minutes about the merits of snow driving, the defensive driving they'd been taught during their special forces training, and whether or not the average Washingtonian could handle the current road conditions. The consensus was no.

"Why do they call you Muffin?" Everly asked

when she'd finished her pizza. She'd been thinking about it again and she'd thought to hell with it, she was gonna ask.

Ryder frowned. "I made the mistake of talking about my grandparents' bakery during training. They make the best damned blueberry muffins you ever had in your life. Pretty much any muffin, really. I may have waxed on a bit too much about missing those muffins."

"That's not the only reason," Zane said, grinning. "Muffin here was a chubby child. In all his kid pictures, he's got one hell of a muffin top."

Ryder dragged his T-shirt up, revealing the same kind of six-pack Gem had. "You see any muffin tops here, my brother?"

Zane laughed. "Nope, which makes it even funnier. If you hadn't gotten so pissed about the name, they'd have picked something else."

"Yeah, yeah, tell me something I don't know." Ryder looked at her, ignoring Zane. "I didn't think the name would follow me from special forces training to my next assignment, but it did. It's never going away now."

"I'm sorry I brought it up," Everly said.

Ryder shrugged. "It's okay. I'm used to it. The only dicks who call me Muffin are my teammates."

"What do you prefer others call you?" Everly asked.

Ryder gave her a grin and his dimples appeared.

He was good-looking, no doubt about it. That grin probably got him laid quite a bit. "Ryder or Ry is fine. Pretty lady like you though? I like hearing you call me Ry."

"How about Ryder?" Gem asked. "Ry sounds a bit personal, don't you think?"

Everly shot him a look. Was he jealous? Ryder swung around to look at him then, and Everly couldn't help but note the dead-serious way that Gem looked back at his teammate.

"And we'll go with Ryder," Everly said. "I mean nobody calls me Ever, right? I don't think I'd like it if they did, quite honestly."

She was babbling. Gem's eyes softened as he looked at her.

Zane's gaze bounced between them. "Well, think we'd better be going, Muff-man," he said, climbing to his feet. "We've brought food and clothing. Nothing more to do here."

Ryder's forehead crinkled. "I thought we were gonna watch a movie and hang out for a while."

"Nah, let's head over to Buddy's. You know that old man never closes up if he thinks anyone will stumble into the bar. Besides, Gem and Everly aren't going anywhere for a couple of days and everything's buttoned up tight here. We aren't needed."

Ryder got to his feet. "Fine. I don't get what the rush is, but if you've got a hard-on for Buddy's, then we'll go."

"I want to shoot some pool. You see a pool table here?"

Gem had stood too, and Everly got on her feet. "You don't have to go on my account," she said. "I didn't mean to start anything with the name business."

"You didn't," Ryder said. "I think maybe I did." He glanced at Gem. "Sorry, man. Didn't realize."

"We're good," Gem said. He put an arm around Everly, and she shivered a little at his touch. Her gaze was drawn to his, and she once more felt that softening that made her belly clench. He pressed a kiss to the top of her head, and warmth cascaded over her.

"Glad to see you two together again," Zane said. "Gem's been hell to live with since you split up."

Everly wrapped her arm around his waist and squeezed. "Has he?"

"Grumpy as shit. No sense of humor. Walks around like he lost his best friend," Ryder added.

Gem only laughed. "Get the hell out of here, dickheads. I need to make up for lost time with my girl."

"I'm not really engaged," Everly added. "In case you were thinking how awful I must be to cheat on my fiancé."

"Wasn't thinking it," Zane said. "We heard the report on his, uh, extra-curricular activities. Glad you aren't with him. You're too nice a person for that kind of bullshit."

"Thank you for saying that."

He shrugged. "You're welcome. Gem," he said, holding out a hand. Gem took it and they shook. "You know where to find us. Call if you need anything. We'll check back again tomorrow."

"Thanks, brother. Be safe out there."

"Will do."

Gem and Everly went to the side door with them, and then they were gone. Gem locked the door behind them and set the alarm. Then he tugged her into his arms and held her close, her head tucked beneath his chin. Everly wrapped her arms around him and sighed. The words she wanted to say stuck in her throat. Three little words that would change everything.

She swallowed them down because there was no going back from something like that. What if he didn't feel the same way? Just because he'd said she was worth fighting for didn't mean he loved her.

GEM and Everly cuddled on the couch and watched television together for a while. He wanted to take her back to bed, but he didn't want her thinking that was all he wanted. So he watched renovation shows on HGTV, and then he watched a documentary with her about elder care and assisted living. That got him a bit choked up if he were honest. Too many elderly people weren't treated with the dignity they deserved.

Made him think of his parents, who weren't elderly, but hopefully would get there someday. He was going to have a talk with his siblings and parents about their plans and wishes for the future at some point. Not the most uplifting topic, but important.

Everly nibbled her lip. It was a worried gesture, not a sexy one.

"What's wrong, babe?"

"I was thinking about the Golden Acres Resort and the folks there. I always stop in on Christmas Eve. I'd like to be there this year, too."

"It's a few days away. There's every chance we'll find these guys before then."

He wasn't so sure. The Buick the intruders had been driving wasn't in the ditch anymore, so that'd been a dead end. If there was DNA in Mal and Scarlett's place, it would take some time to find. A team had gotten out there earlier and was currently going over everything.

He hoped they found something, but he wouldn't hold his breath. There'd been nothing concrete to identify the sender of the threats Everly's mother had been getting, and there'd been no new threat since the last one arrived. Aside from someone shooting at Everly and breaking into Mal's place, there was nothing they could pin down.

"I hope so," she said. "I'm getting tired of not

being able to sleep in my own bed or drive my own car." She tipped her head back to gaze up at him. "However, there is one very wonderful perk about being locked away from the world right now."

His gaze dipped to her mouth. "Oh yeah, what's that?"

"Spending time with you."

He'd thought she was going to say sex with him, so that answer wasn't quite what he expected, but he loved it even more. "I like that part too."

"Do you think we've spent enough time doing other things that we can justifiably go to bed again?"

He grinned at her. "Why leave a perfectly good couch?"

"Oh, good point."

She stood and reached for the hem of his shirt. He let her tug it over his head. She dropped it with a flourish, then knelt on the floor and pressed her mouth to his abdomen. Gem hissed in a breath as she lifted her body up and swiped her tongue across a nipple. Part of him wanted to grab her by the arms, throw her onto her back on the cushions, and take over.

But another part loved seeing the happiness in her expression as she touched and licked him. When she unbuttoned his jeans and spread the fly open, his dick strained against the confines of his underwear. She pushed the fabric down and licked his shaft. His balls tightened.

Gem put a hand in her hair and held her gently. "Babe, you're killing me."

"Mmm, take them off then. I want to suck your dick."

Jesus. Gem lifted his hips and shoved his jeans down until he was butt-ass naked on the couch. Everly cupped his balls in one hand and his dick in the other, and he threw his head back on the cushion and closed his eyes, trying to regain control. Then she took him in her mouth, and he thought he was gonna blow.

He didn't though. He managed to hold on while she put her all into giving him head. He let her take it as far as he could before he reached for her. "Stop, babe. I wanna be inside you when I come."

She stood with a grin on her face and ripped off her clothes, dropping them into a pile with his before she straddled his lap. He wrapped a hand around the back of her neck and pulled her down so he could kiss her.

She sighed into his mouth, her hips jerking back and forth as she rubbed her wet pussy against his cock. When she shuddered, he knew she'd already come. Wasn't going to stop him from making her do it again, though.

After her tremors subsided, he guided her up and she sank down on him with a long, low moan. He felt the same. He broke the kiss then and gazed up at her, at the passion shining in her pretty eyes behind the glasses, and his heart tripped over itself.

"I like being locked up with you," he said, caressing her jaw before tucking her hair behind her ear. "There's nothing boring about it."

"I like it too. Who knew that getting shot at could turn into so much fun?"

He didn't like to think about someone shooting at her, or about those men looking for her. Specifically, on the orders of someone they hadn't named. It made him feel furious and helpless at the same time.

He flexed his hips, surging inside her, and she let out a sound of pleasure that made his balls ache.

"Ride me, Everly. Make us both come."

She did, and he forgot everything except how it felt to be with her like this.

It felt like home.

EVERLY WAS A LIMP DISHRAG. A boneless heap. Nothing on this earth felt as good as sex with Gem did.

No, nothing on this earth felt as good as *being with* Gem did. Just being.

She didn't know how she was going to give him up. But she still had to.

After they wore each other out on the couch, they realized they were hungry so they dressed and went into the kitchen. Gem searched through the pantry and fridge, coming up with ingredients to make spaghetti with meatballs. Everly helped as much as she could, but Gem did the cooking. She'd helped him in the kitchen before, when they were dating, and she'd enjoyed it. She was a whiz at garlic bread, so she prepared that all on her own.

They kissed a lot while cooking, and this time she got to enjoy running her hands over his ass or cupping his package. She'd never gotten to do that before. He put his hands under her shirt and played with her nipples while the sauce bubbled on the stove, and she melted with happiness.

When the food was ready, Gem made her sit at the table while he fixed her plate. He let her dictate how much she got, but he dished it out and set it in front of her. She waited for him to join her before she ate the first bite.

"Mmm, so good. You're a great cook."

He laughed. "It's sauce from a jar, frozen meatballs, and you made the bread. I think we're both great cooks."

She grinned as she speared a meatball. "We make a good team."

"We do."

They were halfway through the meal when his phone buzzed. He'd set it on the table earlier, and she'd eyed it longingly for a moment before telling herself she was having way more fun without her phone. But Gem had to answer.

"Hey, man. What's up?"

She twirled spaghetti around her fork, not sure if she could eat much more. Her eyes were apparently bigger than her stomach. But she was having fun, and it tasted good. She hadn't been so relaxed in months.

Gem's expression hardened. She didn't like that look. At all. Fear danced across her skin, but she told herself not to get worked up. It could be nothing. It might not have anything to do with her. She didn't even know who was calling.

But then he looked at her, and she knew.

"What?" she asked, her throat impossibly tight.

He took her hand and held it. "I'm sorry, Everly. Your mother's missing."

Chapter Fourteen

THE MAIN ROADS HAD BEEN SALTED AND WERE passable, though it took Gem a little bit of time to work his way out of the neighborhood. Everly was belted in beside him, silently staring out the window. She'd gone from chatty and happy to silent and stricken. He hated it. Would do anything to fix it.

He'd begun to think of the safe house as their refuge, the place where they existed in a bubble of orgasmic sex and long conversations about anything and everything. It hadn't lasted long.

Now they were back out in the real world, and she wasn't with him anymore. Her mind was on her mother.

Gem didn't care for Ellen Fairhope, thought she was a cold-ass bitch, but Everly *did*. And Gem cared about Everly. He reached over to take her hand in his. She curled her fingers into his palm.

"We'll find her. It could be a miscommunication somewhere. The weather's affecting everything."

"I should try to call her again."

He'd given her his phone to try her mother, but Ellen Fairhope hadn't picked up. When it went to voice mail, he'd given Everly the slash-across-the-throat signal not to leave a message. She'd closed her eyes, but she'd given him back the phone.

"We'll call her from HOT HQ. Not much longer."

Saint had told him to bring Everly ASAP. The team was gathering. Mendez and Ghost would be there, too.

"If I still had my phone, I'd know if she'd tried to call me." Everly didn't look at him.

"I'm sorry, babe, but I had to ditch it."

"I know. It's just—" She swallowed. "It's a hell of a time not to have it."

"Yep. But if it made you safe, it was worth it to me."

She sighed as she turned and lifted her fingers to his cheek, trailed them behind his ear and down his throat. "Thank you. For everything, Gem. I know it hasn't been easy."

His skin tingled where she touched. As if her fingers were made of sparks. "What's that saying? Nothing worth having ever is?"

She smiled. "That's the one."

Half an hour later, they were in the parking lot at HOT. Twenty minutes after that, he'd gotten Everly through security and into the SCIF. Being a congressional staffer didn't hurt, especially when she worked for the chairwoman of the House Armed Services Committee.

Saint was waiting for them. So were Hacker and Bliss, Dean "Wolf" Garner, Noah "Easy" Cross, Zany, Muffin, and Jake "Harley" Ryan. Mal was in Texas, but everyone else was still in town. Gem's throat knotted to think they'd all come out to help when it was technically their vacation time. Then again, it's what his team did. He could count on these guys—and their women—to storm the gates of Hell if he needed them to.

"Hi, honey," Bliss said, coming over to loop an arm around Everly's shoulders. "You doin' okay?"

Gem sometimes forgot that Bliss was from Tennessee, but then she'd let her mask slip and her drawl came out. He liked it. Made her more relatable in his opinion, especially since she was always dressed in the latest fashion and carrying designer handbags. Not that Gem would know a designer handbag if it fell on his head, but the other women in their circle did and they often commented on Bliss's taste in purses. Hacker was as solid as they came, but he was pretty fancy too. The boy had gone to Harvard. Not that he'd told any of them until Bliss needed their help a little over a year ago. That's when they'd learned all about Mr. Fancy Pants.

"I'm a little numb, I think," Everly replied. "Nothing seems real yet."

General Mendez strolled into the room then, Ghost on his heels. Everyone snapped to attention, except Bliss and Everly, of course.

"As you were," Mendez said, and they all relaxed. "Miss Fairhope." He took her hand in his for a moment. "We aren't quite sure if this is officially a problem yet or not, but your mother's security team doesn't seem to know where she went. One of their people was with her, but he's not been heard from either. They could be stuck in the snow somewhere, but so far we can't get a location from either cell phone."

"Does the president know?" Everly asked.

Mendez nodded. "He does. That's why we're involved. I assume you've tried to call her?"

"Yes. She didn't answer. B-but I didn't use my phone. Gem had to throw mine out the window last night. She might not answer if she doesn't recognize the number. Or she's put hers on Do not disturb. She does that when she's working on something. Has anyone called Bob Schaffer? He's the keeper of her schedule."

"We've tried Bob. He seems to be out of comm range as well."

Gem didn't like the sound of that. Ellen Fairhope, her chief of staff, and a security guard were all missing? Still, the snow had created a mess on the roads and there were always dead spots for cellular service. It could be a perfect storm of circumstances. Except that's not what his gut told him. He didn't think anyone in the room thought that either. They were all concerned or they wouldn't be here.

"We'd like you to try calling her again," Mendez said. "Hacker and Bliss spoofed your phone number so it looks like it's coming directly from you. If nobody answers, leave a message. If someone has taken her, they might call back to make their demands known."

"Okay." Gem could hear the strain in Everly's voice. He wanted to put his arms around her and tug her into the circle of his body, but he refrained for the moment.

Bliss took a phone from the table nearby and handed it to Everly. "We're tapped into the line, so we'll be monitoring the conversation."

Hacker put on a bone conduction headset that sat right behind his ears and nodded.

Everly turned to look at Gem, her eyes filled with pain and doubt. He close the space between them, unable to refrain a second longer. When he looped an arm around her waist and pulled her against him, he could feel her trembling.

"Dial, babe," he said softly. "If anyone answers, ask for your mother. If she answers, act normal. Leave a message if no one picks up. Hacker can hear everything, so don't worry about trying to tell us what's being said."

Everly nodded and tapped in her mother's number before putting the phone to her ear. He knew when her mother answered because he felt the tension leave her body.

"Hi, Mother. … Yes, it's me. … I'm sorry I was out of touch. I lost my phone—"

Her gaze snapped to his, her eyes wide and panicky. He gave her a squeeze. "Charger," he whispered in her ear.

"Phone charger. Sorry, I thought the call went out for a second. I couldn't hear anything."

Gem pressed a kiss to her temple. He didn't care what anyone else thought just then. Everly was smart and sweet and beautiful, and she was his. Damned if he was letting her go ever again. Even if he had to shovel some penguin shit to keep her.

"MOTHER? MOTHER?"

Everly strained to hear anything. Her mother had sounded like herself when she'd answered. She'd assured Everly she was fine, wanted to know why Everly hadn't been answering her phone, and then the sound seemed to go dead. Everly glanced up at Gem.

He was looking at Hacker, who pointed at the screen and mouthed that the call was still connected.

"Miss Fairhope?" a voice said. A smooth voice. Like chocolate poured over cherries. She thought she might have heard it before, but she couldn't recall where.

"Yes," Everly replied. Hacker was still listening, but now Mendez and Ghost were at his side, peering over his shoulder at the computer screen.

"Your mother takes too much time to get to the point, I'm afraid. She's currently my very honored guest during this horrible weather we're having, and we'd love for you to join us."

"I, um… Who is this?"

"I'm an old friend of your mother's, Everly. We're having the best time together. It'll get even better when you're here. I'll send a car to get you."

"I'm sorry, but I need to know who you are. And I want to talk to my mother again." Everly's heart thumped. She didn't like his voice, no matter how syrupy and rich. Something wasn't right about it.

"Sorry, sweetheart, but she just headed to the spa. Her treatment is very expensive and she can't miss it. You come join us. It'll make her so happy."

"The roads are—"

"No arguing, Everly. Join us. If you don't, your mother's stay could be of some duration."

Helplessness hung on her shoulders, all damp and

cold. "I'm not at home," she said. "I'll come to you. Send your address—"

"Not how it works. I'll send a car to the Capitol. Independence Avenue, in front of the Rayburn Building. It'll be there in an hour. I suggest you be there too. Alone. No bodyguards, Everly."

The call ended, and Everly's heart dropped like a stone. Hacker ripped off his headphones, and Bliss cursed.

"I couldn't get a location," Hacker growled. "I think whoever has her is jamming it."

It wasn't right. Whatever was going on, it wasn't right. "I have to get to the Capitol," Everly blurted.

"No." Gem commanded, furious and forbidding. "I don't know who that was, but he doesn't mean for either of you to have a good time. Your mother is *not* his guest."

Everly squeezed his hand. "I know. But I still have to go."

"You don't, babe. If you go, he could hurt you both. If you stay, then we don't know what he'll do. Plus it gives us time to find this dick and go commando on his ass."

"There's no time. He said an hour, and it'll take nearly that to get to the Capitol from here with the roads as they are."

"There's a heliport at the Pentagon," General Mendez said. "We'll get you to the Capitol on time."

"Sir," Gem said, still being stubborn. Still trying to

protect her. God, she loved him for that. "Once she gets in that car, we could lose them both."

"Son," Mendez said, "we aren't losing anyone. Did you forget where you are? We'll put a tracking device on her skin. Your team will track and follow."

"I wasn't talking about tracking them, sir."

Gem's eyes were bright, his jaw set stubbornly. Everly worried he'd put his foot in it, but Mendez seemed to soften. He lay a hand on Gem's shoulder.

"You're right. But this is what we do, Sergeant. We do the hard job so that we can save every innocent civilian, not just the ones we want to save. If she's willing to go, then we have to let her and do everything we can to support her."

"Yes, sir."

Everly slipped beneath his arm. He turned and pulled her tightly against him, his mouth in her hair. "Don't go. We'll find another way."

She closed her eyes and curled her fingers in his shirt. "I can't stand by and do nothing. You wouldn't."

He sucked in a breath, and she knew she'd hit him in a vulnerable spot. "She left you, Everly."

He was talking about Qu'rim, of course. Giving back as good as he got.

"Not fair, Gem. And even if you're right, even if she only cared about her own skin that day, leaving her now is *not* something you would do. So don't ask me to do it."

His eyes glittered, but he finally nodded. "You're

right. I wouldn't leave her either. But I'm trained for this kind of work. You aren't."

Everly smiled sadly. "I know. But I'm the one he wants. And I trust you to save us both."

Chapter Fifteen

GEM FELT ABOUT AS HELPLESS AND IRRELEVANT AS he'd ever felt in his life. He wasn't used to that. He was a special operator in the baddest-ass Special Ops unit in the world. He was accustomed to being in control and having a plan. Being a part of the plan.

This time, the only part he had to play was to deliver Everly to the Capitol and then rendezvous with his team so they could follow her progress via the small patch they'd put on her skin. It was revolutionary technology with a razor-thin GPS transmitter, almost invisible unless you were looking at it. They'd applied it to the back of her neck, right beneath the hairline, and Hacker had verified there was a signal.

The entire team was in the helo that winged its way to the Pentagon. There would be a van waiting for them, and they'd drive across the bridge into DC and drop Everly off a couple of streets away from her destination. Gem would shadow her and observe the car that picked her up, then rendezvous with the team at the checkpoint. After that, they'd follow her signal and find out where she was going.

Gem had his arm around her as they rode the short distance from HOT HQ to the Pentagon. His teammates glanced over from time to time, but no one said much. Everly curled into his side and stayed there. He lay his cheek on her head and stared out the window at the wintery skyline that was growing darker every moment as nighttime approached.

They touched down at the Pentagon, and everyone piled from the military helo and into the van. Moments later, they were in motion. The major streets had been cleared by now, though the snow was still thick on the grass and parts of the sidewalks. Gem felt like time was running faster today than it had for the past week. He'd only just gotten her back, and now he had to let her go into danger? It didn't sit right, but he also couldn't deny that she was correct about what he'd do in the same situation.

He wanted to tell her that her mother wouldn't do the same for her, that there were other ways to find Ellen Fairhope, other methods, but she wasn't going to listen. Worse, if something happened and her mother didn't come back at all, she'd blame him for the things he said.

So he said nothing.

When they reached First Street SE, Muffin, who

was driving, pulled the van over near the curb and Wolf dragged the door open. Gem got down and helped Everly. She turned to face the open door, her breath frosting in the air.

"Thanks, guys. I appreciate everything you've done. And no matter what happens, I've loved every minute I've ever spent with you and your ladies."

Wolf's expression was fierce. "You're gonna be fine, Everly. We've got your back."

"I know."

She turned away, her eyes sheened with moisture, and started to walk up the sidewalk, slipping once in a while. Gem followed, his heart throbbing and throat aching with all he wanted to say. Before she made the left onto C Street, he caught her and spun her around, pressing her back against a Metro sign. It was dark out so he didn't worry they'd be seen. Then he cupped her face in his gloved hands and crushed his mouth down on hers.

She kissed him back, whimpering and shivering. When he let her go, there were tears streaking down her cheeks. He wiped them away, cursing himself for being so fucking impulsive.

"It's okay, baby. I'll be right behind you all the way. We're going to fix everything."

She smiled, but it was shaky. "I'm so sorry for everything I've put you through, Gem. I thought I was doing the right thing at the time." She closed her eyes for a second, then snapped them open again, certainty shining in their depths. "I need you to know something. I can't get in that car without telling you that I love you." She shrugged helplessly as fresh pain stabbed through him. "I've loved you for a long time, but I couldn't tell you. I needed you to be happy and live your life the way you wanted. I couldn't let you be punished for being with me, especially when it was my selfishness that kept you there—"

He put a hand over her mouth, gently. The words stopped. "Why do you think I was with you, Everly? Why the fuck do you think I did everything the way you wanted it? I didn't push you to have sex because of what you told me about your life, but I also didn't push because I wanted to do everything right with you. I've never felt like this with anyone before."

Her eyes were wide as she processed what he was saying. "But you were married once. Weren't you in love then?"

"I thought so. But no, I didn't love her. Because I never felt for her even a tenth of what I feel for you."

She bowed her head, her fingers plucking at his jacket. "Life has a funny sense of humor. I want to stay with you, go back to our safe house, and spend the day in bed. I want to hear you tell me you love me while you're making love to me, and I want to know it'll be like that forever. But we don't have forever. I don't even know if we have tomorrow." She lifted her chin and her watery gaze met his. "I'm running out of time. I have to go. But I love you, Jax. So fucking much."

He put his arms around her and held her hard, one hand on her head, pressing her cheek to his chest as the snowy DC landscape blurred before his eyes. She never called him Jax, always Gem. For some reason, that made everything feel more final than he liked.

"You're killing me, Everly. I love you and I don't want you to go."

"I know. But I have to. Kiss me, and then do everything in your power to get us out of there."

Their mouths met, warm tongues seeking, breaths mingling, until he had to let her go so she'd make it on time.

"Go, Everly. I'll be behind you, watching. I love you."

She took a couple of steps backward. "I love you, too. Find us, Gem."

She stopped, then fished beneath her jacket, pulling her locket up and over her head. She rushed back to him, pressed it in his hands, then turned and hurried away, disappearing down the sidewalk toward South Capitol Street. Gem squeezed the locket tight then put it around his neck, beneath his shirt, feeling her warmth against his skin.

"Not losing you, Everly," he growled as he started down the sidewalk. "Not ever."

HER TEARS left frozen tracks on her skin. Not literally frozen, but it didn't matter. Everly felt like everything inside her had frozen and would never be warm again.

And not because of the weather. Because of this. Because of her mother's mystery assailant, who'd been threatening to make her pay if she didn't make it right. Whatever *it* was. He hadn't won yet, but he certainly had the upper hand.

If her mother had only *listened* sooner. If she'd taken the threat more seriously in the beginning, maybe Everly would be with the man she loved instead of trudging across snowy sidewalks, moving toward a meeting she didn't want and couldn't avoid.

She wanted to turn around and see if Gem was back there, but she knew she wasn't supposed to. He was there, following and watching. She didn't need to see him to know. She felt naked without the locket she wore so often, but giving it to him had been right. A promise that she was coming back. That he would find her.

He'd said he loved her. Her heart should be soaring, and it was in some corner of her soul where danger wasn't occupying her every moment. But right now all she could think about was what would happen when she got in the car.

Not that she knew what that was yet. She reached

Independence Avenue and walked over to stand in front of the Rayburn Office Building, watching for traffic on the streets. Though it was Saturday and the roads weren't very busy, especially in light of the snow. It was also dark out, and there was a danger of freezing on some of the less traveled roads.

A white sedan approached. Everly hoped that was her ride, but the car kept going, moving up Independence Avenue toward the Capitol Hill neighborhood. She kept her hands in her pockets and thought about the patch on her skin. She hoped it was enough. She'd never seen, never heard of, such an inconspicuous GPS transmitter before. But HOT was the best, and she knew they wouldn't use it if it didn't work.

Two more cars inched past as the minutes ticked by. She wanted to look for Gem. Eventually, she let herself turn and look at everything, because that was a normal thing to do. Someone waiting for a person who was late would look at her surroundings.

Wherever Gem was, she didn't spot him. She stomped her feet and then started to pace for warmth. Her toes were cold, her nose, even her fingers, though she wore gloves and kept her hands in her pockets.

Fifteen minutes after the appointed time, another car came up the hill toward her. It was dark gray, a Toyota Sequoia, and this time it stopped. A man in a ski mask got out as Everly's heart pounded. He was big and broad and he was there for her.

"Everly Fairhope?"

She breathed in and out as panic throbbed to life inside her. What if he killed her right here? What if he shot her and left her for dead? What if it wasn't about taking her to where her mother was at all?

She had no choice, though. "Yes."

"Need you to get in the car, ma'am."

"How do I know you have my mother?"

"Your mother is a guest of Mr. Rooney's, nothing more. As are you. Please get in."

Mr. Rooney? Everly racked her brain, but she didn't come up with anything. She hoped Gem was close enough to hear the name, too. She went over to the vehicle. The man opened the back door and she got inside. There was a man in the driver's seat and one in the seat beside hers. They were also wearing ski masks. The one who'd spoken to her shut her door, then got into the front passenger seat. The locks clicked shut, and her stomach knotted.

The man beside her opened a laptop computer and started typing as the Sequoia slid away from the curb. Everly didn't look back, though her heart beat in her ears as panic began to set in. The man on the computer waved something in her direction.

"She's got a transmitter on her. I'm getting a signal coming from her body."

The one who'd let her in the car turned in his seat and regarded her with cool eyes. "Either you remove it or we will, Miss Fairhope."

She stared at him, but there was no way around it.

Once she peeled the patch off her skin and they disposed of it, Gem and his team would lose her. That kiss they'd shared on the sidewalk had felt more like goodbye than she'd cared to admit. Now she knew why.

She reached up beneath her hair and peeled the edges away. The patch took a few strands of hair with it. Her skin stung as she held it up.

Computer man whistled. "I've heard of those but haven't seen one yet. Wow. Those special ops guys get all the cool toys."

"Yeah, well, you don't get to play with it. Toss it out the window."

Computer man lowered his window and took the GPS transmitter from her fingers. Then he tossed it out. Everly wanted to cry, but what would be the good in that?

"Anything else?" the man up front asked. "We're going to find it, so you'd better tell us now."

"Nothing."

"You sure?"

She didn't like the growl in his voice. It made a little kernel of fear flare to life. But there was nothing else. "I'm sure."

Computer man was still waving his wand or whatever it was in her direction. "She's clean."

Everly let her breath out slowly. She had a feeling that if he'd pronounced her not clean, the consequences would have been painful.

"Where are we going?" Everly asked. "Is my mother safe?"

"Your mother is a guest, like I've said. She's fine, and so are you. You'll know the destination when we get there. Mr. Rooney is a private person."

"I don't know any Rooneys," Everly said.

"He knows you. That's all that counts."

Chapter Sixteen

EVERLY STARED OUT THE TINTED WINDOW AS THEY looped around the Capitol building and headed toward Massachusetts Avenue. The driver sped up, whipping into side streets, emerging again, back-tracking a bit until she was utterly confused. Which, she suspected, was the idea. Not for her, but to shake off a tail. She prayed they weren't successful.

It wasn't until they reached the area around the National Cathedral and hooked west that she began to get an idea where they were headed. They drove into Wesley Heights, traversing down snowy streets with gated houses that sat back off the road under cover of trees. Some houses weren't visible from the road at all. Finally, they turned into a drive with an iron gate and a guard shack out front.

Everly was still scared, but she felt like she could breathe a bit easier. They were still in the city, and that was something. Maybe Gem and his team had been able to follow her after all.

The gates swung open and they drove up a twisty drive until a beautiful Mid-century modern mansion appeared. Windows were the first thing you saw all along the front of the house, followed by the smooth stucco façade in a white that blended with the snow. The windows blazed with light.

The SUV pulled into one of the open garage doors, which rolled slowly down behind them. Everly curled her hands into fists, her nails digging into her palms.

The man in the front seat got out and opened her door for her. He'd removed his ski mask. Recognition hit her, and her stomach twisted. This man had been shadowing her mother for the past few days. Her bodyguard, she'd said. Everly had so many questions. He reached for her and she shrank back against the leather.

His expression didn't change as she recoiled from him. He took her by the arm, dragged her out of the SUV, and propelled her toward a door that led to the interior. Her arm hurt where he'd wrenched it to drag her from the vehicle, but Everly still jerked it from his grip. He let her go and she followed him through the house. It was every bit as stark and modern inside as it was outside. He stopped in front of a gorgeous wooden door and rapped on it softly. Someone said to come in, and the man opened the door and stepped to the side, motioning her through.

Everly's gaze landed on the man sitting on a leather Chesterfield sofa, a glass of whisky in his hand.

"Everly!" Her mother jumped up from a chair opposite.

Everly hadn't noticed her at first, but now she cried, "Mama!" reverting to her childhood name for her mother.

The name she'd used before Ellen Fairhope became a United States Congresswoman and changed everything about herself so that the sweet, attentive mother had faded into memory.

Her mother rushed over to hug her. Everly wrapped her arms around her, thinking maybe she'd had it all wrong. Maybe everything was fine and this had been a misunderstanding. Her mother was clearly well, not a mark on her, and this Mr. Rooney, whoever he was, seemed like anything but a villain as he sat on his couch and watched their reunion.

"You shouldn't have come, Everly," her mother said sternly. "You should have stayed away."

Everly frowned. "But you were missing, and we were worried. The president is worried too, Mother. Why didn't you let anyone know where you were?"

"Ah, that's my fault, I'm afraid," Mr. Rooney said. "I wouldn't allow her to make any calls except to you.

But you, naughty girl, lost your phone. Threw it out a car window, actually, but no matter. You're here now."

Everly's stomach clenched. There was only one way he could know that…

Before she could say anything, her mother gripped her hand, pushing Everly behind her. "Leave her out of this, Josh. I told you before that I'd do as you asked."

Josh Rooney. Everly still wasn't sure when she'd heard the name, but it was familiar. And then it hit her. She'd been pouring over documents lately, and that one was prominent.

"JLR Enterprises," she said. "You're competing for the base contracts for Qu'rim and the middle east. Maintenance and base oversight."

Those were lucrative deals where private firms came in and took over the infrastructure. They were responsible for disposing of military equipment and waste, and they had access to tens of millions of dollars in construction and equipment loans. They also had access to cash, which was designed to grease the way with local authorities and informants. Untraceable, large amounts of US dollars. Easy to divert some of it to your own coffers if you were unscrupulous about stealing money that rightfully belonged to every US citizen.

"Smart girl. See, Ellen? I told you she wasn't oblivious to your dealings."

Everly didn't know what he was talking about, but

she wasn't about to give him the satisfaction of asking the question that hung on the tip of her tongue. Her mother's fingers were tight around hers. Tight and cold. Everly squeezed back, wanting her to know it was okay.

Her mother turned to her and gripped her shoulders. "I'm sorry, Everly. I made a mistake, and I never wanted you to be a part of this. I'm going to fix it, I promise."

Everly frowned as she looked into her mother's eyes. "Whatever it is, I'm sure it's going to be okay."

Her throat was a knot and her stomach churned, but her mother nodded, her eyes closing before she spun back to face Josh Rooney. "Let her go, Josh. I'll get your votes. I promise you."

He stood. He wasn't especially tall, but he was built like a bulldog. Like a former military guy who'd let at least a little of his muscle go slack. Like maybe he worked his upper body more frequently than his lower, but still ate hamburgers on a regular basis.

He wasn't hard and fit like Gem, but he wasn't fat either. And yet he was completely intimidating as he closed the distance between them, whisky still in hand, ice cubes rattling as he finished off the last dregs. He was almost to them when he moved to the bar instead, placing the glass on the smooth mahogany wood and taking the stopper out of a bottle of Scotch.

Bushmills. Not cheap stuff.

"You promised me that a month ago, Ellen. I'm tired of waiting, honey. Now you go get in the car with Tony and trot back to the Capitol. I expect a favorable outcome before Congress leaves for the holiday, or Everly's stay with me could be of some duration."

"I'm not going without her." Her mother was still standing in front of her as if she could shield Everly from harm with nothing more than her body.

Josh Rooney sighed. Then he motioned to Tony, who still stood in the door. Tony walked into the room and stopped in front of her mother. Then he punched her in the stomach. Everly's mother dropped to her knees, sucking wind, and Everly screamed, dropping with her, arms around her mother's shoulders.

"Mom. Mama." She closed her eyes, anger and fear churning inside. "Don't fight. Just do what they ask. It'll be okay. Everything will be okay."

Tears ran down her cheeks as hatred burned hot in her soul. But she was helpless to do anything. She just needed to get her mother to go, and then she could pray that Gem found her like he'd promised.

Her mother's gaze met hers. Her eyes were watery and pain pinched the corners of her mouth. "I'm sorry," she wheezed. "Didn't want you to come."

"I had to."

"As charming as this is, it's time to go, Ellen. Think about doing anything but getting my votes, think you can call the FBI or those HOT soldiers or the fucking Girl Scouts, and your daughter will never be found. Get my contract awarded, and she'll be home in time for Christmas."

Everly stood and helped her mother to her feet. Tony waited, hands crossed in front of his body, calmly waiting to be called on again to commit violence against a woman half his size and nearly twice his age. Disgusting prick.

"Go, Mother. Do what you need to do. I'll be fine."

Her mother hugged her hard. Something she hadn't done in years now. Then Tony dragged her from the room and Everly was left alone with Josh Rooney. He sipped his drink then motioned her to sit. She didn't want to, but she did it anyway, straining to hear sound from outside the room. Was Gem coming to get her? Was that his team breaking in? Or was it a door slamming as Tony took her mother to the SUV?

There was a noise behind her and she turned as another man walked in. A moment later, a sharp pain pricked her arm and she spun around. Josh Rooney stood over her, a syringe in his hand.

"Sorry, sweetheart, but it's good night for now."

"THEY FUCKING FOUND THE GPS," Hacker said. "How did they know to look for it?"

Gem ground his teeth together and didn't say a

word. He was incapable of speech just now. He'd watched Everly get into that Toyota Sequoia, dying a little inside as she did. Letting it happen went against everything he'd wanted to do in that moment.

But he had, and now they'd lost a vital link to her. The signal was somewhere in the street near the Capitol, not moving, but the Toyota was. Muffin followed it at a distance. And then the driver whipped onto a side street.

"Motherfucker." Muffin hit the gas and skidded around the same corner. Taillights slid out of sight down another side street. "Hang on, bitches," Muffin said. "It's gonna get bumpy."

And slick. That was a given with the slush and snow.

"You're sure the name you heard ended with knee?"

Hacker again. He'd closed his computer while they held on for dear life, but his mind was always turning.

"Mr. Knee. That's what it sounded like. Dude's voice was too low on the first part of the name, but I heard the last part. He said Mr. Something-knee." Gem raked a hand over his head. "Trust me, I keep trying to reason it out and see what I can come up with, but the first syllable is lost."

"Fucking hell," Muffin said a few tense minutes later. "Do you see them?"

Saint was beside him in the passenger seat. "No.

Keep going. They can't have gotten all that far. They kept going down side streets, backtracking, then always back to Mass Ave."

"We can't lose them," Gem said, low-grade panic starting to unfurl within. "We don't have a GPS signal, and we can't just lose Everly like a bunch of fucking amateurs."

"I'm sorry, Gem," Muffin said, not taking his eyes off the road. "I'm trying."

"They aren't amateurs," Saint threw at him. "There's some training there and you know it."

True. Didn't make it any better though.

"I'll hack into the traffic cams," Hacker said, opening his laptop again now that they weren't careening down side streets. "Maybe we can work out the route that way."

Gem put his head in his hands and told himself to breathe. Beside him, Wolf lay a hand on his shoulder and squeezed. "We'll find her. Might take a little longer than we'd planned, but we'll find her. This is what we do."

Gem nodded. If they didn't find Everly, if he didn't protect her like he'd promised, he didn't know if he'd be able to wake up every day knowing he'd failed the woman he loved. Knowing he hadn't been good enough to save her.

Chapter Seventeen

GEM STILL HAD HIS BADGE TO GET INTO THE RAYBURN Office Building. At seven a.m. sharp on Monday morning, thirty-six hours since Everly had disappeared, he was strolling through security like he owned the place, ready to break some heads. Zany was with him, having also procured a badge thanks to HOT and Mendez.

Gem hadn't slept much over the past thirty-six hours, and he was pissed as hell. Fire-breathing pissed. Frantic, too. Hacker had accessed the street cams. They'd found the Sequoia at different points, enough to tell it was headed into Northwest DC.

After that, they'd lost track because there'd been no more street cams to access.

Gem had allowed himself a real first class freak out. He'd gotten out of the van and screamed his anger to the cold, dark, snowy landscape until he was hoarse. If he'd been any less well-trained, he'd have pulled his pistol and shot every fucking round he had into the night air.

He'd needed to shout, to rage, to grieve the loss of his woman. Not the permanent loss, never that, but the fact they'd lost her when he'd promised he would come for her. Promised he would save her.

Fucking hell.

Now, Gem was determined. Everly's locket lay against his skin, beneath his shirt, burning a hole in him. He had a mission and he wasn't going to be deterred. Not two hours after they'd lost Everly, Ellen Fairhope had returned home with her security guard. She'd called the president, who'd let Mendez know.

Bob Schaffer had turned up, too, though he hadn't been missing at all. He'd simply turned his phone off because he and his wife were going through marriage counseling and he'd promised the weekends to her. When he'd checked his phone late Sunday night and saw the flurry of calls, he'd responded immediately. His wife and two sons were proof he'd been home with them, so that was a dead end.

But Ellen Fairhope? She was fair game so far as Gem was concerned. She hadn't answered any calls, either, at least not from him. He hadn't had a prayer's chance of getting close to her before now, but he fucking wasn't stopping until he had answers.

Wendy looked up as Gem entered the suite. Michael was there as well. He glanced Gem's way, but quickly dropped his gaze again. Gem would have stalked over and ripped the guy up by his tie, but he had bigger fish to fry. And Michael Franks wasn't capable of kidnapping Everly, evading pursuit, and disappearing with her. The guy was standoffish, but he wasn't a mastermind and he didn't have the resources. Professional opinion.

"Hi, Gem," Wendy said brightly. "I have some things for Everly to sign—"

Gem kept walking and Zany went with him, though he heard Zany say, "Sorry, ma'am, important business."

At the end of the corridor, Ellen Fairhope's office loomed. Her secretary, Abby, looked up as Gem and Zany walked into the atrium.

"Hi, Gem. Can I help—"

Gem ignored her, too, twisting the knob on Ellen's door until it swung open. Ellen's head snapped up. She was on the phone, and she didn't look anywhere near as polished as she usually did. Her blond hair was lanky and limp, she had dark circles under her eyes, and the whites were red. Her nose was red, too. She still managed to look outraged, however, and that set Gem's teeth on edge.

"Abby!" she called, jumping to her feet. "Get these men out of here."

"Yes, ma'am. Sorry, ma'am," Abby said, rushing into the room.

But one thing they hadn't learned yet was that

Gem wasn't going to be deterred. He crossed his arms and stood still as a stone while Abby hovered over him, trying to shoo him away. Zany apologized and Gem glared at him.

"This'll go faster if she leaves," Gem growled.

Ellen looked fierce and determined, and then she looked defeated. She waved a hand and Abby left, closing the door behind her. "Sergeant Stone, you are really trying my patience," Ellen said, giving a superior sniff. "What do you want?"

"Everly," he snarled. And then he was at her desk, lunging across it, his face in hers before she could blink. "Where the fuck is she?"

A thousand emotions crossed her features before she went stone cold again. "You mean you don't know?" she asked. "What a bodyguard you are."

Her voice nearly broke on that last. He paid attention. "What aren't you telling me, Ms. Fairhope? You know something."

Her hand shook as she reached for the phone again. "I don't know what you're talking about. I have to make some calls. There are important government contracts that need to be finalized before the recess. Please see yourselves out."

Gem closed his eyes. Told himself he wasn't going to throttle this woman. "She disappeared, Ms. Fairhope. She took a phone call and she went to save *you.* She didn't come back, but you did. And I want to know where. The. Fuck. She. Is."

He finished that last on a hard growl. Ellen Fairhope blinked at him. And then she burst into tears.

"Please," she cried. "You have to go. Before he sees you. If he knows you're here—"

She cried even harder then. Gem was taken aback. "What are you talking about? You have to tell me."

She dropped her head onto her arms, then sat up again and swiped angrily beneath her eyes. "I don't have to tell you anything. You can't help her. I have to get this contract approved, and then she'll be safe." She grabbed his arm and squeezed it hard. "He'll kill her if you're involved. If HOT is involved. You can't go after her."

Shock reverberated through him. Shock and horror and anger. She knew what had happened to Everly, but she was too scared to share it. "We can get her back safe. But we have to know—"

"No! Now go, before Tony comes back from the men's room. He's here to watch me, to listen. If he sees you, if you move against Josh, she's dead. Please, Sergeant. If you care about her, you'll *go.* I'll fix everything, and she'll come home."

Josh.

"Ellen," Gem said, "you have to tell me everything. We won't make a move if it's not safe, but we have to know. I'm the good guy here. I swear it."

Her fierce expression collapsed. She nodded as

she swiped beneath her nose. "Go, please. Now. Be in Statuary Hall at ten a.m. Stand on the plaque that marks where John Quincy Adams's desk was. I'll be there, but don't approach me. I'll tell you everything then if you'll trust me."

Gem didn't want to wait until ten o'clock, but it was clear Ellen wasn't going to say anything further. She was fearful, and Josh Something-knee had someone stationed here to watch her every move. He'd give her until ten.

"If you aren't there, I'm coming back. And I won't go away until you tell me what I want to know."

Her face was pale. "I'll be there."

WHEN EVERLY WOKE AGAIN, she was in the dark. She lay still and did an inventory of her body. Everything *felt* okay. That was something.

She pushed herself upright. Her head throbbed and her mouth was dry, like she'd been drinking alcohol. She hadn't though. She remembered Gem kissing her on a dark street, and then she remembered getting into an SUV with three men and being taken to an exclusive area of the city where her mother waited with a man named Josh Rooney.

A man who wanted a contract to manage bases in the Middle East, and who seemed as if he would stop at nothing to get it. She didn't understand why. It was lucrative, sure. There could potentially be a lot of unmarked cash that moved through his hands. But Josh Rooney was already living pretty well. So what else was there?

A chill slipped through her as she remembered what was at stake in Qu'rim. Uranium. Having access to a mine could be very advantageous for someone with questionable morals. Life-changing.

Everly swung her legs around to put them on the floor. But the floor was only a couple of inches away, which meant she was lying on a mattress with no frame.

She rolled to her knees and tried to stand. It took a few tries as she gripped the edge of the mattress with her fists, but she made it. She locked her knees and stood until the queasiness subsided. Her legs wobbled as she moved, but she was determined to make it to the small window high up on the wall a few feet away. She didn't know why, except it was the only light she could see.

When she reached the wall, she put her palms against it. Cold concrete. The window was above her head, which meant she was probably in a basement. She turned, trying to make out shapes in the dark. Her glasses were long gone and she wasn't wearing contacts, so things were both blurry and dark. There was the mattress on the floor, but the rest of the space appeared empty from what she could see of it. Except for a bucket not far from the mattress. She wondered if that was meant to be her toilet, and she sucked back a whimper.

She would *not* crumble. Gem was coming for her. She knew he was coming. She had faith. If she had to pee in a bucket, then she would. Gem had to endure worse deprivations on missions. She could endure this. For him. Because he was coming for her.

Everly made her way around the room, feeling her way, peering into dark corners, but there was nothing. She found a door, but it wouldn't budge. There was no food, no water. She was alone in a cold basement with a bucket and a mattress. She had her coat and gloves, but no blanket. No pillow.

Everly went back to the mattress and sat down. She stared at the window, at the meager light coming through, and prayed that Gem was on his way. She didn't know how he was going to find her without the GPS tracker, but he would. She knew he would.

She just had to believe.

AFTER GEM and Zany left Ellen Fairhope's office, he called Saint and gave him the name.

Josh Something-knee.

That was more to go on than they'd had before. Hacker would find something. He had to.

Gem didn't like walking out of Ellen's office without answers, but she'd been scared. He believed that she thought she was protecting Everly by doing what this Josh person wanted, but he had to convince her it wasn't true. Somehow, he had to convince her to trust him instead.

It was an hour later, when he was stalking the halls of the House and Senate office buildings while Zany kept an eye on who came and went from Ellen's office, that something she'd said triggered a thought. He dialed Saint.

"She said she had to make calls about important government contracts that needed finalized before the recess. That Everly would be safe if she got a contract approved. That's what this guy's involved in. We need to take a look at contracts up for bid right now."

Saint whistled. "Corruption? Ellen Fairhope? Wow."

"I don't know if it's corruption or not, but why else would she be at the office when her daughter's missing, looking like death warmed over, and making calls to finalize contracts if a contractor wasn't involved somehow? I thought she was burying herself in work, making excuses, but that's not what she meant. She meant *this* contract—whatever contract it is. We need to find it."

"We'll get it figured out."

Gem closed his eyes for a second. "We have to, Saint. I promised I'd keep Everly safe, and every second she's not with me—fuck, it kills me to think she's scared and alone and wondering where I am."

He didn't say the rest of it because he couldn't. That she was hurt. That if he didn't find her in time, she'd be dead. He couldn't think those thoughts and make it through the day.

"I know, buddy. I really do. We'll find her."

Gem knew that Saint had been through his own hell when Brooke and a little girl she cared about were kidnapped by a drug cartel and taken to Colombia. Didn't help him feel any better now, though. Saint knew it, too, but Gem appreciated the gesture.

"I'm going a little crazy here," he said. "I feel useless."

"Not useless. You've gotten us a name and a motive. We didn't have that before. Look, these guys are professionals too. They knew to look for a tracker, and they knew to do evasive driving to shake off a tail. That narrows the field a bit. We're going to find this motherfucker, and we're going to get Everly back."

"Yeah, all right. I gotta go. It's almost time for the meeting. If she doesn't come, I'm going to track her ass down and pin her to the fucking wall with my hands around her throat until I get some answers."

Saint, the ever-patient team leader, sighed. "Gem, honey, promise Daddy you won't do that. Ellen Fairhope is still a powerful congresswoman, and Capitol security will shoot your ass if you do something so asinine."

Gem almost laughed. Almost. "Fine, Daddy, I

won't choke the congresswoman. Yet. Get us some answers though, or I can't promise a thing."

AT A FEW MINUTES TO TEN, Gem walked into Statuary Hall to wait. There was a tour group standing near the John Quincy Adams plaque, so he had to wait. Once they were gone, he walked over to the spot and stood on it. Words dropped down on him as clearly as if someone was standing right beside him and speaking in his ear. He looked around the room, wondering what the hell was going on, and saw a young woman on the other side of the room talking to the boy beside her.

Every word she said was as clear as day. Gem was transfixed. The woman and boy moved away, and a few minutes later Ellen Fairhope came into the room. She looked haggard. Nothing like the confident woman of power she usually was. He was struck again by the circles beneath her eyes.

She didn't acknowledge him. But she did look his way, presumably to make sure no one else was standing near. There weren't many people in the hall anyway. The tour group had moved along, and there were only a couple of stragglers who were making their way to the exit.

"It's a trick of the dome," she said softly, her words in his ear. "It was thought that John Quincy

Adams heard everything his opponents were planning simply because of where he sat. But it's unlikely, as the room was a bit different during his time, and the dome as well. There were probably also rugs, which would have dampened the effect. Anyway, it works for our purposes."

She clasped her hands together and watched him, though she pretended to look at the statues as well. "I don't have a lot of time. And I'm not sure it's a good idea to tell you anything, but if you can get my daughter home safe, then I'm willing to try. But if she dies, Sergeant Stone, it'll be on your head as much as mine. You must take care with what I'm about to tell you, and you mustn't allow any of your fellow military persons—team, whatever—to go off half-cocked. Josh Rooney means business, and he will kill her if he knows you're coming. He'll pass it off as an accident, an unfortunate accident, and everyone will believe him. He's had practice at this, I assure you."

Gem's insides were winding tighter and tighter with every word. He didn't know if she could hear him in return, but he spoke anyway. "Everly's safety is the most important thing to me. I want to know where she is, who took her, so I can figure out how to get her back. This isn't about military heroics, Ms. Fairhope. I love your daughter. I want to marry her. And even if that isn't possible, then I want her alive in the world so I can keep living too. That's all that matters to me.

That she is alive and well, even if she can't be with me."

Ellen bowed her head. He wasn't sure she'd heard, but then she nodded. "I'm entrusting you with this, Sergeant, knowing I'm sealing my own doom. But I don't care. Get her back safely. Bring her home, and you will have my eternal thanks."

She sucked in a breath. And then everything spilled out in a rush until Gem could hardly contain it all. When she was done, she walked away and he was alone.

There wasn't a lot of time, but Gem knew what he had to do.

Chapter Eighteen

Time ticked slowly when you were locked away with no distractions. There was no phone to scroll, no television to watch, no books to read, no window she could actually see out of. Everly's belly gnawed itself from the inside out, and her mouth was dry. She'd peed in the bucket once, but she had nothing left to give. She thought she'd kill for a bottle of water right about now.

She tried to sleep, and did in snatches, but mostly she was awake. Roaming her prison at first, but then lying on her back and staring up at the ceiling. There were steel beams and concrete above her head. She didn't know if that meant she'd been moved to another location, or if she was still in Josh Rooney's house. His house was industrial enough that it could be his basement. It could also be a basement in a different building. Commercial, maybe. Or a warehouse, though did warehouses have basements?

By the time Everly heard a key scraping in the lock, she thought she was hallucinating the sound. But light flooded her prison, and her heart leapt with joy. Gem had come to get her!

She struggled to push herself up. She knew she had to look like hell, but Gem wouldn't care. He'd carry her out of there and make sure she got food and water, then he'd wash her tenderly and tuck her into bed beside him so she could feel his heart beating next to hers and know she was okay.

Except it wasn't Gem. It was one of the men who'd been in the SUV, though not Tony. She still cringed because she wasn't sure if this one was coming to hit her the way Tony had hit her mother. He stopped near the mattress and dropped something on it.

Then he shined a light in her face, and Everly threw a hand over her eyes.

"Your mama's running out of time, sweetheart," the man said. "Maybe she doesn't care what happens to you now that she's free."

Everly didn't respond. She had a feeling he wanted her to. Like he wanted an excuse for violence. She didn't know why he'd need one, but she kept her head down and didn't say anything.

He made a disgusted sound and walked away. The door scraped shut behind him and the lock clicked.

Everly searched for what he'd dropped. A large bottle of water and a package of crackers. She twisted the top and drank greedily before telling herself she needed to make it last. The crackers were peanut butter, which meant she'd need to drink more, but she was hungry so she ate three of them and sipped a little more water.

Then she lay back and closed her eyes. Where was Gem? Why wasn't he here yet?

A tear slid down her cheek and dripped onto the fabric of the mattress. She dashed it away angrily and told herself not to cry.

It didn't work, though.

GEM AND ZANY returned to HOT HQ where the rest of the team gathered in Strike Team 2's ready room. Mendez and Ghost were there, too. Everyone looked as pissed as Gem felt.

"Josh Rooney," Mendez said, and a slide appeared on the screen overhead. "JLR Enterprises has a few base security contracts overseas. He's looking to push beyond that and into base maintenance, construction, and procurement. That's top to bottom control of the structure, with a lot of power over what gets done and by whom. It's pretty much a pipeline for money laundering. Not only that, but there's the uranium mine in Qu'rim we helped secure a few years ago. Might not have anything to do with his plans, but it might. Can't rule it out."

The slide changed. There was a photo of Rooney from a few years ago. He wore an Army uniform and held a service rifle. The background was the Afghan high desert, and he had a big grin on his unshaven face as he perched on the hood of a dirt-colored Humvee.

"Former Army Ranger Lieutenant Josh Rooney. He left the military after four deployments in Afghanistan and Iraq, and founded his own company focusing on private security in war zones. He recruits from all the services, special forces and otherwise, and most of what his people have done until now is provide base security, especially for civilian contractors. He's made a lot of connections, and he's worked his way into the Washington scene over the past five years or so. He is, by all accounts, also very charming. Which probably explains what happened next. Gem?"

Gem was still reeling from everything Ellen Fairhope had told him, but it certainly made a lot more sense than a random attack by a stalker who wanted her to pay for crimes they'd failed to elaborate upon in any of the messages she'd gotten.

"Yes, sir." He cleared his throat. "Congresswoman Fairhope and Mr. Rooney had a romantic relationship they kept secret. It went on for a little over a year, and Ms. Fairhope nudged contracts in Rooney's favor during that period. He kept detailed records. He recorded all their conversations and, uh, liaisons. He's been threatening to expose the relationship to keep her in line. She said it ended months ago, about the time she made that trip to Qu'rim. He's probably the one behind the attack on the convoy, but there's no proof. Still, her no longer being with him doesn't really matter. Her position on the House Armed Services Committee, and the fact he had contracts up for discussion and vote before the committee while they were still seeing each other, means she's in a bad position should it come to light."

"Corruption at its finest," Saint muttered.

"She said he's been pushing hard for this contract, and when she told him there was opposition on the committee, he started threatening her with violence. The shots fired at me and Everly were a warning meant to intimidate Congresswoman Fairhope into getting him what he wanted. He called her the next day and told her as much."

"Explains why they missed," Muffin said.

"And why they came after us at Mal and Scarlett's. Still not sure how they knew where to find us, but I suspect he's got contacts who helped him. According to Ms. Fairhope, he intended to put pressure on her by taking and holding Everly. When he failed, he went the somewhat trickier route of abducting a sitting congresswoman and using her to get Everly to come to him."

"Sick fuck," Zany muttered.

Gem hadn't liked Ellen much, but the way she'd begged him not to risk Everly's life, and how disheveled and scared she looked, made him think Everly was right after all. Her mother loved her. She just had a shitty way of showing it with her overbearing interference in Everly's life. He still wasn't prepared to forgive her for that stunt in Qu'rim, but maybe Everly had that right, too, and her mother had thought she was putting the country's interests first.

Mendez folded his arms and stared at the photo of a smiling Rooney. "His people found Everly when they shouldn't have been able to, they found the tracker we put on her, and they evaded pursuit. I'm thinking a guy like that is feeling pretty cocky right about now. He successfully abducted Ellen Fairhope, and now he has her daughter so she'll do his bidding. Which she's doing. What about this Tony guy?"

Ghost clicked to the next slide. "Anthony Borelli. Also a former Ranger. Been working for Rooney since he went into business."

"That's Ellen's bodyguard," Gem growled. "I never heard his name, but I saw him with her a couple of times last week. Fucking hell, I didn't recognize him when he picked up Everly because he had on a ski mask."

"Explains why he disappeared when she did," Saint said.

Mendez shook his head. "I gotta be honest here

and say I have no idea how deep Rooney's connections go. It's a risk to move against him, but I think we have to take it. We need to grab Borelli in such a way that Rooney isn't alerted and interrogate him."

Mendez frowned, thinking. Then he started for the door, calling over his shoulder, "Get a plan for infiltrating Rooney's property. Find out everything you can about his movements for the past seventy-two hours. I've got a phone call to make."

Mendez was gone, but Ghost remained. "You heard the man. Let's get busy finding out where this dickhead soldier of fortune's been going. Trace any and all vehicles belonging to Rooney or his company, find any buildings or warehouses he owns. Let's find all the possible places he could stash Everly Fairhope."

TWO HOURS LATER, a HOT team waited inside the White House's west wing for Congresswoman Fairhope to arrive for her meeting with the president, something Mendez had asked him to set up. Naturally, she'd complied with the request, taking her security guard along for the ride. Not that she had a choice about bringing him since his orders were to shadow her.

When Anthony Borelli walked into the Oval Office, unarmed and unaware, he was handcuffed and taken out a different entrance than he'd entered. Mendez enjoyed the expression on the man's face, especially when he got a look at the stars on Mendez's shoulders and the Special Operations badge on his pocket. Ellen Fairhope had stared as he was led out, her jaw opening and closing like a fish's, before tears sprang to her eyes and she had to be helped to one of the couches flanking a coffee table in front of the Resolute Desk.

"M-my daughter?" she'd asked.

"We're working on that, Ellen," President Campbell said gently as he took a seat beside her. "But we need your help. I want you to tell General Mendez everything you know about Josh Rooney, okay?"

Ellen turned to look at the tall, handsome man with salt-and-pepper hair standing nearby. A man she hadn't seen when she'd first entered the room. She'd met him on a few occasions, but they'd never spoken more than a few words.

Ellen nodded as the general took a seat across from her. The president squeezed her shoulder as he stood, then left via the outer door that would lead him back to the Residence. Her career was over, but that no longer mattered. In a way, she was relieved. The grief would come later, but not right now. There was no room for it.

She sniffled as she gazed at the man across from her who could save her daughter. Or doom her if he got it wrong.

"I understand your fear," he said softly. "I'm a

parent myself, and I worry every day. But I don't think Josh Rooney intends to let her go, ma'am. I think she's in grave danger, and I believe you are as well should he get what he wants. That's why I need your help."

Ellen closed her eyes for a brief moment. She had to dig deep for the dignity she'd squandered the day she'd allowed her loneliness to take charge of her life and let the wrong man in, but she found it. She always found strength when she needed it most.

"What would you like to know, General?"

IT WAS dark when the men came to get her. Everly didn't remember falling asleep, but she had. She'd eaten all the crackers, peed in the bucket, cried until her eyes swelled and her throat ached, and now she was being rudely hauled up off the mattress and thrown over a man's shoulder.

"Put me down," she said, but her voice didn't work the way it should, and the words came out as a single whispered sound.

"Did she drink all the water?" a man asked when the one carrying her reached the top of the stairs he'd been walking up.

"Not all of it, but a good amount," the other man trailing after them said.

"Good. Should be enough sedative to keep her quiet. Put her in the car."

"Nooooo," Everly cried.

But the men paid her no attention. She was tossed into a trunk, and the lid slammed shut. They didn't bother to tie her, though, which she thought was a mistake.

Or maybe not, since they'd drugged her and she couldn't command her arms or legs to do anything at the moment.

She'd needed the water so badly she hadn't questioned it. She hadn't even noticed if it'd tasted weird or not. She'd just been thirsty, and she'd drank, conserving what she could since she'd had no idea how long it would be before someone brought more.

Soon the car was in motion. Everly lay on her side, trying to will herself to stay awake, to fight when next they opened the trunk, but it was a losing game. Sleep was easier because she didn't feel any pain. Besides, when she slept, she saw Gem. She clung to the hope he'd find her, but a part of her was beginning to think he might fail. That he was only human after all, and that his promises, no matter how sincere, were empty.

No! She wouldn't listen to that despairing voice. Wouldn't let it poison her hope.

"Gem," she muttered. "Please."

And then she was gone again, sleep dragging her down into a comforting silence.

When next she woke, her mind sharpened a little quicker than before. She blinked as she tried to focus on her surroundings. There was light this time, not much, but she could see she was somewhere different than before. A room she didn't think was a basement. It didn't feel as damp for one thing. The walls looked like they could be made of plaster or drywall, though it was hard to tell without her glasses. There was carpet beneath her feet. A bank of windows let in lights she assumed were from other buildings.

There was a chemical smell to the air, too, but she didn't know what it was.

Her neck ached. It took her a moment to realize she was sitting in a chair, her hands duct taped together, her legs duct taped to the chair legs. Everly lifted her chin and the room spun a bit before it stopped. She gently rolled her neck from one side to the other, trying to ease the kink.

"Careful how much you move, sweetheart."

Everly jerked. Josh Rooney came into view, holding a cell phone. "Pretty sure the detonator won't trigger if you fall over, but it might."

He grinned, and her heart thumped. "Why are you doing this?" came out as "Whyudoooos?"

He tipped her chin up and looked into her eyes. His were blue, but not the pretty blue of Gem's. No, they were without depth. Shallow, self-absorbed. Superior. Like he never lost and never would.

"Too bad we don't have more time. It'd be kinda

fun to fuck you, too. See who's better. Mother or daughter."

Everly shuddered.

"Don't worry. I've got someplace to be, and you'll see stars of a different kind when this IED explodes."

"Noooopeas...."

"It won't hurt. You won't know it happened, not really. I mean I don't know for sure since nobody ever tells you about it after, but it definitely doesn't last. Boom, gone. This whole place is gonna burn hot, so there won't be anything left of you to find. Shame."

He hunkered down in front of her. "I can see you want to know why. Tony missed the last check-in, which ain't good. That means your mother has probably betrayed me, and she's betrayed you. If she'd just done what I told her to do, none of this would happen. But they come looking for you here, they'll trip the wire. Or maybe I'll trigger the detonator by calling it. Just for fun."

She couldn't turn her head away when he smashed his mouth down on hers. His tongue was in her mouth, gagging her, and then he pulled away, laughing.

"Now if she calls me with good news, or Tony shows up, I'll deactivate the trigger. We'll all laugh about this together, and life will be good. If she doesn't call, well, kaboom. Lights out, sweetheart."

He kissed her again, then stood and turned away. She was still gagging as he strode across the room.

The door opened and shut, and she was alone with the silence ticking in her ears.

Or maybe that was the bomb. Everly was scared to move at first. She tried to find the sound, to see the bomb, but it seemed to be behind her. She looked for any thin wires near her chair legs, but saw none. Tentatively, she lifted her hands. Other than being taped together, she could move them. It took her a few tries, because she was still a bit groggy, but she finally managed to bite into the tape at her wrists.

Once she had it, she wasn't letting go. If she could get her hands free, maybe she stood a chance.

Unless Rooney called and triggered the bomb before she succeeded.

Chapter Nineteen

TIME WAS RUNNING OUT.

Gem and his team scaled the warehouse in Maryland where they thought Josh Rooney had taken Everly. They didn't know for sure, but they had to act or risk losing her for good according to Anthony Borelli. He'd told them they had two hours max, and that was over an hour ago.

Gem didn't completely trust Borelli's information, but Mendez had put the screws to him pretty hard. Given the choice between cooperating and helping to get Everly back, or being a traitor to his nation and charged as a co-conspirator in the kidnapping and murder of a Member of Congress's daughter, Borelli had flipped his allegiance pretty damned fast.

He'd given them Rooney's burner number for this job and told them the plan as far as he knew. Rooney liked to keep his plans close to his chest, which meant

Borelli didn't know everything. He was an hour past his check-in time at that point, which would likely trigger action.

If Rooney didn't hear from Borelli within three hours of a scheduled check-in, he'd assume the plan had gone wrong and have Everly disposed of as a big fuck-you to Ellen. He'd do it in such a way there was no evidence and he'd walk free. Then he'd go after Ellen.

Gem had almost leaped over the table and ripped the man's throat out, but Zany had wrapped his arms around Gem and kept him from doing it.

They'd debated having Borelli call Rooney with an excuse for being late, but Borelli told them Rooney wouldn't buy it and he'd have to go in person. No way in hell were they letting that happen, which meant that option was officially off the table.

Hacker had traced the burner and found Rooney at his house. Shortly after, the burner had been on the move while his official cell stayed put. When he ended up at a warehouse facility in an industrial area near Baltimore, Hacker went to work searching for traffic and security cameras so they could see what happened when Rooney arrived.

Rooney was smarter than that, though. There was nothing to look at because he'd clearly known where to avoid cameras. His phone was on site for no more than thirty minutes before he'd left again. They'd had to decide whether he'd taken Everly to the warehouse, kept her at his house, or if she was somewhere else entirely.

When they'd asked Borelli, he'd said Rooney wouldn't keep her at his house. He wouldn't take the risk of Ellen Fairhope crossing him and getting caught red-handed. That meant HOT was breaking into the warehouse.

Mendez and Ghost had sent another Strike Team to shadow Rooney while Gem's team went to Maryland. Only after they confirmed they had Everly safe would the other team take Rooney into custody.

Gem and his team entered the warehouse from the roof. Immediately, they were hit with a strong odor of jet fuel emanating from the warehouse floor. They were a few miles from the airport, and this wasn't exactly a fuel storage facility.

The hairs on Gem's neck prickled. Something wasn't right about that. His team felt it too, because they exchanged looks, silent, frowning, before they crept along the gallery at the top of the warehouse to the bank of storage containers stacked three stories high.

There, they split up and dispersed into smaller teams of two. On one side of the warehouse, there were offices and smaller storage rooms. Everly could be in one of those, or she could be in one of the many containers stacked one on top of the other. Despair rose hot and heavy inside him, but he tamped it down and moved as softly as possible toward the second-floor offices.

The steel staircase creaked under his weight. Zany was behind him, also trying not to make noise, but there was only so much they could do. On the warehouse floor, something dropped and struck with a metallic clang. Gem held his breath.

"Fucking bumped into a shelf and a box of tools fell off the edge." It was Muffin's voice coming through the comm.

"Nobody's shooting, so I guess we're good," Saint replied.

Gem let out a breath—and then there was another sound. A voice.

"Gem? Is that you? Are you coming for me? Please, please, please. Someone. Anyone. Please!"

The voice came from one of the rooms above. Every emotion he had told him to run, to find her, to get her out of there. But his instincts said no. They also said *wait, easy, careful*.

Zany shook his head, a short sharp gesture. Gem acknowledged the signal.

The rest of the team converged quickly and they moved up the stairs, heading toward the sound.

"Building's clear," Saint whispered in their ears. "But something's not right."

"Agreed," Wolf growled. "I don't like this. It's almost too easy. And that jet fuel. Shit, it's strong."

They moved down the gallery and into a hallway,

coming closer to the door where her voice was. Last room at the end. They shined their lights, searching for things out of place. Wires where there shouldn't be any. Booby traps.

"Please," Everly sobbed, louder now. "I don't want to die. I haven't gotten to live yet. I want to go home."

Gem's heart was breaking. He looked at Saint, who nodded.

"I'm here, Everly," Gem called. "I'm here, baby."

"Gem? Gem! Oh my God, I heard a noise but I didn't think— Don't open the door! There's a bomb. He said there was a tripwire, but I don't know where. I got loose, but I'm afraid to move. I can hear something ticking, but I don't know where it is. Oh, Gem. I love you. I just wanted to say that again."

Gem's throat was tight. Tears pressed against his eyelids. He wanted to howl. "I love you, too, Everly. I'm going to get you out of there. It may take time, though."

She was still sobbing. "I don't think we have much time. He could call any minute and trigger the bomb. If he knows you're here, he will. I know I said I wanted you to save me, but I want you to save yourself more. It's enough knowing you came for me."

"Fucking hell," Gem growled. "I have to go in there. I have to try."

Saint looked troubled. "We don't have a lot of time to figure this out. Hack, we need to jam that cell signal."

"On it," Hacker said.

"We could go back up on the roof, in through the window," Muffin said. "That room is against the exterior wall."

"What if he's got someone watching for that?" Zany asked. "Hell, they might have seen us scale the building. Maybe they're waiting for us to trigger the bomb."

"We can go through the wall," Gem said. "Go in the room beside this one, punch through the motherfucking wall. He couldn't set a trigger for every option. He expects us to come through the door or the window."

"And he could trigger the bomb any second before we jam the signal," Wolf said. "If we're going, we gotta do it fast. The longer we take, the more likely something's gonna happen. For all we know, he has a timer on it as well."

"Anybody who doesn't want to go with me, I understand," Gem said. "You have wives and fiancées to go home to, and kids," he added for Easy. "It's nearly Christmas. I won't ask you to go with me."

"Are you fucking kidding me right now?" Hacker replied. "We're a team. We could bite the dust on any given day with this job, but we keep doing it. I'm not leaving you, asshole."

"Nope, me neither," Easy said. "And I appreciate the thought about Jenna and Alice, but Jenna knows what the stakes are every time I go out the door."

Saint cut them off. "We're moving. Now. There's no time to waste."

"Hang on, Everly," Gem called. "We're coming. Don't be alarmed by anything you hear, okay? We're coming."

"No, Gem! Don't do it."

"We're coming," he yelled back. "Don't argue, Everly Elizabeth, or I'll put you over my knee when I get you back home."

"Kinky," Muffin said as they pushed into the room beside the one Everly was in. "I like it."

"Shut up," Gem said. "Start cutting."

"With pleasure."

EVERLY WAS SHAKING SO HARD she feared she might set off whatever mechanism controlled the bomb if she didn't stop.

But she couldn't stop. Fear and adrenaline and hope coursed through her all at once. She could hear sound in the room next to the one she was trapped in, and then a wicked-looking knife punched through the wall. Several knives, actually. Long, serrated, working together to dismantle the structure.

The drywall disappeared as they cut, punched, kicked and pulled, until she could see the shapes of men. They were dressed all in black so it was hard to see them very well. She couldn't tell which one was Gem yet.

When a man stepped between the studs, she thought it had to be Gem. Who else would be first when she was in danger?

"Careful, Gem," another voice said, confirming it. Lights shined into the room and across the floor.

"There's fishing line," someone else said. "There's an O-ring on the support beam in the middle of the room, and the line goes through it. Motherfucker probably rigged it to go when anyone opened the door."

Gem shined a light. "I see it. The line goes to the door. He probably taped it in the jamb, then hooked it around the knob." He made a noise. "Never fucking saw it when we stood on the other side."

"Signal jammed." She recognized Sky Kelley's voice. "Make it quick."

"What's that mean?" she asked.

"Means Rooney can't call the bomb," Gem said. "But it doesn't mean we're out of danger yet, so don't move."

"Okay. Please hurry."

"Doing my best, baby."

Gem moved slowly, sweeping light in front of him, presumably looking for more wires. Everly was crying. She hated feeling weak and helpless, but there was a bomb beneath her and this might be her last few moments on Earth even if Rooney couldn't trigger it remotely. A girl could be forgiven for crying under those circumstances.

Gem didn't look at her. His gaze was on the floor, his feet shuffling forward slowly. They'd been careful to pull as much of the wall back into the other room as possible. There weren't huge chunks of it littering the floor in this room, which had to make it easier to search.

"Anything?" Wolf asked.

"I don't see anything. No cuts or indents in the carpet, no wires. Baby," Gem said, his voice pitching softer for her. "I need to shine this light on you, so close your eyes. Don't move unless I tell you to, okay?"

"Okay. But Gem, I'm shaking. I can't stop."

"I know, baby. I know. You're brave and beautiful, you know that? And I'm so fucking sorry I wasn't there for you sooner."

She could hear the anguish in his voice. She couldn't look at him, though, because the light was on her face now. She hated to think what he saw. How dirty she was, how disgusting. It'd been more than a day, or so she thought, since she'd gotten into the SUV with Tony and the other men.

"Is Mother okay?" she asked, guilt throbbing to life as it finally occurred to her to ask.

"Your mother is fine. She's safe. Worried about you, but safe."

"Thank God."

"I'm walking behind you, Everly. Don't move."

"Okay."

The trembling came in waves. She tried to relax, tried to make it lessen, but it wasn't happening.

"No other tripwires besides the one on the door," Gem said to his team. "Device on the floor behind the chair. Jesus, looks like C4 with a cell phone detonator. There's an analog clock making the ticking noise, but it's not attached to the bomb."

Everly closed her eyes. Josh Rooney had wanted to terrify her with every breath she took while sitting in that chair. He'd succeeded.

"Is it attached to her? Is there a pressure detonator on the chair?"

There was silence for a long moment. "Not attached to her. Doesn't look like there's a pressure detonator. I can't see any other wires coming out of this thing, but I need to look closer."

Gem's breath sucked in alarmingly fast, making the hairs on Everly's arms prickle.

"Holy shit, there's a countdown alarm. Thirty seconds left. Move!"

Everly didn't get a chance to ask what was happening because Gem snatched her off the chair and sprinted for the wall opening. He shoved her through the studs, into someone else's arms, and that person started to run. She didn't know who had her, but she clung to him and squeezed her eyes shut. He pounded down the stairs, then someone else took her at the bottom. She didn't know where they were going, or if they'd make it.

The chemical smell was stronger down here, and it made her dizzy. Booted feet struck the warehouse floor hard as the team ran. There was a bang, as if two objects had collided. Someone swore. "Fucking door's locked! Help me kick it open."

There were more grunts and more bangs. "Fucking steel shit! We have to get out of here!"

More cussing, more kicking—and then fresh air flowed across her cheeks. She was tossed to another man, and they rushed outside into the night air, putting distance between them and the building.

Sudden heat surrounded them. And then the concussion of the explosion swallowed them, booming everything into silence.

Chapter Twenty

Everly felt like she was underwater. She could hear, but her ears were ringing. She could still feel the shockwave reverberating through her, too. It hadn't been there, and then it had, knocking them to the ground. Or maybe they'd fallen on purpose. She wasn't sure.

A wall of heat beat at them from behind, a physical thing with no mercy. So much heat. Another explosion boomed, and the man holding her stumbled to his feet and kept going. Away from the burning warehouse, which she could see over his shoulder wasn't that far away at all. They'd made it out the door and barely across the parking lot before the building exploded.

Any closer, and they might not be getting up at all.

"Gem," she cried out. Had he made it? What if he hadn't? What would she do?

"Got you," he said, and her gaze snapped to the greasepainted face of the man holding her. "Hang on, Everly. You're going to be okay."

She clung to him, her head bowed to his chest, breathing him in and cursing the weakness that didn't allow her to stand on her own two feet. She was a burden to him, and she hated it.

His team converged on a van, opening doors and piling inside with weapons and equipment. Everly was plopped on a seat and belted in, then Gem was beside her. The engine roared to life and they were moving, rolling away from the site of the continuing explosions. The sky was bright orange behind them. Red and blue lights raced toward them as sirens blared. Everly held her breath, thinking they would be stopped, but the emergency vehicles raced past them and kept going.

"You okay, baby?" Gem asked. He brushed her hair from her forehead, and she flinched. She didn't want him looking at her until she had a shower, until she didn't look like an unfortunate vagrant living on the streets. Until she didn't smell like one. She was very aware of the odors of urine and sweat that emanated from her, and it mortified her.

"I'm okay. Just feel like shit."

"We're taking you to Riverstone," Gem said. "Gonna get you checked out properly."

"No, I just want to go home. With you," she begged. "Please."

"No can do, babe. Riverstone. If the doc clears you, then you go home."

"Your leg's bleeding," Zany said as they passed beneath a street lamp.

Everly thought he meant her at first, but it was Gem who responded.

"It'll be fine. Just a little shrapnel. I'll get it checked out at the hospital."

"Let me see," Wolf ordered. Everly didn't know a lot about their structure, but she knew Saint was in charge and Wolf was second. Which meant that Gem had no choice.

Gem hissed as Wolf did something Everly didn't see. "Fucking hell, man," Gem said.

"That's a pretty good sized piece of warehouse embedded in your thigh, Gem. Why the fuck didn't you say anything?"

"Everly," Gem said. "She's more important."

Everly gazed up at him, at the sweat on his brow. He looked a little green. Alarm flared as his eyelids drooped. "Gem, what's going on? Are you okay?"

"Fine, honey. Just fine."

She would have believed him if he hadn't chosen that moment to fall backward in slow motion.

"WERE you trying for matching thigh wounds?" Dr. Stacey Puckett said when Gem opened his eyes. Her hands were on her hips, and she was frowning at him.

"Uh, no, ma'am. Just kinda happened."

"I see that, soldier. Maybe you need to reconsider your life choices before you lose a leg instead of just damage it."

"Yes, ma'am."

Gem wasn't feeling a lot of pain at the moment, probably because of the IV dripping pain meds into his veins. The last thing he remembered was riding away from the explosion with Everly safe beside him. Dr. Puckett was talking about the surgery they'd done to remove the shrapnel and repair the tissue. Gem was only half listening.

"Everly," he said when she stopped talking.

"Mm-hmm, knew that's what you were thinking about. She's fine. A bit dehydrated and weak, but we've given her IV fluids and kept her for observation. Just like we're keeping you."

"I want to see her—"

Dr. Puckett held up a finger and he stopped talking. "I figured that. If you'll just listen to what I'm telling you, you can see her right away."

"Yes, ma'am."

"No more heroics, Sergeant Stone. Not for a month at least, you hear me? You're going on light duty and you're going to do your PT as ordered, or I'll declare you unfit for duty for the next quarter.

That wasn't a tiny piece of metal embedded in your leg, and you need time to heal."

"Yes, ma'am."

Dr. Puckett was more than just a doctor. She was the director of the hospital, and when she was busy chewing your ass, you'd better listen. It was like being torn a new one by a much smaller version of General Mendez. There was no room for argument or disagreement.

"All right then, I guess you can see Miss Fairhope now." Dr. Puckett took hold of the privacy curtain and whisked it open.

There was another bed in the room, and this one contained a smiling Everly. Gem's heart squeezed tight at the sight of her. There were dark circles beneath her eyes, and her face looked a little hollow, but her hair was shiny and her eyes sparked with health.

Thank God.

It hit him how close he'd come to losing her. How close they'd all come to dying. All the fear and despair and self-loathing he'd felt for not finding her sooner came crashing back down on him. Add to that his whole team had almost been taken from their loved ones because they'd been helping him rescue her, and emotion threatened to overwhelm him.

"Everly," he croaked.

Her eyes were glassy. "Gem."

He started to move, but Dr. Puckett cleared her

throat. He jerked, surprised to find her still standing at the end of his bed. "No, sir. You don't move a muscle. If you try it, I'm having her moved out of here. You got me, Sergeant?"

"Yes, ma'am."

"Mm-hmm. Miss Fairhope, you're cleared to move. And please do remember that you are in a public place, subject to the comings and goings of hospital staff and visitors. There. I've said my piece. Good evening, both of you."

Dr. Puckett breezed out of the room. Gem held his breath, waiting for her to return. She didn't, and he relaxed a little. Then he turned to look at Everly. She pushed out of her bed and rolled her IV over to his bedside. Then she bent down to kiss him.

He put a hand behind her head, threaded it into her hair, and kissed her with everything he had. He never wanted to go through another forty-eight hours like the ones he'd just lived ever again. Worst two fucking days of his life.

Everly pulled away first. Her fingers traced his lips, his cheek. "You found me. Just like you said you would."

Gem closed his eyes tight, fighting the guilt and pain. "Not fast enough, Everly. Can you forgive me?"

She blinked as she looked down at him. Then she frowned and hitched herself up onto his bed, turning on her side to lie facing him. He didn't move because he was half convinced Dr. Puckett was lurking outside the door just waiting for it. But he turned his head to watch his woman as she settled herself.

"First of all, if they hadn't let me shower after they checked me out, I would *not* be in this bed with you. I was totally disgusting. And second—" Her eyes filled with tears, and she shook her head. "My God, Gem. Forgive you? For what? You found me, you got me out of there. I'm alive because of you."

He felt like crying. What the hell had Dr. Puckett put in that IV anyway? He swallowed the hard knot in his throat and willed the tears away. Fucking baby. He wasn't going to cry.

"You're amazing, Everly. I fucking love you like, I don't know, the best damned thing to ever come into my life. I promised to protect you, and I failed. You were held captive, and he put a fucking bomb under your chair. A bomb that nearly killed you—"

"And you," she said softly, putting a finger over his lips to stop him. "All of you."

Like he didn't know that. He'd been willing to risk himself for her, but his teammates? They shouldn't have done it, but he was damned grateful they had. Without them, he and Everly would have been incinerated along with the warehouse.

"I shouldn't have let you get in that SUV. I should have found another way."

"There wasn't another way, babe, and you know it."

He did know it. But that didn't mean he didn't

wish he'd kept her cocooned from the shit that'd happened. He sucked in a breath to cool his emotions. A chain glittered around her throat and he reached out to touch it.

"Your locket."

She nodded and dragged it from the neck of the pajamas she wore. "You kept it safe. They brought it to me when you were in surgery—"

"Everly! Oh my God!"

Gem jerked toward the unwelcome voice coming from the door to their room. Ellen Fairhope stood there, looking far more put together than she had the last time he'd seen her. Like her old self, except for the lines of worry creasing her face.

"Mama!" Everly cried.

Gem had a selfish urge to stop her from leaving his bed, but he didn't do it. She scrambled to her feet and went into her mother's arms. Ellen closed her eyes and bowed her head, sobbing quietly. Gem was conflicted. On the one hand, he despised the woman. On the other, she truly did love her daughter. She may have left Everly behind in Qu'rim, but she'd sacrificed her career and her reputation to get her daughter back safe. That wasn't nothing.

"Oh, honey. I'm so sorry," she said. "It's all my fault."

"It's okay, Mother," Everly said, reverting to her customary formality. "Josh Rooney made his own choices. That's not your fault. Thankfully, Gem found me. He risked his life to save me, and he was wounded doing it, but I'm alive. Everything's going to be fine."

"I've made so many mistakes," Ellen said, brushing Everly's hair behind her ear.

"You're human. Like the rest of us."

Ellen nodded. Then she met Gem's gaze. She didn't look any softer toward him than she ever had, but he didn't care. "Thank you, Sergeant Stone. I'm grateful for everything you've done to bring Everly home."

"You're welcome, ma'am. But I didn't do it for you. I did it for her. Because I love her."

Everly smiled at him, and he felt the warmth of it like the sun breaking through clouds on a cold day. She left her mother's side and returned to him, twining her fingers with his. "I love you, too, Jackson Stone."

She gazed down at him, and he wished like hell he could sweep her into his arms and hold her tight. But, Dr. Puckett. The crazy woman was somewhere close, and she'd know if he tried it. She'd come barreling into the room and chew him another good one, and he really didn't want that.

Everly squeezed his hand. Then she looked at her mother. He saw her straighten, saw her spine stiffen. *Good for you, baby.* He didn't know what she was about to say, but whatever it was, he thought it might be the first step toward standing up for herself.

"I'm not marrying Stuart," Everly said. "I'm

marrying Gem, if he'll have me. I don't want to run for political office. I never have. I don't want an advantageous marriage, either." She finger-quoted *advantageous*. "I want to marry a man who'll walk into a burning building for me. Since Gem willingly walked into a room with a bomb about to explode, just to save me, I'm pretty sure he'd do the burning building thing too. I'm sorry, Mother, but I'm tired of trying to be all the things I'm not. You're a brilliant congresswoman, and you'd make a brilliant senator or president, but it's not me. It's not what I want."

First step, hell. Everly had gone the whole way. Gem wanted to cheer. She didn't know everything about her mother's dealings with Josh Rooney yet, but Gem and Ellen both knew she wasn't running for those offices anytime soon. If ever. Ellen looked at him, waiting for him to say something about her affair or her dirty deals, but he wouldn't do that to Everly. It was up to Ellen to tell her daughter the truth.

Everly squeezed his hand tight, as if gathering her courage. "If you intervene at all, if you get Gem sent to Antarctica or a remote base anywhere else, I'm going with him. I'll shovel penguin shit beside him before I'll work another moment in your office if you interfere in my life again."

The corners of Ellen's lips had tightened during this speech, but for once she didn't say anything to contradict her daughter. "I've only ever wanted what's best for you, Everly."

"I know. But I think it's time I get to choose for myself. I never wanted to disappoint you, but I can't live the life you want me to live. I have to live my own. I have to be *me*. If I stumble and fall, I'll get up again. All I need is for you to support me, but if you can't do that, then I'll still make my own choices. I'm done trying to be the perfect daughter."

Ellen nodded, her stiffness returning. "I've never expected perfection, Everly. A mother wants her children to have the happiest life possible, and it's hard to watch them make mistakes. I've tried to keep you from making them, but I see I've not done the best job of it."

"Gem is not a mistake, Mother."

He heard the hard note in Everly's voice—for him, in defense of him—and wonder filled him. He'd always thought, deep down, that he wasn't good enough for Everly Fairhope, Esquire. That she didn't think he was enough for someone like her. Just like his ex-wife had been searching for more, he'd assumed Everly felt the same way. He was a soldier, a warrior, and what he did was important. But it was a hard life in many ways, and it took a special kind of woman to accept it. To accept him.

Sleeping with a guy like him was easy. Living with him was hard.

"It's okay, baby," Gem said, pressing a kiss to her small hand where it rested in his. "Your mother doesn't have to like me. Don't try and force her."

"We will be having Christmas dinner at our family home in Roanoke," Ellen said, her chin lifting. "Please join us, Sergeant Stone. I would be delighted to have you there."

Gem didn't know how sincere she was about the delight part, but Everly looked so hopeful that he knew he wouldn't say no. He'd been looking forward to joining Saint, Brooke, and his other teammates who'd be there with their spouses, but he thought they'd understand why he had to bow out. He hoped Ellen's dinner was as good as Brooke's prime rib.

"Thank you, ma'am. And please call me Gem, or Jackson if you prefer."

She seemed like a Jackson person to him. Jax or Gem was too informal for a woman like Ellen Fairhope to say.

"I should be going so you two can rest." She hesitated in the doorway. "I didn't mean to suggest my daughter is making a mistake with you, Jackson. I was speaking about my mistakes in trying too hard to guide her. I apologize for any misunderstanding, and I look forward to seeing you at Christmas."

A politician to the last. Gem nodded. "Understood, ma'am."

"Before I go… Everly, may I speak with you for a moment?"

"If it's about Gem, then no."

"It's not. He already knows what I want to tell you. It's about Josh Rooney."

Everly looked confused. Gem kissed her hand again. "You need to listen to your mother, babe. I'm not going anywhere. Dr. Puckett would have me tied down if I tried."

"There's a couch outside this door," Ellen said. "It won't take long."

"I'll be right there," Everly replied.

When her mother was gone, she turned to look down at him. Fuck, he hated being in this hospital bed. He wanted to make love to her, let her know how much he loved her. How much he would always love her. How right his life was now, and how much he looked forward to every moment with her. But right this second, she was looking at him with worry lines marring her pretty forehead. He wanted to fix it for her, but he couldn't. Only talking to her mother would help.

"I'm not going to like what she's about to tell me, am I?"

He hesitated. "Maybe not, but I think you'll get through it. You love each other, and even if I don't understand your mother, I admire that she did the right thing when it came down to it."

Everly took a breath. "Oh boy. Okay. Thank you…" She twisted her fingers together. "Um, I know I kind of sprung that whole marriage thing on you. I was inspired, but you don't have to agree to marry me yet. Or ever if it doesn't work out."

"Everly Elizabeth Fairhope," Gem said, grabbing

her hand and tugging her down to him. “Of course I’m marrying you.”

She giggled as he kissed her nose and cheeks, then sighed into his mouth when their lips met. “I love you,” she whispered. “You make me better, braver, and I can’t imagine life without you. I can’t believe I almost let you go for good.”

He brushed her hair back and kissed her forehead. She inspired him to say the kind of things he’d never thought he could. “You fill all the empty pieces of me and make me whole. I want to go through this life with you beside me.”

“Then that’s what we’re going to do.”

He grinned. “Yep, that’s what we’re going to do.”

Chapter Twenty-One

"YOU SURE THIS IS OKAY WITH YOU?" EVERLY ASKED.

Gem gave her a mock frown. "Babe. I'm on crutches. It's not an issue. Let's get in there and bring some Christmas cheer to these folks."

She opened her car door and went around to get Gem's crutches from the back seat. She'd wanted to keep her promise and visit the Golden Acres Resort on Christmas Eve, but she hadn't wanted to leave him. He'd said he would go with her, and here they were.

Tomorrow, they were making the four-hour drive to Roanoke, staying the night, and returning the next day. Part of her didn't want to go at all, but her mother needed the support more than ever. Ellen Fairhope had resigned her seat on the House Armed Services Committee, and there was talk of her resigning her seat in Congress, though nothing had been decided yet.

Everly wasn't worried about her own job, but she was worried about the other staffers in her mother's office. They'd all looked a bit shell-shocked when her mother gathered them up and announced her plans a few days ago. They were even more rattled when the FBI arrested one of their own yesterday for sending threatening messages to a sitting Member of Congress.

More secrets coming out of the shadows. So many of them lately.

Everly had been as shocked as anyone when Michael Franks was cuffed and led away. When Michael was ten, his parents' farm was seized under eminent domain to make way for a new highway interchange to ease traffic around Roanoke.

The land had been in the family for four generations. His parents fought the government in court, but it was eventually decided in the state's favor. His mother was compensated for the land since his father had died of a heart attack, which his doctors said was brought on by stress, and the family had to move.

Michael had started sending the messages because he'd only recently discovered that Ellen Fairhope had been one of the government attorneys who'd fought the case twenty years ago. She hadn't been the lead attorney, but she'd been on the team. That was enough for him.

The FBI had gotten a tip from someone in his family that he'd become obsessed with the case. When they'd obtained a warrant and searched his premises, they'd found envelopes, card stock, and a printer that turned out to be the same one the messages had been printed on. Michael had been careful with sealing the envelopes and mailing them, using gloves and wetting the adhesive with a sponge. He'd known that any of his non-saliva DNA found on the messages could be explained away by his working in the office where they were opened.

What his endgame had been was anyone's guess, but he wasn't going to get the chance to carry it out. Threatening government officials was a felony, and Michael wouldn't be out of custody anytime soon. Thank God.

He wasn't the only one currently in custody. HOT had picked up Josh Rooney the night of the bombing and found the chemicals and equipment in his basement. He'd had residue on his clothing as well. Anthony Borelli made a deal and told everything he knew. Rooney was being charged with kidnapping a government official, as well as a host of other crimes, and all his contracts for providing base security overseas had been rescinded.

Also not someone walking free anytime soon.

Then there was J. Stuart Morrison. That slimy weasel had been involved in Rooney's shady shit, too. Like Borelli, he'd cut a deal to avoid prosecution.

He'd been working for Rooney through a shell company, getting richer, and he'd started dating Everly as a way to keep tabs for Rooney when he was making plans to use her against her mother. She didn't know where the rumored engagement came from, but Stuart had probably oversold his interest to her mother.

He was the one who'd slipped a tracking device into her computer bag the last day they'd had lunch together. That night, two of Rooney's employees had found her and Gem at Mal and Scarlett's place. If Gem hadn't made her leave the bag behind, they'd have likely followed her to the next location, too.

The next time she saw Stuart, since he was presumably free to continue doing what he always did, she thought she might punch his lights out. Probably not really, but it was a nice thought that made her happy to imagine.

"Everly! You made it!"

"Wouldn't miss it, Edna." Everly said, giving the old woman who'd greeted her a hug. The foyer of the home was decorated with a blinking Christmas tree and poinsettias, and everything looked festive. "Are we in time for dinner?"

"You bet. We're having ham tonight and turkey tomorrow." Edna's gaze slid past her to Gem. "Oh my, who is this tasty morsel of arm candy you've brought along?"

"Behave, Edna," Everly said, keeping her arm

looped around the woman's shoulders. "This is my fiancé, Gem."

God, she loved saying that. Gem was her fiancé. The man she was going to marry. Not until summer, though. They were going to have a wedding with all the trimmings. She'd asked Gem if he minded letting her mother throw a big fancy wedding or if he wanted to get married quicker.

Everly would have married him at the courthouse the way Noah and Jenna had done, but he said a big wedding was fine with him. Meant he could invite his parents, three brothers, two sisters, their spouses and kids, and wear his dress uniform with the medals. Since nothing could be sexier than Gem in uniform—unless it was Gem out of uniform—she'd told her mother they were happy to accept, though Everly was going to be front and center in the planning. Her mother agreed, and they'd already started discussing venues.

"Pleased to meet you, ma'am," Gem said, extending a hand to Edna.

She took it coyly and then giggled. "What a big strong man you are."

Everly laughed. "Laying it on thick, Edna."

Edna pretended to be affronted. Then she laughed, too. "Honey, when you get to be my age, all you can do is look at the goods. Maybe touch them if they let you. They don't let you, unless it's those strippers that come out of the cake like at Bonnie's birthday party last week. He let us all fondle his muscles. Dreamy."

"Sorry, Edna," Gem said. "I can let you fondle my biceps if you'd like me to escort you to dinner, but be warned I'm gonna hop there on these crutches."

"What happened, dear?" Edna asked, wrapping her hand around his arm and squeezing. "Oh my, better than the stripper."

"Gem's a soldier," Everly said. "He got injured on a mission."

Edna gasped. "Dear boy, I'm so sorry. And thank you for your service. My Ronnie was a Marine. He died twenty years ago. Agent Orange."

"I'm sorry," Gem said. "It's good men like him who made it better for us who serve today."

"Thank you for saying that." Edna cleared her throat. "Well, shall we go into the lounge? Everyone's waiting. When we heard Everly would be here for our annual Christmas Eve feast again, we decided to do a little something special. Didn't know we'd *really* have something to celebrate though."

"What have you all done?" Everly asked. She kept pace beside Gem and Edna as they slowly moved toward the lounge.

"You'll see," Edna said.

They made it to the big double doors that fronted the lounge area, and fifty seniors burst into *Joy to the World*, accompanied by a piano, a violin, and a cello. Everly's eyes grew misty and she had to take off her glasses to wipe the tears away before they blurred everything.

"Surprise," Edna said. "We've prepared you a little concert. Now you and Gem sit down over there" —she pointed to a sofa—"and we'll sing a few songs before dinner."

Edna left and Gem sat, putting the crutches on the floor beside him. Everly sank down beside him and he looped his arm around her. She snuggled into him, happiness blooming in her soul as the chorus serenaded them.

"I see why you like coming here," Gem said in her ear.

"There are so many wonderful people in this place. People who've had unbelievably rich lives, and who might be alone now. I like hearing their stories and helping where I can when they need legal help. I wish I could do more, but I'm just one person."

"Interestingly enough, I happen to know a sitting Congresswoman," Gem teased. "Maybe she needs something new to focus on."

"She might not be there much longer," Everly said sadly. "You know that."

"She's there now, baby. She has connections and resources, and so do you. You know people. If your mother resigns, you still know people. You don't need her help, though while she's there you might as well use it."

"You know, you're pretty smart for arm candy," she teased.

"Honey, I'll have you know I'm flipping brilliant. I made you fall in love with me, didn't I? My best move yet."

TWO MONTHS LATER...

"THIS IS GONNA BE GOOD," Mal said, snickering. "So good."

"Shhh," Gem replied, trying not to laugh as Muffin came strolling into the locker room, whistling after his shower. Mal and Gem were hiding behind a row of lockers. Saint and Wolf were sitting on the bench. Easy, Zany, and Harley were still in the shower. Hacker was perched on top of the lockers, holding a bucket.

If Muffin looked up, they were done for.

He didn't look up as he went to his locker and opened it. "What the—" he began, but he was cut off by goop slopping down from above.

The guys hooted. Mal and Gem stepped around the lockers they'd been hiding behind. The other guys came bounding in from the shower, towels wrapped around their waists, laughing their asses off.

At Muffin's feet were a dozen muffins that'd fallen

out of his locker when he opened it. Those were the distraction. But it was the blueberry batter dripping down his head, the main event, that was the funniest thing of all.

Muffin wiped the batter from his cheek, sniffed it, and stuck his finger in his mouth. "Mmm, good shit right there. Fuckers."

"Sorry, Muff, but you asked for it," Hacker said. "Never swipe my laptop and pretend to stick a refrigerator magnet on it."

"It was your turn," Muffin said. "And you have to admit I scared you."

He wiped batter from his face. Dude looked hilarious with blueberries and yellow batter sliding down his head and over his shoulders.

"Definitely." Hacker levered down from the lockers and faced Muffin. "Might need to shower again, man."

Muffin wiped more batter from his head, then flung it at Hacker. "Oops."

Hacker looked stunned. He was in uniform because he'd showered and dressed first. And now he had batter dripping down his ACU shirt. Muffin laughed as he headed for the shower, leaving muffins on the floor and thick batter splattered everywhere.

"You saw that, right?" Hacker asked.

"Saw it," Gem said.

"Maybe I should hack into the county real estate

records and jack up the property taxes on his new place…"

Saint snorted. "No. Do not do it. That's an order."

Hacker sighed. "Fine."

He started to unbutton his shirt. Of course the anal-retentive dude had another shirt in his locker, starched and ready to go. He shrugged it on and buttoned it up.

Wolf's phone rang and he snatched it up. "Baby, what's up? What? Now?" His face went white. "I'll be there. Don't do anything without me!"

"Is the baby coming?" Saint asked.

"Yeah. Holy shit, holy shit," he muttered as he threw on his boots.

Mal's phone rang. "Yeah, baby? … Mm-hmm. Okay, I'll tell him. Love you too. Bye… Yo, Wolf," he said after he'd put his phone down.

"What?"

"Scar says to cool your jets. Actually, Haylee says to cool your jets. Scar's with her and she's taking her to the hospital. You are to meet them there, and you are to drive at a reasonable speed and not get a ticket or hurt yourself. Haylee's words. Yes, her water broke, but it could be hours yet. So calm your ass down, button your shirt up the right way, and get moving."

Wolf gaped. Gem laughed as he slapped Wolf on the shoulder. "Dude, the ladies have it. Do what you're told and go be with your wife while she gives birth to your child."

"Yeah, and be sure not to hold her hand during contractions," Mal said. "I read that was a bad idea. Also, don't let your balls get anywhere near her hands, or she's likely to rip them off for knocking her up."

Wolf kept getting dressed, but at a more reasonable speed that allowed him to make sure he had his clothes on right. "I'm sure that's good advice. Thanks. Shit, I wonder if I should call her mother?"

"Ladies," Gem reminded. "Trust me, they've got it."

"You're right, you're right," Wolf said, buttoning his shirt and grabbing his cover. "Permission to leave?" he asked Saint.

"Granted. And let us know what we can do to help. I'm sure Brooke's on it now, but if you think of anything, call."

"Copy. Thanks."

Wolf jogged for the door and was gone. "Man," Gem said. "Just think, next time we see him, he'll be a dad."

"Pretty cool, right?" Zany said. "Hey, how are your wedding plans going?"

"Based on the fact Everly's happy, I'm assuming they're going well. She and her mom are planning everything, and Everly isn't upset when she comes home. Doesn't get much better than that."

Ellen was still a bit of a control freak, but whenever Everly pushed back, she gave ground. She was navigating a new landscape as much as her daughter, but they seemed to be finding their way. Ellen was friendly to him, but he wouldn't say she approved. Maybe she did, but she'd never said so. She spoke to him, called him Jackson, and he called her ma'am or Ms. Fairhope. He doubted he'd ever call her mother, though he was positive Everly would call his mom by that name.

Ellen was still in Congress, but she'd announced her intentions not to seek reelection. It'd shaken up the Hill for a while, but things were settling again. Everly was still working in her mother's office, but she'd successfully started to turn Ellen's focus to the issues Everly was passionate about. And she was advocating for seniors with other congressmen and women, which made her feel good.

They went to see Edna and the gang a few times a month, and Gem had even managed to get his friends to go, too. It was always a hoot because Edna and the ladies were salty and didn't mince words. Gem loved it.

He loved everything about his life with Everly. When it was time to go home for the day, he texted Everly he was on the way and drove the miles to her house in town. They'd discussed moving, but the truth was she had a great home and there was plenty of room. He'd given up his apartment, and now he lived with her.

He parked in the garage and went inside. Soft jazz played on the speakers throughout the house. His senses prickled because that was the kind of music they often had sex to. "Everly?"

"I'm in here, honey. I fixed you something to eat."

"Okay, great." He walked into the kitchen and stopped dead. The blinds were all closed, and Everly sat on the kitchen island, butt-ass naked, legs spread to show her glistening pink pussy. Her nipples were hard and she had a rose in her teeth.

Gem's cock was hard in half a second. He threw his hat down and went over to the island, running his hands up the insides of her thighs. "Damn, baby. You know all my favorite things to eat, don't you?"

"I hope so," she breathed, tickling his chin with the rose.

Gem dropped to his knees on the cushion she'd helpfully placed there and tugged her to the edge of the island as she squeaked in delight. "Hang on, baby. I'm about to blow your mind."

"Ohhhhh," she moaned as he proceeded to do just that.

Much later, when they lay in bed naked in each other's arms, her phone buzzed. She reached for it lazily, then sat up when she got a look at the text.

"Haylee and Dean have a healthy baby girl. Yes!"

"That's awesome." He hesitated. "We've never talked about kids. You want any?"

She slid against him again and kissed his chest. "I

think so. But not for a while yet. I want time to be together first. I want you all to myself. What about you?"

"Kids are work, but I think it's something we could handle. Someday."

She stretched and threw a leg over his abdomen. "Someday is good. For now, though, we can practice how they're made."

He flipped her onto her back and settled between her thighs. "I need a lot of practice, babe. To make sure I get it right."

"I think that's a good plan. I love you, and I love the way you think."

He slid inside her, groaning at how right she felt. "Love you too, babe. So much. Gonna show you as often as I can."

She smiled that beautiful smile of hers when they were connected as intimately as they could be. "I already know, Gem. You're my burning-building person. And I'm yours. Always."

"Always," he said, his throat tight with emotion. And then he didn't say anything at all for a long time.

HOT LIMIT Sneak Peek

Ryder Hanson had no desire to dive into a frigid lake on a cold, windy, gray-ass day, but he was gonna do it anyway. The woman floating face down, arms spread out, body bobbing in the choppy water, made the choice for him.

Ry peeled his sweatshirt over his head, toed off his hiking boots, and swore a blue streak as he got a running start down the dock. He had no idea how long she'd been there. He'd noticed her from the kitchen window just moments ago. He'd gone to get a cup of coffee and there she was. Like a piece of drift-wood. He'd thought he was seeing things at first, but fuck all if she wasn't real.

Ry dove into the water, arms out in front of him, body arcing the way he'd been taught during all the brutal hours of combat swim training. The lake wasn't deep, no more than four feet at his dock, but he knew how to dive into much shallower water if need be.

The water was cold enough to shrivel his balls and make him scream like a little girl if he let it. He wasn't about to let it. He'd bobbed in colder water than this waiting for a pickup after a mission, and he'd trained in colder water too.

He just hadn't expected to go in today.

Ry powered through the water until he reached her. He flipped her over so her face was no longer submerged. There were cuts and bruises on her skin. She was deathly pale and her lips were blue, but there was a pulse. Shallow and thready.

Fuck. She wasn't even wearing a coat. Probably lucky since that would have weighed her down.

Ry turned her head to the side so water could drain from her nose and mouth and then put his mouth over hers and breathed. He did it four times and waited. Her chest moved, thank fuck.

He put everything he had into swimming for the dock again, one arm wrapped around her and the other stroking for all he was worth. He'd been so damned happy and proud when he'd put an offer on this place just last month. He'd been saving, looking for the right property, and he'd found it. One of the pluses about it was how remote it was for being within fifty miles of DC.

Where the fuck had this woman come from then?

Ry reached the dock, managed to push the

woman onto the weathered wood, and followed her up. Her chest was still moving and her pulse was stronger. He turned her to the side again. When she started to cough, he breathed a little easier. Not that she was entirely out of the woods yet, but it was better than a few moments ago.

He needed to get her warm, and he needed to get her to a hospital. He had combat medicine training, so he wasn't entirely clueless about what to do, but he didn't want responsibility for her any longer than he had to have it.

He scooped her into his arms and carried her inside, kicking the door closed and heading straight for the bathroom. He lay her on the floor and started the water running in the bathtub. He hadn't even used the tub yet. Funny this would be the first time.

Once the water was the right temperature, he put her in the tub and let it keep filling. She lay back against the rim, her eyes still closed, her chest moving. She started to whimper as he peeled his jeans and T-shirt off. He grabbed a towel and scrubbed himself dry, then hooked it around his hips. He couldn't leave her to get more clothes, and he couldn't shower yet either. Not until he had her warmed up and out of the water.

He wouldn't take a chance of her slipping beneath the surface while his back was turned. He took the time he had now to study her. She looked to be about thirty or so, with dark brown hair slicked against her skull. It fell to just below her shoulders.

There was a cut on her left cheekbone, some scrapes on her chin and cheek, and a bruise beneath her left eye. She had finger marks on her collar bone and at the base of her throat. Her fingernails were torn and ragged, and one had ripped partially off. It was starting to bleed again now that the water was warming her.

"Jesus, sweetheart, what happened to you?"

She wore what looked like leggings and a sweatshirt with Princess Leia on it. She had no shoes or socks, and nowhere to stash any ID. He wouldn't know who she was until she woke. He could do a search for missing persons, maybe that'd turn something up. He could also snap a pic and send it to Sky "Hacker" Kelley, see if maybe Hack could find something.

But that seemed to be a bit too intrusive just now. If she didn't wake after he got her warm and dry, maybe he'd do it then. Except he'd be taking her to the hospital by then, so maybe he'd just wash his hands of the whole thing. Let them figure it out.

She was still whimpering, only now he could understand words. Words that tore his heart in two.

"No, please, no…"

He hunkered down beside the tub and frowned. "It's okay, you're safe. I've got you. No one's going to hurt you."

She shuddered, her head moving back and forth as if denying what he was saying. He thought she might be convulsing and he reached for her to stop her sinking under the water.

Her eyes snapped open. The terror he saw there stunned him at first. Then it angered him.

"It's okay," he said again. "You're okay."

She opened her mouth. And then she screamed.

Books by Lynn Raye Harris

The Hostile Operations Team ® Books

Strike Team 2

Book 1: HOT ANGEL - Cade & Brooke

Book 2: HOT SECRETS - Sky & Bliss

Book 3: HOT JUSTICE - Wolf & Haylee

Book 4: HOT STORM - Mal & Scarlett

Book 5: HOT COURAGE - Noah & Jenna

Book 6: HOT SHADOWS - Gem & Everly

Book 7: HOT LIMIT ~ Coming May 2023

The Hostile Operations Team ® Books

Strike Team 1

Book 0: RECKLESS HEAT

Book 1: HOT PURSUIT - Matt & Evie

Book 2: HOT MESS - Sam & Georgie

Book 3: DANGEROUSLY HOT - Kev & Lucky

Book 4: HOT PACKAGE - Billy & Olivia

Book 5: HOT SHOT - Jack & Gina

Book 6: HOT REBEL - Nick & Victoria

Book 7: HOT ICE - Garrett & Grace

Book 8: HOT & BOTHERED - Ryan & Emily

Book 9: HOT PROTECTOR - Chase & Sophie

Book 10: HOT ADDICTION - Dex & Annabelle

Book 11: HOT VALOR - Mendez & Kat

Book 12: A HOT CHRISTMAS MIRACLE - Mendez & Kat

The HOT SEAL Team Books

Book 1: HOT SEAL - Dane & Ivy

Book 2: HOT SEAL Lover - Remy & Christina

Book 3: HOT SEAL Rescue - Cody & Miranda

Book 4: HOT SEAL BRIDE - Cash & Ella

Book 5: HOT SEAL REDEMPTION - Alex & Bailey

Book 6: HOT SEAL TARGET - Blade & Quinn

Book 7: HOT SEAL HERO - Ryan & Chloe

Book 8: HOT SEAL DEVOTION - Zach & Kayla

HOT Heroes for Hire: Mercenaries

Black's Bandits

Book 1: BLACK LIST - Jace & Maddy

Book 2: BLACK TIE - Brett & Tallie

Book 3: BLACK OUT - Colt & Angie

Book 4: BLACK KNIGHT - Jared & Libby

Book 5: BLACK HEART - Ian Black!

Book 6: BLACK MAIL - Tyler Scott

Book 7: BLACK VELVET - Dax & Roberta

The HOT Novella in Liliana Hart's MacKenzie Family Series

HOT WITNESS - Jake & Eva

Who's HOT?

Strike Team 1

Matt "Richie Rich" Girard (Book 0 & 1)
Sam "Knight Rider" McKnight (Book 2)
Kev "Big Mac" MacDonald (Book 3)
Billy "the Kid" Blake (Book 4)
Jack "Hawk" Hunter (Book 5)
Nick "Brandy" Brandon (Book 6)
Garrett "Iceman" Spencer (Book 7)
Ryan "Flash" Gordon (Book 8)
Chase "Fiddler" Daniels (Book 9)
Dex "Double Dee" Davidson (Book 10)

Commander

John "Viper" Mendez (Book 11 & 12)

Deputy Commander

Alex "Ghost" Bishop

Strike Team 2

Cade "Saint" Rodgers (Book 1)
Sky "Hacker" Kelley (Book 2)
Dean "Wolf" Garner (Book 3)
Malcolm "Mal" McCoy (Book 4)
Noah "Easy" Cross (Book 5)
Jax "Gem" Stone (Book 6)
Ryder "Muffin" Hanson (Book 7)
Zane "Zany" Scott (Book 8)
Jake "Harley" Ryan (HOT WITNESS)

SEAL Team 1

Dane "Viking" Erikson (Book 1)
Remy "Cage" Marchand (Book 2)
Cody "Cowboy" McCormick (Book 3)
Cash "Money" McQuaid (Book 4)
Alexei "Camel" Kamarov (Book 5)
Adam "Blade" Garrison (Book 6)
Ryan "Dirty Harry" Callahan (Book 7)
Zach "Neo" Anderson (Book 8)
Corey "Shade" Vance

Black's Bandits

Jace Kaiser (Book 1)

Brett Wheeler (Book 2)
Colton Duchaine (Book 3)
Jared Fraser (Book 4)
Ian Black (Book 5)
Tyler Scott (Book 6)
Dax Freed (Book 7)
Thomas "Rascal" Bradley
Jamie Hayes
Finn McDermot
Roman Rostov
Mandy Parker (Airborne Ops)
Melanie (Reception)
? Unnamed Team Members

Freelance Contractors

Lucinda "Lucky" San Ramos, now MacDonald (Book 3)
Victoria "Vee" Royal, now Brandon (Book 6)
Emily Royal, now Gordon (Book 8)
Miranda Lockwood, now McCormick (SEAL Team Book 3)
Bliss Bennett, (Strike Team 2, Book 2)
Angelica "Angie" Turner (Black's Bandits, Book 3)

About the Author

Lynn Raye Harris is a Southern girl, military wife, wannabe cat lady, and horse lover. She's also the New York Times and USA Today bestselling author of the HOSTILE OPERATIONS TEAM ® SERIES of military romances, and 20 books about sexy billionaires for Harlequin.

A former finalist for the Romance Writers of America's Golden Heart Award and the National Readers Choice Award, Lynn lives in Alabama with her handsome former-military husband, one fluffy princess of a cat, and a very spoiled American Saddlebred horse who enjoys bucking at random in order to keep Lynn on her toes.

Lynn's books have been called "exceptional and emotional," "intense," and "sizzling" -- and have sold in excess of 4.5 million copies worldwide.

To connect with Lynn online:
www.LynnRayeHarris.com
Lynn@LynnRayeHarris.com